MW01133670

# GRAY'S HARBOR

## Finding Refuge Among
## Shorebirds and Saints

# MARTHA L. HENDERSON

Gray's Harbor
Finding Refuge Among Shorebirds and Saints
All Rights Reserved.
Copyright © 2021 P Martha L. Henderson
v2.0

This is a work of fiction. Names, characters, businesses, places, events, locales, and incidents are either the products of the author's imagination or used in a fictitious manner. Any resemblance to actual persons, living or dead, or actual events is purely coincidental.

The opinions expressed in this manuscript are solely the opinions of the author and do not represent the opinions or thoughts of the publisher. The author has represented and warranted full ownership and/or legal right to publish all the materials in this book.

This book may not be reproduced, transmitted, or stored in whole or in part by any means, including graphic, electronic, or mechanical without the express written consent of the publisher except in the case of brief quotations embodied in critical articles and reviews.

Outskirts Press, Inc.
http://www.outskirtspress.com

ISBN: 978-1-9772-4605-9

Cover Photo © 2021 www.gettyimages.com. All rights reserved - used with permission.

Outskirts Press and the "OP" logo are trademarks belonging to Outskirts Press, Inc.

PRINTED IN THE UNITED STATES OF AMERICA

*FOR*
*EVER DEDICATED TO*

*DR. STEVEN G. HERMAN*

*ORNITHOLOGIST, PROFESSOR, AND ICONOCLAST*

# PRELUDE

Lekmaltch dropped his hook into Water on the big bay. He was salmon fishing. Really, the fish were waiting for the hook. He watched large numbers of salmon fight their way up the river channel that ran out to the ocean through the big bay. The salmon were rushing upstream where they would go through the transformation from swimmers to carcasses that nourished the river's edge. Ferns that framed the forest would pull the nutrients into the trees. Today, Lekmaltch needed a fish to feed his family.

"Become my fish," said Lekmaltch looking into Water. He thought of his granny who taught him to fish and hunt with a grateful heart.

"Feed my family," said Lekmaltch, "so that we may live with Water."

The sun caught the silvery skin of a salmon as it rose to the surface of Water. The fish leapt toward at the hook. Just as its piercing teeth grabbed the hook, Lekmaltch felt the ground shake. Earth moved up and down, rolling like waves. For a moment, Lekmaltch wondered if it were Water rolling, and somehow the fish had pulled him into the river. Earth rolled again, this time with a booming sound like thunder. Lekmaltch felt the sound in his feet. He fell to Earth trying to hold on to a large rock that protruded from Earth at Water's edge. Nothing seemed to act in its normal way. The rock moved from side to side until freezing cold Water began to pour in around Lekmaltch's feet. Water stiffened his feet and he could not find a way to be grounded on Earth. The bay began to churn, waves thrown upward only to crash into Water that seemed to be rising all around him. Water roared over him as it began rushing toward the bay as if pulled by the ocean.

Lekmaltch saw many salmon tumbling past his feet, pulled up and over themselves back towards ocean. The bank gave way to the pressure of Water. Lekmaltch sank into the roaring slurry of mud, ferns, trees, and the salmon. In the last moment of his present time on Earth, Lekmaltch saw a wall of Water, taller than the sand dunes, coming toward him. He felt a huge pull on his legs as Water reached up and grabbed him like a bear pulling him into a killing embrace. He sank into the afterworld still holding his fishhook.

Many of his relatives greeted him in the afterworld. Each whispered an account of their journey.

"I was getting Water at the stream."

"I was walking along the beach."

"I was following a deer."

Their Earth language became the singing of spirits, and as spirits, they floated back to their accustomed places, continuing to live in the afterworld, as they had before. The dead lived among those who survived Earth Acts Like Water, helping the living find food and shelter, singing to let them know they are not alone. In the afterworld, Lekmaltch returned to the boundary between Earth and Water, his spirit drifting from one rock to another until he came rest on a rock rooted in Earth at Water's edge. The rock became known as Lekmaltch. Among the Quinault people, Lekmaltch became a guiding spirit for those fishing at the end of the long sand spit that curled out into the bay from its north shore.

To tell the story of Earth Acts Like Water also requires the telling of Time between Terrible Waters. Since the last time Earth Acts like

Water, many changes had come into the bay. First, people living near the bay began to die of diseases their medicines could not heal. Then white people came, claiming to have 'discovered' the bay while looking for wealth that they claimed as theirs. White men killed animals living in Water and on Earth. Beaver, sea otters, mink and whales were butchered without thanks to their spirits. More white people came, building docks along the rivers, cutting down forests, and clearing land where they could. The bay was their way in and out of Quinault land. Larger ships came to dock near the mouth of the bay. For these ships to sail in the bay, the white men dredged the bottom of the bay. They left the mud in the shallows, creating tidal basins. Towns were built on the mud banks that formed at Water's edge. Few white people thought about the mudflats as unnatural.

Tidal Water now covers the mudflats and creates shallows where once deeper Water was found. Those who entered the bay are never sure when Water was more than a thin layer of brine covering the mudflats or when there was enough Water to keep a ship afloat. The bay and its mudflats have become dangerous places. King tides are the most dangerous, hurling Water into the channels and covering the mudflats at much greater depths than usual. Buoys and massive tree trunks, their roots exposed as a tangled mass, are laid out on the mudflats to warn ships of their expanse and the changing Water levels.

Normal tides bring life into the mudflats. Water seeps into the mudflats, refilling the heart of the bay with lifegiving brine like blood refilling a beating human heart. The brine brings tiny germs of life, full of proteins and sugars that push into capillaries to feed the heart. In response, the heart pumps bits of plant life back into the brine. When briny Water covers the mud, small fish swim to meet the plants and animals that have returned to Water from the muds.

Shorebirds fly close to Water, diving for fish from high above Water. Ducks, flying low and then landing on Water, turn upside down into the brine to feed on life in the muds. Peregrine falcons dive at great speed from the sky to carry off ducks to feed their young. Larger fish weave their way into Water in search of the smaller fish. Above Water fly eagles and osprey, all waiting for the moment when they spy a large fish close to Water's surface. The strong birds turn in their silent flight and dive straight down through the air into Water to clutch the fish with their strong talons. Pulling the fish upward, out of Water, the large birds climax the story of life and death along the narrow edge between Earth and Water. The cycle begins again when the next incoming tide feeds the heart with the brine. Seasons change, birds migrate, the mudflats wait through storms and constant rain for the birds to return.

Today, Lekmaltch sits on his rock just beyond the sand spit now called Damon Point. He watches the bay with all the spirits of his people, both those in the afterworld and those who still inhabit the land of the Quinault. His people hold a piece of paper, a legal document, that says they own the bottom of the bay and its mudflats. Now they control the dredging and creation of more mudflats. They can say what happens to Water in the bay and who uses the mudflats. Lekmaltch wonders how you could own a heart. The heart owns you, and you must listen to it for the cycle of life to endure.

# *1*

# CONSTRUCTION DOWN

*I*closed my desk drawer, switched off my computer, and adjusted the sleeves of my new sweater. Bob, my boss and owner of Harbor Insurance, was always looking at numbers. Sales rates, changing policies, and extra years of coverage meant everything to Bob. He took the business byword "Be safe, harbor your assets with Captain Bob" seriously. He had been pacing the floor in front of the door all week. I could tell he was less than happy with the end-of-the-week numbers.

My desk calendar said September 15, 2010. The date was circled in red to remind me it was payday. Beside the calendar stood a coffee-stained greeting card, its edges worn with age. The inside message read 'YOU ARE GREAT.' The card was signed, Love, Your adoring brother, Bruce. I winked at the card as Bob locked the front door and made his way to my desk. It was 5:00, the end of the day and the end of the week.

"Here's your pay," Bob said. As usual, his outstretched hand offered a stack of twenty dollar bills fresh from the ATM at Grays Harbor Savings and Loan down the street. Something seemed a bit different this time. I reached forward and took a taller than usual stack of twenties from across the desk. I raised a questioning eye to see Bob's face turn downward.

"I'm sorry, but I have to let you go. I hope the extra pay will help you out until you find another job," he said. "I'll give you a good recommendation."

Bob stepped back from my desk and looked out at the rain blowing against the window. "It's just that the economy around Aberdeen is getting worse. The recession is hitting everyone. There's just not enough interest in buying insurance. People are getting rid of everything they can." Turning, he dusted off his gray pants, and walked briskly back to his office firmly closing the door behind him.

"But…" my voice trailed off. I starred at my desk in disbelief. Bob's words slowly sank in and around me. They settled around my heart. Immobilized, I sat, starring at nothing. Bob's words rose from my heart and into my head. I was not going to be sitting at my desk, answering phone calls or smiling at clients anymore. I looked at Bruce's card. This isn't supposed to be happening, I thought.

Bob was right, of course. Businesses in Grays Harbor County were suffering. Timber jobs were gone. Commercial fishing was nothing compared with what it was ten years ago. The national, and some said global, recession had found its way into Aberdeen and Hoquiam. Like the tidal waters that drained away from the mudflats and channels of the harbor, the dollars that flowed through the county had drained away. It would be a long time until the tide turned for this remote space on the Washington coast. Somehow, I never anticipated the receding economy would find me. I was happy working in the insurance office. My source of security wasn't supposed to end, but now it had.

I slowly gathered my personal belongings from my desk. A packet of postage stamps, a granola bar, and a small bag of makeup essentials went into my tote bag. I picked up the small framed photo that always sat beside my computer. The photo was of Bruce. "I so miss you," I whispered. The photo and card were the last things to go into my tote bag.

Unlike most people in Aberdeen, I did not belong to a large extended family. It had just been Bruce since high school. Bruce had been my best friend since we were kids. He steered me away from bullies in school. He pushed me to take math classes and learn to type. He was the most disappointed when I started working in restaurants and motels. "You've got more to offer, don't settle for less," he would chide.

I watched Bruce work hard on commercial fishing boats and charters at Westport, the fishing community on the south side of the entrance into the harbor. I saw more of him when I started waiting tables at the Shore Galley on Westport's main street that bordered the docks. Bruce lived aboard *The Alaskan Mermaid* when it was in port.

The *Mermaid* was one of the last big commercial trawlers that made Westport its home port. Nine years ago, the captain informed the crew that it would be their last trip up the coast to the Gulf of Alaska. "Just not making enough money now that the environmentalists have gotten the salmon haul reduced," he said. Bruce had warned me that there were big changes in the fishing industry. "Westport won't be the same. They'll have to find something else for people to do out here."

A week after the *Mermaid* left Westport, I got a telephone call at the Shore Galley. It was the captain of the *Mermaid*.

"I'm really sorry to have to make this call," he said in a hushed voice. "Your brother was in an accident. We were pullin' lines and one of them slipped off the roller."

"He's OK, right?" I said with a sinking feeling in my stomach.

A stillness settled over the phone line. "I'm sorry," said the captain. "We did everything we could, but he didn't make it."

The stillness turned into the silence of death. "We'll pay to have his body flown back to Aberdeen. Just tell us what funeral home you use."

Bruce's death left me numb for months. I couldn't believe he was gone. I'd be waiting for a phone call from him, a chance to hear his voice and laugh over some raunchy joke or just wish each other a good day, but the call never came again. My world got a lot smaller after that. My world got even smaller today. It felt like a noose was being drawn closer and closer around my neck.

With one last look at my desk, I put on my coat and stepped out into the constant Aberdeen rain. It felt colder and more fierce than usual. Instead of turning right to walk down the street to my usual Friday dinner spot with my friend Connie, I turned left and trudged through the blowing rain to my small apartment. A gray-winged white Caspian tern squawked over my head as it flew towards the harbor. Late to begin its migration south, the tern seemed as lonely and displaced as I felt.

Turning the key to unlock my door, I wondered how long I would be able to pay for the apartment. It wasn't much but it had been my home for nearly five years. There had been many years of living on the road, traveling between clusters of houses along US 101 while I had worked as a waitress. Other years I slept in shambles of an unrentable hotel room while I spent in the day cleaning the rooms rented to beachgoers from Olympia. My pay always came in an envelope. Men came in and out of my life.

My hope for an apartment began nearly six years ago. I had paged through the Aberdeen paper, "The Daily World" and found a small ad at the bottom of the sports section. A boxing center was opening on Simpson Avenue. They needed someone to keep track of the boxers' health insurance records. The hours were slim; not a full-time job, but the ad promised consistent work. I put on the best clothes I had and went downtown to the storefront that had been transformed into the boxing club.

"You must be here all the time. Can you keep careful records? Nothing fancy here. You'll get paid every Wednesday," said the club manager.

I was thankful for the work. I quickly learned the record system on the club computer. My pay envelopes had enough money to create a tiny savings with occasional bonuses that added a growing sense of self-awareness. Every night I spent in the stale studio room I had rented in an old boarding house added to my sense of homelessness. The goal of an apartment became my overarching reason for getting up every day.

One Saturday night, the main bout was between a boxer from Hoquiam and another from the nearby town of Elma. The Elma boxer showed me his medical insurance card, and I made the required notations in the computer file. Turning to the local fighter, I expected to him to hand me his card. Instead, he had a form with a set of numbers on a line as if to indicate an insurance policy had been purchased.

"Do you have anything else to prove your insurance?" I asked.

The fighter shook his head. I laid the form on table. I could hear the crowd starting to get wound up over the scheduled bout.

"I can't take this number without better identification and a real insurance card," I said.

"I'm here to fight, don't get fuzzy over some paperwork," he said with a hiss.

The thundering sound of his fist hitting the table caught the crowd's attention.

"Hey, let him fight!" yelled someone in the crowd.

"I'm sorry. Unless you have a card…" my voice was interrupted by the club manager.

"What's going on, I?" he asked.

"He doesn't have a medical insurance card," I answered.

"Let him fight!" yelled the crowd.

The club manager waved me aside.

"Let's see that form," said the manager. He paused at every line of the form, slowly working his way down the form.

"OK, this will do," he said, looking at the computer system, carefully avoiding the fighter's eyes.

"Go suit up," he said to the boxer.

The crowd shouted their approval. "Fight! Fight!" echoed through the hall.

The manager gave me an angry look and jerked his thumb towards the door.

"No need for you anymore," he in a defiant voice.

I stared at the manager. I was not sure what had happened, but it looked like a crime had just been committed. I sat stiff, barely able to take a breath. The manager closed the computer file and slide the form into the wastebasket.

I reached under the desk and found my purse. I looked around the room again as if it were a foreign place instead of the sense of security I had always felt in that space. Now the crowd seemed cold and distant, their shouts turned inward on the exchange of jabs and hooks to take place once the fighters met in the ring. I heard the bell for the first round sound as I pulled the door open. The damp Aberdeen air quickly surrounded me, filling my lungs with a mist.

The damp air was cold, and smelled of dead fish and boat fuel. Small fishing boats were bobbing at the docks that lined the Wishkah River. Grays Harbor was only a short distance away. The tide must be out, I though. There was no sound of waves or the bumping of driftwood along the embankment. Everything seemed to be out now, even my luck. The dismal damp depilating collapse of my hopes and dreams moved over me like a fog enveloping one of the isolated rock islands off the coast.

"You okay?" ask a male voice from behind me.

The unexpected voice sent a shiver of fear through my body.

Before I had a chance to react, the voice came again, "I saw what happened in there," said the man. "You did the right thing. Too bad you were overruled."

"Well, thanks for the compliment, but now I'm out of a job." I responded.

"How much do you know about medical insurance?" he asked.

"Only what I learned in there, but I enjoyed my work and tried to do a good job."

"I could see that, paying attention to insurance legalities requires a desire to do a good job."

Coming closer, the man stuck out his hand. "Hi, I'm Bob. I own Harbor Insurance."

"Oh, the office downtown on Simpson Street?" asked I.

"Yes," said Bob. "That's right. Do you really need a job now?"

"Yes, I do," I said.

"Well, come by my office on Monday and let's see what we can do."

I stood for a moment. The offer dazed me as much as the club manager's bad behavior.

"Okay, thanks. I'll be there."

On Monday, I put on the best clothes I had, a pair of slim black slacks from Walmart and a white shirt I had left over from my last waitressing job. I added one of two scarves I owned, a blue and yellow checked square that I folded on the diagonal. I wrapped the triangle around my neck hoping the knot at my throat and draping corners would cover up the bits of stain on the blouse collar. I pulled my rather longish blond hair back in a low ponytail and ran a glaze of semi-pink lipstick across my mouth. My grey-blue eyes were a bit brighter next to the blue scarf. A few crowfeet wrinkles crinkled away from my eyes into the margins of my face. I put my nearly empty wallet, a plastic comb and the tube of lipstick into the black purse bought at Goodwill. I looked in the mirror. A tall, attractive middle-aged woman stared back.

"Head up, smile, and believe in me," I said to myself. Walking down the steep flight of stairs from my room to the street, I thought once again how much I wanted my own apartment. I arrived at the office at nine o'clock just as Bob was unlocking the door.

"Here you are already!" he said. He showed me into the office, motioned to the desk closest to the door. "You can start there by greeting people and finding out what type of insurance they are looking for. Send them back to me, and I'll take care of them."

That's how my work at the insurance office began. Every month Bob added another task to my work and eventually, I learned to help people determine their insurance needs. After six months, Bob enrolled me in an on-line class on insurance requirements and legalities. I worked through the class and moved on to the next. Within the year, I took my first exam. When the score came back, Bob grinned. "You did well," he said. My weekly envelope of cash had a bonus in it. Finally, I had enough to make a deposit on a tiny apartment a few blocks away.

The Cove Apartments had been on my radar for the last couple of months. They were located between a tire shop where all the signs were in Spanish, and an abandoned sport fishing shop. The street had once been lined with respectable single-family houses, but over the years the commercial traffic along Simpson Street had spilled into the neighborhood. The Cove stood perpendicular to the street with doors facing the parking lot. A red and white For Rent sign had just appeared on the street. I copied down the phone number scrawled across the bottom of the sign.

The phone rang several times until I wondered if it was all a mistake. I had started to put the receiver back in the cradle when I heard an older woman's voice gasping on the other end of the line.

"Hello," gasped the voice.

"Hello," I responded. "I'm calling about the apartment at The Cove. Is it still available?"

"Oh yes," came a calmer voice. "Sorry, you just caught me shooing a dog away from my yard. He was looking to make my poor Ziggy his next meal."

"Ziggy?" asked I, trying to be polite.

"Ziggy's my turtle, the only kind of pet to have in this wet country. Now, do you want to see the apartment? I can show it to you now if you want."

"I would love to see it now," said I. Optimistic that the apartment was move-in ready, I was anxious to see it as soon as possible.

"I'll be right there. I live just around the corner," said the turtle owner.

I walked to the apartment complex and stood on the street waiting for the woman to arrive. As promised, the woman came from across the parking lot. I wore baggy gray pants and a sweatshirt with "Save Aberdeen Stop the Olympic Wilderness" stitched across the front. I had seen racks of similar sweatshirts around town when I would occasionally buy a used blouse or new scarf to add to my "professional wardrobe." As soon as I had an apartment, I intended to start buying new, more fashionable clothes at JC Penney's.

The woman waved her hand at the last apartment door, furthest from Simpson Street. "This one is the quietest," she said. "The previous tenant got married and bought a house."

"Oh, that's nice," said I.

"I guess," said the woman. "I think she needed a nursery."

The woman unlocked the door and stepped aside to let me enter the apartment.

"It's small but easy to heat and clean," said the woman.

The apartment was typical of those built in the '70's. A small living room across the front of the apartment with a window and door to the parking lot, a narrow kitchen separated from the living room by a tall counter with cabinets above a pass-through space, and refrigerator, sink, and stove all along the back wall. It followed the apartment's interior wall. The hallway led straight back past a small bathroom behind the kitchen wall to a small bedroom. A closet lined the interior wall and a window looked out on an empty yard behind the empty fishing shop next door. All the walls were painted buff white. The living room and bedroom were carpeted in tan, and yellow linoleum covered the kitchen and bathroom floors.

"It's lovely," said I in a soft voice. I turned to the woman with hope in my heart.

"How much is it?"

"Its $450 a month with a $450 deposit. You'll pay your own utilities. There's no laundry but there is a laundromat down the street. If you can pay the deposit and first month's rent, you can have it now."

I stood for a moment, silently thinking through whether I could afford this. Nine hundred dollars was just about all I had. The bonus had pushed up the savings just enough. If I spent it all now, I would have nothing for a rainy day. But every day is a rainy day in Aberdeen, I thought.

"Ok, yes. I do have the money. I can pay for it now."

"Alright, let me go get my lease form and the key," said the woman. "I'll be right back. Don't go anywhere."

"Oh no, don't worry," said I. I'm not going anywhere, I thought to myself.

While the woman trudged out of sight, I walked through the apartment again. This time I noticed the short cream pleated drapes in the living and bedroom, the tiny linen closet tucked into the bathroom, and the double sink in the kitchen. Electric heaters lined the wall below the windows in the living room and bedroom. There's wasn't much daylight in the apartment, but it was always grey in Aberdeen. Ceiling lights would be on all the time anyway. My own bathroom and kitchen, I marveled.

"Here you are," said the woman as she entered the apartment. "Fill out this form, and the apartment is yours."

I filled in my name: Saron Lindquist
Marital Status: Single
Age: 58

Occupation: Insurance clerk

Weekly Pay: $500

I signed the agreement clause to keep the apartment clean and in good shape. I had no one to list as next of kin so I wrote down Bruce's name as my contact person.

"You work at Harbor Insurance?" asked the woman.

"Yes," I responded with a bit of pride in my voice. I pulled an envelope out of my purse and counted out nine one hundred-dollar bills. "I'll pay you in cash, if that's alright."

"It's okay today" said the woman. "Rent is due on the fifth of each month. Please pay with a check next time. Here's the key. I hope you enjoy the apartment. Don't forget to call the PUD and have them put the power in your name."

"Oh, I won't," said I. It would take the last bit of savings, but I would make it. I would have my own place. A dream come true!

I moved my few belongings, mostly clothes and a set of sheets and towels, to the apartment that night. That first wonderful night in my own place was one of the happiest times in my life. Gradually, I furnished the apartment with finds at thrift shops or special sales at the downtown antique stores. I went once a month to Penney's to shop their final sales rack for nice work clothes. Kitchenware came from the Dollar Store as did most of my cleaning supplies and personal needs. Once a week I went to Safeway for food and anything else I needed. Occasionally, I splurged on a woman's magazine or bought coffee at the adjacent Starbuck's.

Every Friday, Bob gave me an envelope with pay and occasional bonuses. I saved the cash, making sure I had enough money for the rent and utilities. I got used to a dinner out on Friday nights and eventually, a movie or coffee with acquaintances. In the last few months, I had been able to set some money aside in my new bank account. I felt comfortable and sure that my life had taken a turn for the better. I could think about retirement like the people who walked into the insurance office.

But tonight, when Bob had handed me the envelope, everything in my safe and predictable world changed. I still couldn't quite grasp what had happened. I forgot all about my dinner date with Connie. Walking slowly back to the apartment, I felt the old fog of loneliness, doubt and disappointment surround me. Once inside the beige room, I tossed my bag into the easy chair. The nearly empty refrigerator offered only a bottle of beer. Opening it, I headed to the bedroom, crawled into the bed, and pulled the covers up to my arms. It would be a long weekend of sorting out my unemployed life.

Maybe it was time to just stop working. Maybe I'll just retire. I'm old enough to get Social Security, I thought. I'll go on Monday and see. I closed my eyes and tried to remember Bruce's love and encouragement. I really need help this time, Bruce, I whispered into the dark room.

# 2

# ABERDEEN

*T*he weekend was sad and lonely. I went for a long walk on Sunday afternoon desperate to know what Monday would bring at the Social Security office. I had heard only angry and passionate stories from a few clients in Harbor Construction about the detachment and coldness of clerks at Social Security. It was a funny game, people balancing their futures on investments either with the government or with Bob. And here I was, facing my own future based on calculated risks that disappeared like a high tide abandoning Grays Harbor.

I walked through Aberdeen to Morrison Park along the Chehalis River. The Chehalis River began its merger with tidal water at this point. From Morrison Park, on the north side of the river, I could see the large river channel from the massive Weyerhaeuser sawmill and processing plant at Cosmopolis to just beyond the US 101 bridge that spanned the river in Aberdeen. The area on the southeast end of the bridge was dedicated as a National Historic Seaport. The dock was used by the *Lady Washington*, a tall ship that called Aberdeen its home port. When she wasn't in Aberdeen, the *Lady Washington* was sailing on the Pacific, sometimes as part of movie sets. She had been in "Pirates of the Caribbean." Her sailors tended to stick together, dressed in period costumes. Some townspeople thought they were real pirates. I knew they were.

There were three other large rivers that entered the estuary, the Wishkah where the inter-harbor fishing boats tied up, the Hoquiam River just west of Aberdeen where ocean-going tugs and fishing boats found moorage, and the Humptulips River that entered the bay west of the City of Hoquiam where only sports fishermen took their boats. The rivers and tides created the eastern end of Grays Harbor. The entire estuary covered ninety-four square miles. When the tide was out, the estuary was a massive mudflat with a narrow channel for the Chehalis River kept open by dredging. In turn, the dredging spoils renewed the mudflats' sediment and hubris. Dead to the casual observer, the mudflats were full of life for the more judicious eyes of shorebirds.

The dredging process created a constant state of renewal, mud brought up from the bottom rebuilt mudflats across the shallow harbor that then slowly eroded away with the tides. It was hard to say what was natural anymore, the old Chehalis channel was lost under decades of mud. Most people thought the mudflats had always been there and did not realize they lived on old mudflats. It was only when a new commercial building was constructed along the bay that people re-learned that nearly everything in Aberdeen was built on soft ground. Forty-foot timbers, twelve inches in diameter had to be pounded into the mud in order to support a new building. Even then, a large truck passing the building would cause the building to shake. After a while, no one noticed the vibration and forgot all about the mud on which they lived.

To me, the mudflats were massive feeding areas for migratory birds. I had learned to identify birds, understand the ecology of the mudflats, and become accustomed to the changing tidal conditions. I had taken a class at the community college taught by two rather crazy faculty members of The Evergreen State College in Olympia. We learned all sorts of things about the natural and political ecology of Grays Harbor. The faculty tried to get us to see that everything was interrelated, dependent upon each other. If one part of the total eco-system failed, other parts would as well.

Looking at the river channel now, I wondered what the failing economy would do to the channel and the mudflats. A black bobbing head, floating up and down with the river current caught my attention. White-speckled black wings were folded against a white body. The white speckled black beak and white eyes helped form my opinion that it was a common goldeneye duck. The duck dove into the water, searching for a snail or mollusk on the river bottom. The duck was as dependent on mud as we who lived along the river.

At one class meeting, an ornithologist from the Olympia campus came and spoke about the significance of the mudflats for migratory birds. He talked a lot about the fact that the presence of peregrine falcons had required Washington state biologists to work with the federal government biologists to protect the basin as habitat for the falcon. The peregrine falcon was identified by the federal government as a threatened and endangered species. With the urging of the ornithologist, the basin mudflats and surrounding alder groves, the falcon's habitat, had been set aside as a wildlife refuge to be managed by the US Fish and Wildlife Service. The ornithologist then told us some stories about how the residents of Aberdeen and Hoquiam had tried to stop the basin from being designated as a wildlife refuge. "But we won!" he had said with great gusto. After he spoke, we went on a field trip to Bowerman Basin on the west end of the bay. The ornithologist taught us how to keep a field journal and document the wildlife especially the migratory birds we observed. I loved the challenge of seeing new birds and documenting them in my field journal.

I tried to tell Bob how excited I was about what I was learning in the class.

"Evergreen State?" he asked. "I wouldn't spread that around if I were you. I do not want people thinking we are some sort of radicals.

We need to buy cheap lumber, not promote the environment."

After that, I kept what I learned about the history and ecology of the bay to myself. I learned to identify the birds around the bay and keep field notes. I tried to practice naming birds on my walks, but eventually lost interest and the self-discipline to keep notes. Who would read them anyway? I wondered.

The class included a history of the Grays Harbor and the surrounding area. I loved learning how the harbor was named by the British explorer George Vancouver for Captain John Gray, an American explorer who had seen the bay while sailing up the West Coast. The beauty of the bay and the ability to see Mount Rainier on the eastern horizon had given Vancouver hope for the elusive Northwest Passage. Vancouver had sailed into the bay just far enough to see that it was not navigable during low tide. Gray had bypassed the bay and sailed further north. He anchored off the Quinault River near an Indian village named Taholah. Here he and his crew went ashore for supplies. They stayed long enough to meet some of the Indians who called themselves Quinault. Gray named a nearby river after the Indians.

Remembering the class and how much I loved birdwatching distracted me enough to stop worrying about my current situation. Everything had to go well at the Social Security office on Monday, I told myself. I would find the money to pay for the apartment and enjoy the benefits of retirement everyone talked about. I could spend time birdwatching, I thought.

Monday morning arrived after a sleepless night. I spent half the night starring at Bruce's photo, searching for a message of reassurance. Twisting round and round in my sheets, I spent the other half in denial, sure that I would wake from a bad dream. Between search for a paranormal message and an alternative reality, I managed to convince myself that Monday was federal holiday and I had it off. Tuesday would be back to normal.

I faced reality at 8am, got up and showered, drank a cup of coffee over the kitchen sink, and turned to face the door to my apartment. Coat on, I grabbed my bag from where I had tossed it last night and took a deep breath. One way or another, today held my future.

The Social Security office was in a strip mall in Hoquiam. I took a number at the door and waited my turn. The room was about half full of older men wearing worn brown Carhart jackets and faded blue jeans. Others in the room were a mix of younger women trying to keep track of toddlers and anxious looking newly married young women hoping to claim their new name and legal status. After a 54-minute wait, my number was finally called.

"How can I help you?" barked the clerk from behind the counter.

"I think I want to retire and collect my Social Security," said I with a bit of embarrassment in my voice.

"Number?" barked the clerk. "What's your Social Security number?"

I pulled out my card and gave it to him. He looked at the card and typed in the nine-digit number into the computer. He watched the screen filter through the stored data. His face began to turn cross, wrinkle lines protruded from his nose, and his eyes began to squint at the screen.

"Have you been working?" he asked me in a cheerless voice.

"Yes, I have been working at Harbor Construction for five years and before that," I hesitated. "I worked at the Bullring. Before that, well, restaurants and motels."

"Well, according to this, you haven't gotten a paycheck or earned Social Security benefits since 1993. You've only earned $329.00 in monthly benefits."

"But how can that be? I got paid every week..." my voice trailed off.

"You must have gotten paid in cash because there's no record of any recent employer paying into your account. Here, fill out this form to start receiving the bit you have earned. It will take a month to have the first check deposited into your bank account."

I was stunned. It took all my energy to turn away from the counter, form in hand, and drag myself back to the chair where I had been sitting. I sat down, feeling like the lump I surely looked like. 'How would I survive?' I wondered.

"Okay?" asked a voice beside me. A bit surprised, I looked at the source of a voice, a slight middle-aged man with dark hair and a strong chiseled face. He wore baggy blue jeans that needed to be washed, an old woolen shirt, and a pair of well-worn work boots. "It can be a little depressing here. I bet you just got some bad news."

His voice was wry but kind. I slowly turned to face him. He attempted a smile. "It's always bad news here," he said again.

"I guess I really didn't know what to expect," I said in a quiet voice. "I thought I was going to get enough Social Security to live on, but I guess not."

"It happens to all of us," he said. "I keep hoping for some disability, but it just never works out. Always one more form, one more doctor's appointment, one more 'No.'"

He looked straight at me with kindness in his eyes. "Hang in there, kid, we all keep hoping."

The man at the counter yelled again. "Gray Quinn"

"That's me," he said. "See you around."

Gray got up with a bit of a struggle. I noticed his need to hold on to the arm of the chair while raising his tall thin frame. He had a bit of a shake in his walk to the counter.

"Okay, Quinn, what's your story?" said the clerk.

"Okay," said Gray in a patient voice. "I'll tell it one more time."

Gray reached back into his memory of the day his life was altered forever. To tell the story of the day's events, and all the pain that had followed, was like opening a plane's black box from a crash site. When the box was opened, the stench of decaying human flesh emerged like a mushroom cloud. The beat-up old box held shreds of red and black plaid flannel, fir tree needles, a prescription for a pain killer, cigarette butts, and beer bottle caps. Underneath all the odd bits of a destroyed identity was a tribal identification card. Gray Quinn, Member of the Quinault Indian Nation. Date of birth: May 23, 1960. Everything else was washed out from sweat and years of collected dampness. On a piece of first aid tape pasted on the bottom of the card was a name. "Aggie Quinn – Grandmother," it read.

The box also held a hard and difficult story to tell. Noisy vibrations of chain saws, log trucks, and men's voices that brought Gray back to a brutal day. He heard again the slow sputtering sounds of bark wrenched from timber became a creaking, groaning sound of ripping tree trunk that became a crescendo of splintering fir stem. Gray heard the gravelly shout from the machinery operator below him on the steep slope.

"Watch out! It's coming down on you!"

Darkness and silence descended on Gray. While his fellow crew-members called down the mountain for support and medical attention, Gray passed into another world where his body became numb to the weight of the top twenty feet of the tree struck him across his right shoulder. His arms flared out before him as he was slammed into the serrated edges of the sword ferns that covered the moist, dank ground. The tree trunk rolled to one side, leaving rigid fir needles and prickly branches to cover his limp body. Blood slowly began to drain from his mouth.

The machine operator swung the cab of the tree snipper around. Gray lay out-of-sight, entombed in tree limbs and slash left behind by the machine. The operator slammed the gears of the snipper into a lock and hold position. Idle, the massive claws hung like a beetle's attack pincers. The operator turned off the diesel engine. Silence, already a part of Gray's deafened consciousness, filled the rest of the forest. The operator unzipped his stained nylon vest and fumbled through a big piece of pocket in his plaid flannel shirt. Finally, he found the company issued cell phone to be used only in emergencies. The connection was not good, only one filled hole in the five that indicated full reception.

"Hello," he yelled into the phone. "Quinn's down. Hit by the top of a tree. Can you come and get him?"

"Is he Okay?" yelled the receiver on the other end of the call back to the snipper.

"He's not moving, just down on the ground. Better send the helicopter, we're way up north on Burnt Hill."

"I'll call the company office. Try to figure out your exact location."

Time stood still for Gray. For the machine operator, the dispatcher, the company office, the emergency response team, and the helicopter pilot and medic, time sped by. Every second was another drip of blood out of Gray's body. His exact injuries were unknown. Not knowing the extent of the damage done by the falling tree, the medical support system in Aberdeen could only prepare for the worst and hope for the best.

When the helicopter arrived at Burnt Hill, the only possible way to rescue Gray was to lower a stretcher to the ground. The machine operator rolled his body on to the stretcher and the pilot hit the Up button on the cable roll. Once inside the helicopter, the medic slowly felt Gray's body. Bones that should have been connected were either broken or disconnected. Blood continued to ooze out of his mouth indicating punctured organs and internal hemorrhaging. The medic eased a painkiller into Gray's arm. Morphine surged into Gray's bloodstream, numbing nerves and further dimming Gray's touch with the real world.

"Let's get him to the hospital," he shouted.

The pilot turned the helicopter and started the flight back to Aberdeen. He had seen too many of these logging accidents to have much faith that Gray would survive the flight. Still, he took the shortest route he could back to the landing pad at the Aberdeen Community

District Hospital. He pushed the helicopter forward, flying just above the treetops. When the helicopter crossed the boundary between the second-growth forests and recent clear-cuts, the pilot had to fight to keep the helicopter heading south against the wind gusts. Knowing that larger birds sought refuge in the few isolated "wildlife trees" left in random spots across the clear cuts, the pilot edged his craft away from the spars. The medic loaded another syringe of morphine in case Gray regained consciousness.

Gray entered the dark coma of unconsciousness and remained there for eight days. When he opened his eyes, all he could see was white. White walls, white drapes around his bed, white lab-coated doctors, and white tubes that connected his body to white machines with blue flashing lights. He watched silently while a nurse changed a bag of fluid draped between the white tubes.

The nurse looked into his eyes. "Welcome back," she said sweetly.

A doctor arrived at his bedside soon after the nurse left the room. The doctor looked carefully into Gray's eyes.

"Can you hear me?" he asked. "If you can, blink your eyes."

Gray blinked his eyes.

"You've been in a bad accident. You have several broken bones and internal damage. I'm afraid you will be here for a while. Are you in pain?"

Gray blinked his eyes again.

"I'll take care of that," said the doctor in a matter of fact way. "We'll make sure you don't experience pain."

Gray slipped back into a thick sleep. The seemingly endless days in the hospital were filled with memories of sleep, painkillers, and tubes tied to machines that kept him alive. The story merged into a reality that seemed to repeat itself daily. Gray's life had never been the same since the accident.

"Then I slowly got to physical therapy," Gray said, returning to the man behind the counter. "But I can't work. I need disability."

The man behind the counter handed Gray a set of forms. "Fill these out," he barked.

"I already did this," said Gray.

"Well, do it again," he said. "I don't have a record of them."

Gray went back to his chair and starred at the forms. I watched him a bottle of prescription pain killers from his pocket and slam several into his mouth. His shoulders sagged as he worked on the forms.

I sat for a minute, taking in Gray's apparent resignation in having to deal with un-ending forms and his use of pills to face them made my reality of poverty even more desperate. I walked back to the apartment in a daze.

# 3

# PIRATES

*W*hen I got back to the apartment, I found a note from Connie tucked into the door. You alright? Read the note. Missed you last night. I closed the note, unlocked the door and collapsed into the chair. Would I have to give up my friends? Would they give up on me once they knew I had not much to live on? Aloneness and homelessness were everything I had hoped to avoid, and here they were, alive and well surrounding me like Halloween witches. The dark side of life in Gray's Harbor was sucking me into its deadly ways. I doubted Connie could throw me a life line now, although she once had.

I got to know Connie when I worked at the Shore Galley in Westport. We waited tables during the same shift. When tables needed to be cleared especially after a large group or families with more than one screaming kid, we helped each other as much as possible. Sometimes we tried to make a game of it, seeing who could fill the dish bin the fastest. The spring beach days had brought more families out than usual. I doubted I would get a break long enough to go for a short walk in the June sunshine.

"On to the next, you wench," cried my dark-haired partner.

"You make this so much fun," I said. "As if we are pirates hunting for gold on a desert island on these wretched tables."

"I am a pirate," said Connie.

"What?" said I. "You're not a pirate. There aren't women pirates. There aren't any pirates anyway."

"No?" said Connie with a shit-eating grin. "Yes, there are, right here in Grays Harbor. I sail on *Maiden's Curse.*

"Sail? What does that mean?" I looked askance. Was this for real? I thought. Maybe this was one of Connie's tricks to make the work go faster.

"I'm a member of *Maiden's Curse* crew. We sail the ship under Captain Ham. We're sailing this weekend here in Westport for the Pirate Daze Festival. If you're interested, why don't you come along? We always need another crewmember during the festival."

"What will I do?" I asked.

"It's a tall ship. That means old-fashioned sailing ship. You'll help with the sails, wind ropes, polish the wood. Except we're pirates, and we really don't care about the gleam of the trim. We care more about sneaking up on *Lady Washington* when she's in port. Captain Ham says we'll own that ship someday. Arrrrgh!" Connie said with a mischievous look.

"I guess that sounds like fun," I ventured.

"Fun?! It way beats the heck out of sitting in taverns in these beach towns," stated Connie. "Meet me at the Westport marina on Saturday. Be prepared to sail, no matter what the weather. And be prepared to save your maiden virtues below deck, if you know what I mean." She winked and I giggled.

"Okay," said I in a brave voice. "I'll be there."

As directed by Connie, I was at the Westport marina early Saturday morning. I dressed for wind and weather. My clothes included warm leggings under rain pants, a low-cut ruffled blouse under a tight-fitting wool sweater, tall rubber boots, and a brimmed rain hat. I carried a leather backpack I had bought at a garage sale a while back. I thought it would come in handy for something but had no idea it would be the ideal bag for impersonating a woman pirate.

Large ocean-going fishing boats down from Alaska and the north Pacific were tied up on the southern end of the marina. Charter fishing boats that ran out Grays Harbor out to the edge of the continental shelf were tied up along the docks open to the public. On the north end of the marina were private boats, half cruisers and half sailboats capable of crossing the Pacific or sailing down the coast to Mexico for the winter.

The sight that attracted the most attention today was *Maiden's Curse*, a seventy-five foot two-mast ship with a thirty-foot cabin between the masts. A bridge stood above the cabin toward the stern. The ship was painted black to its keel and brilliant blue from the keel to the deck. The deck was the same blue as well as the two masts and crow's nest on each mast. The bow was extended with a bust of a woman, the cursed maiden. She was painted wearing a bright green low-cut blouse. Fiery red hair surrounded her pink face. Dark green eyes looked out over the sea before her. A gold amulet was draped around her neck, and large round bangles hung beneath her earlobes. She carried an air of defiance that created a shroud of mystery. Seeing the ship for the first time created a sense of adventure with a high dose of fear for the observer. I was aware that I felt the dual emotions of erotic passion and pathological fear.

*Maiden's Curse* was tied up along the seawall, bow set toward the channel, away from the marina as if ready to leave at a moment's notice. Her gangplank bridged the ship to seawall, the tide held them at the same height for the moment. A crowd had developed around the gangplank, hoping to get a taste of pirate life and grog. I headed toward the ship, hoping to find Connie.

"Keep back!" scowled a pirate. "We've got business here. We're in port for a reason, and it ain't to be nice to a bunch of landlubbers like yourselves!" he yelled. The crowd booed and the pirate reached for his knife.

"Enough, matey," came a booming voice from the bridge. "Leave them alone. We'll be goin' to sea soon and show 'em the work of a pirate ship. *Lady Washington* has been spotted tied up to her dock at the Seaport. She will be sailing down the channel this morning. We'll see how far she makes it," bellowed the voice.

I scanned the bridge to find the source of the voice. Standing on the bridge, his hands at his waist, was a white-shirted, bearded man. He towered over the bridge. Black breaches and heeled boots gave his figure an air of authority. His wide leather belt held a gold-studded knife in his waistcoat. His demeanor made it clear that using the knife was a common thing to him, it backed up his capacity to control the ship, the crew and the crowd.

Standing next to him was a woman, dark hair billowing behind her in the wind. Her ruffled blouse, while of the same cut as the bearded man, hung loosely about her shoulders and gapped to reveal a pushed-up bosom of some size. She wore red breaches, heeled black boots, and gold chains around her neck and arms. In her hair were bright feathers and large gold hoops hung from her ears. Her stance seemed familiar to me. From where did I know this person? I gasped with I realized it was Connie.

At the same time, Connie recognized me. She swung her head, with all its billowing hair and gold trappings, around to whisper to the bearded man. Together, they engaged me with their piercing eyes. The crowd followed their gaze and those around me stepped back.

"You're ours!" cried the giant captain. Three bearded, booted pirates bounded off the ship into the crowd and took me by each arm. "It's a pirate's life for you, missy!" yelled the leader of the trio. They picked me up and ran through the crowd, over the gangplank and dropped me to the deck of the ship. "Welcome to *Maiden's Curse*, you wench."

Was it a game or was it for real? I wondered. Whatever it was, it was fun and different, and much more exciting than another day in dull Aberdeen. Without any further questions about responsibilities or schedules, I joined in the work on board. I loved the sailing and comradery of the crew in *Maiden's Curse*. We acted out the roles of pirates, answered questions from kids in our best pirate voices, took part in some antics that fulfilled everyone's dream of pirate life, and drank gallons of grog, some flavored water and some bad rum.

We set sail with the incoming tide. Captain Ham put the ship into the channel and headed upstream toward Aberdeen. There were other ships in the channel including a car carrier waiting to go out with the tide and a freighter loaded with wood chips also waiting to maneuver out of the harbor. *Maiden's Curse* was dwarfed beside each of the ocean-going vessels. Their crews came to the edge of each respective ship and waved down at the sails and sailors on the deck of *Curse*. The freighter blew its horn as we edged past it.

We zigged and zagged from one side of the channel to the other as we went further inland. From the ship's deck, the bay seemed immense. Shallows were marked with buoys and huge cedar trees that were anchored to the floor of the bay. Islands not visible from the shore stretched out along the channel. Captain Ham steered the ship further inland until we neared the arc of the US 101 bridge that marked the end of the bay and the entrance to the fast-flowing Chehalis River.

The tide lost its power in opposition to the river's volume of water that was headed out through the channel and entrance to the harbor. The river's course was marked by the high levels of sediment it carried down from Mount Rainier and through its watershed. So much logging, land clearing, and pasture grazing along the river's course had led to erosion. Flooding was a common spring event. Water levels this spring had been high with near breaching of the sea walls along the Aberdeen shore.

*Lady Washington* was tied up at her dock just inside the 101 bridge. There was a lot of activity on the dock beside her. From *Maiden's Curse* position in the channel, it looked like the Lady was getting ready to take out a large group of school aged children.

"Arg," bellowed the captain. "We won't be taking hostages today. Turn this tub around. We'll wait for another time to take *Lady*."

At this point, *Lady Washington* fired her starboard cannon. The plastic 'shot' fell about 100 feet from her deck, into the middle of the river.

"She thinks that will scare us?" laughed Captain Ham. "Pull those sails, you maidens!"

*Maiden's Curse* turned slowly to face the harbor. The river's current pushed us past Aberdeen's old docks and boat ramps. Finally, the wind caught our sails. Captain Hamundarson commanded the crew to hoist or drop the sails as needed to tack against the still incoming tide. We made our way back to Westport and the festival.

Connie looked convincing in her costume. There were other pirates on board that I thought I recognized from Aberdeen, but I wasn't sure given their costumes and jovial antics. By the time we got back to port, I was tired. All the work of sailing in the wind plus learning so many new things had worn me out.

"You're not headed home are yea?" yelled Connie. "There's lots more to do tonight."

"Okay," I said with a bit of disbelief in my voice.

"Let's go walk through the vendors and get you some more pirate gear," said Connie. "You could use a skirt and maybe a leather belt. And then we can get some grub and watch some belly dancing."

Connie ran up the gang plank and met me on the dock. She slid her arm through mine at the elbow and nearly pulled me along. "It's great that you want to be a pirate," she said. "There's lots more than just playing at the docks. We go for longer sails in the harbor. Sometimes Captain Ham gets a bit of work for us. It helps pay for the upkeep on *Maiden's Curse*. We usually call him Captain Ham when he's not around," she whispered.

"What do I have to do to become a member of the crew?" I asked.

"I'll nominate you at the next meeting and we'll all vote. The fact that you worked so well on the ship today will make it easy to vote you in. Then there's a monthly membership fee, not much. You can afford it. Besides, where else will you get so much fun for so little?" she said.

Connie pulled me along through the vendor shops. I bought a billowing black skirt and a couple of sashes. The leather belt was too expensive for my budget.

"You need a hat, too," said Connie. She plopped a three-corner hat on my head. "You look great! I'll find you a feather for the hat."

We stopped at a vendor for some beans and a tough piece of meat. We headed to the tent that admitted everyone over twenty-one and ordered beers to go with our food. Other pirates in various costumes came into the tent. Several red-panted, black vested men came and sat at our table.

"You must be from *Maiden's Curse*," one growled at us.

"We are," stated Connie. "Any problems with that?" she growled back.

"Only if you think you can take up this whole table," hissed another vested pirate.

"Hey," said one of the pirates from *Maiden's Curse*. "Leave them alone."

"Oh, we like to eat with the ladies," sang out another vested pirate.

"Is that so?" yelled another *Maiden's Curse* crewmember. "We'll see about that."

Connie grabbed my arm. With a wink and a gentle pull, she said, "We better get out of the way. They are all going to have some fun. They're just play-actin' for everyone."

We left the tent just in time to hear some shuffling of feet. I looked back to see two pirate groups squared off over the table where we had been sitting. The yelling grew quieter as Connie and I walked past more vendors.

"Are you going to stay for the dancing?" Connie asked.

"Maybe not tonight," I said. "This has been a super fun day, but I think I'm worn out."

"Okay," said Connie in a friendly tone. "I'll nominate you at the next meeting. Start thinking of yourself as a pirate. Captain Ham expects us to be fit and ready to sail any time of the day. There is always some reason to be putting *Maiden's Curse* under sail. You'll see."

That was my first day as a pirate. Connie stayed true to her word. I was voted in as a full member of *Maiden's Curse* crew. I paid my monthly dues and kept my pirate garb ready to sail whenever Connie called. I started attending the bi-monthly meetings and meeting more pirates' sans costumes. I was right, I recognized many of the pirates as leading businesspeople in Aberdeen and Hoquiam. The pharmacist at the Hoquiam Rite-Aid was a member, one of the firemen from the fire station in downtown Aberdeen participated, and a grocery store manager I knew from shopping at Safeway was a member of the crew. Over time, I became more familiar to them as well and we would greet each other on the street or in shops downtown.

After Pirate Daze and my formal membership, I felt more and more comfortable on *Maiden's Curse*. I volunteered for every sail. Some days were easy, others a bit more work to follow Capt. Ham's demanding voice. It took a strong wind to carry *Curse* through Grays Harbor, under the span of the 101 bridge, and into the main channel of the Chehalis River. A sail back to home port at Westport was much easier. The river had a powerful current that would carry *Maiden's Curse* back out into the harbor, they just had to tack and get the ship turned around. Capt. Ham called out the sailing orders and the crew pulled hard on the mainsail. The ship came around, the crew steadied the sails. I watched the shoreline in between orders from the captain.

Sailing downstream in the Chehalis channel, Aberdeen passed by them on the north side of the ship. Most people in Aberdeen had no idea that there were old docks, landing sites, abandoned piers, and half sunk loading docks along the waterfront. The waterfront exposed the older buildings, most of them abandoned. Streets led into the older route of US 30. I could imagine barges and tugs pulling up to the old docks, their cargo unloaded and sorted for truck transport to places along the old highway.

Just past the old docks, the Port of Grays Harbor had begun to build newer facilities. The story went that a large cargo ship was fighting to stay afloat off the coast during a bad storm. They radioed the Port and asked if they could enter the harbor and find safe moorage. They needed repairs and wanted to unload their cargo. Grays Harbor was not known as an international seaport, so the captain did not have much hope for the safe moorage, but something had to be done. Amazingly, the Port dispatcher replied that there was good moorage if the ship stayed in the Chehalis channel. A tug was being dispatched to tow the ship up the channel once it crossed the harbor bar. The captain managed to get the crippled ship over the bar and the tug pulled them to a moorage off Aberdeen. With that simple act, the last international port on the West Coast was rediscovered.

As I sailed up and down the harbor on *Maiden's Curse*, I imagined seeing the ghosts of earlier pirates. Whispers of hidden treasure, silent meetings between pirates and carriers of contraband goods and stolen Indian slaves, and raiding parties swirled around sailors aboard ship. There was enough evidence in ship's logs and diaries to believe that Sir Francis Drake had at least approached the entrance to the big bay. Drake, although sanctioned by Queen Elizabeth I to claim territory and bounty for England, was also a menacing pirate who filled his ship's hold with furs, captured slaves, and terrorized indigenous populations. Indigenous tales told of Chinese pirates who had also made themselves known along the coastline.

Captain Ham was equal to the stories of ruthless pirate captains. He kept a stern lip and barked orders to the crew.

"Keep your eyes on the water," he would yell. The crew scattered back to their positions along the ropes. I followed orders and kept her portion of the deck tidy, ropes neatly coiled below the sail rigging.

One afternoon, Captain Ham called me at the insurance office. "We need you to crew this afternoon," he barked. "Cooper can't make it and we have to be out on the water. Be at the Westport dock at six o'clock." The line went dead before I could respond.

I left the office at 4:30, saying I had an appointment in town. Once out of the office, I strode to my apartment, pulled off my dress and redressed in a pirate costume. At the last minute, I grabbed a wool sweater. It seemed a good idea against the possibility of sailing after dark. They had never sailed past dusk before, I was not sure what the evening schedule was going to be. I boarded the five o'clock bus for Westport sure that I would arrive in time to meet ship.

At five forty-five, I exited the bus at the Westport dock where Maiden's Curse was tied up. I waved at a smaller group of fellow crew-members that usually went out on a cruise. There were three men that I did not recognize. Capt. Ham started giving sailing orders. The usual group meeting before a leisurely sail was not held; instead, the men and I took our positions on the deck and waited for orders from the helm.

Captain Ham ordered the ropes that tied the ship to the dock to be undone. The ship turned away from the dock under motor power and inched its way out of the Westport marina. We glided past large fishing boats that worked in the Alaskan fishery, smaller fishing boats used by the charter fishermen, and pleasure boats and sailboats that docked in the marina. No one said where Maiden's Curse was bound or what the sailing schedule was. The other crewmembers seemed to be intent on their work as if they knew.

Once out of the marina, Maiden's Curse hoisted her sails and started a slow tact across the main channel. I could see the long sandy arm of Damon Point curling out into the bay from the north shore. A group of coots bobbed in the water, their white beaks acting like beacons against the dark blue water. A narrow entrance to an empty marina became where the point connected to the mainland at Ocean Shores, the town that had developed on the sand spit. A faded sign with some lettering was posted at the rocky edge of the marina entrance. The words "Welcome to the Quinault Nation" were barely visible. The word Lekmaltch was also on the sign, but I did not know what it meant.

"How odd," I thought. "I don't know why we are here."

Following the captain's orders, Maiden's Curse nudged into the first slip. There was barely enough light to see the dock. It was not until we were alongside the dock with lines cast overboard that I saw two men with large plastic bins on the slip. As soon as the ship was tied up, the wooden gangplank was lowered to the slip and the men carried the bins up to the deck. The men struggled with each bin as if they were heavy. Once on board, the bins were covered with an old piece of canvas. The men returned to the slip and the captain ordered the gangplank pulled back on board. The whole operation took only fifteen minutes. Maiden's Curse powered away from the slip using a motor I did not know she had. We slipped out of the marina. No one had seen us sail in and out of the marina. The wind caught the ship's sails and we glided back across the harbor back to the dock at Westport

While crossing the gangplank to the dock I heard Captain Ham say to another pirate, "That will pay your month's dues." I wondered if that would be true for me as well. It would be a welcomed relief to my slim budget.

"Don't go talking about this evening to anyone, Missy," I heard Captain Ham yell.

I turned and saluted. "Aye, aye, Sir," I yelled back. If this was a way to make a little bit more cash, I was not going to complain if this extra-legal work paid my pirate dues. I did not want to drop out of the pirate crew. But it was odd, whatever cargo we had just delivered to an abandoned marina. I looked back at the marina as we sailed back into the main channel. The sky began to turn with the approaching dusk. We had to get back across the bay to our berth at Westport.

# 4

# MAIDEN'S CURSE

*Maiden's Curse's* suspicious trip might have appeared to have gone un-noticed, but in fact, there was an observer. Gray Quinn and an old childhood friend, Roger, were sitting down among some rocks fishing. They had come to the old marina to fish for salmon. In Quinault tradition, the fish were more easily caught in a moonless sky. Both men had learned these traditions from their Quinault families. As a boy with no real father to train him, Gray's granny had taken him fishing and taught him the old ways.

Watching *Maiden's Curse* slip into the old marina, laden with plain brown boxes, and sail back across the bay, the two men knew something wasn't quite right. A group of noisy coots raised out of the water in the ship's wake as if to confirm the men's suspicion.

"That must be some good stuff," said Roger with a wry smile. "We'll have to keep our eyes on that ship. It tied up either at old Randolph's fishing dock or out at Westport. They must take being pirates pretty serious."

Old Randolph was a shirttail relative of Roger's. The Randolph fishing dock was on the bay between Hoquiam and the Bowerman Airport on Moon Island. Piles of old lumber, sawmill equipment, and abandoned fishing boats created a jungle around Randolph's weather-beaten gray house. Tidal changes exposed the mudflats under the house twice a day. Rotting old docks lined the shore on either side of the house. *Maiden's Curse* could tie up at the dock during high tide or when storms flooded the mudflats.

Gray pulled his fishing rod up and tried to give the line a bit of play.

"You're welcome to keep an eye on the ship," he said. "I'm not so interested."

"You givin' up the path to a quick fortune?" asked Roger with a sly grin.

"I'll give Granny some peace. She's not doing so well," Gray answered.

"Yeah, I hear she's pretty sick and staying close to home at Taholah," said Roger. "Indian Health Service isn't doing much for anyone up there."

"Same old story," Gray said with disgust. As far as he was concerned the federal government was always making promises to the Quinault but never keeping them.

Gray started thinking about all the times Quinault Nation members who lived up at Taholah had asked for help. They needed better schools, paved roads, emergency care, and fire protection. It always seemed to take a long time for the US government to respond. The Nation offered some help, but they weren't as rich as some people would think. The casino at Ocean Shores was starting to make a difference, but there were so many needs everywhere on the reservation.

"You going to go up and see your granny?" asked Roger.

"Maybe," Gray replied. "You know I'm not welcome up there."

"They still mad at you for not seeing your father?" asked Roger.

"Yeah. I guess they expect us to go see wife beaters, even when they're in the state prison over at Walla Walla. I'm not going over there," said Gray.

"Well, good luck helping your granny," said Roger.

"I was hoping she could help me. I'm not having any luck finding a job, it's getting difficult to pay for prescriptions and eat," Gray said. After a while he added, "Once Granny's gone, so am I. I won't be going to Taholah anymore." After another silence he said, "Or anything else tribal."

"You can't stop being a Quinault," said Roger. "Let's get out of here before it gets any darker. That ship has spooked the fish."

"Naw," said Gray. "I bet old sasquatch Gee Keek has fished out this spot."

"Don't say that," said Roger. "He could still be around these woods." There was a bit of apprehension in Roger's voice as he looked around. "I wouldn't be surprised. They can be anywhere."

About a week later, Gray heard his granny had died. Roger told him when tribal members were gathering to help her soul travel to the next world. He couldn't bring himself to make the fifty-mile trip north to the old Indian town. He didn't want to make his granny's soul suffer in its journey to the next world. He knew his granny loved him. He went and sat by the water near Randolph's dock. A flock of common murre flew at him, then they circled back toward him. The murre turned in unison from side to side revealing their white bodies and then their black heads and backs. It was a moment of suspended joy to see them rotating in unison. At the last possible moment, they turned and flew out to sea. Granny must be taking up residence out on one of the bird islands off the coast, Gray thought. He watched the birds until they were black dots against the blue sky.

Gray looked out over the shallow mudflats and across the channel to the hills that lined the southern side of the bay. On one of the hills was a tall painted water tower. The tower, Gray knew, was part of the Stafford Creek Correction Center. Gray knew some of the prisoners held at Stafford. He went there occasionally, to visit old friends, people he had met while working in the woods. There were a few friends from his detention days at Naselle Youth Camp down the coast at

Willapa Bay.

One of his friends behind bars was working on a project to grow frogs that could be released down in Oregon. It was all part of some larger project that was supposed to make the prison and the inmates familiar with sustainability, whatever that was. His friend told him about listening to lectures from Evergreen State College faculty. Gray didn't quite understand it all. But if people were into the projects, he was happy for them. There was not much else to bring happiness to the life of an inmate.

Looking across the bay, Gray could also see the entrance to the Elk River estuary. The mouth of Elk River was a rich oyster producing area. The marsh and river just inland from the bay were abundant with all types of fish and marsh plants. Gray remembered a day his granny had taken him there to gather reeds. They also found several plants that Granny collected for her medicine bag. Gray remembered a lot from that day, what plants were good to collect, what plants could only be collected at a certain time of the year, and what plants never to collect. One day, while he and Granny were collecting some plants, a guy with an Evergreen baseball cap on approached them. Granny didn't want to talk to him. "They're always looking over an Indian's shoulder," she said. "Too many wannabes out here."

Elk River entered the harbor at a place known as Bay City. The Elk River estuary met South Bay, a bay within the harbor. Two narrow strips of land reached towards each other at the point where the estuary and South Bay met. From 1911 to 1925, the American Pacific Whaling Company had operated a large whale processing facility. Between two and three hundred humpback, finback, and sperm whales had been flensed during the years of plant operation. The whales were harpooned in the ocean, pulled by ship over the bar at the harbor's entrance, and brought to Bay City for processing. Now all that remained of the plant were a few piers from the old docks. Today, an oyster company operated at the site.

Gray and his granny had often parked Gray's old pickup, which he didn't own anymore, below the bridge that connected the strips of land. Granny shivered every time they went there. "Whale spirits," was all that she would say. Perhaps in the afterworld, Granny would find the spirits of the all whales killed and torn apart at the whaling station. Gray's arthritic pain seemed worse when he thought of her. He took another painkiller to try and forget his sadness. Without Granny, he was all alone.

Gray took the city bus that ran out to Westport one day in early October. He got off at the stop by the Elk River estuary and went down to the water. He felt closer to his granny. He sat for a long while, remembering her stories and always her reminder that the Quinault owned the bay.

Looking out across the bay to Lekmaltch's rock, Gray began to detect some movement out in the bay that he couldn't quite make out. Reflections off the shallow water especially late in the afternoon could make any object of the water look like a ghost ship. He watched intently, hoping to get a clue as to what was moving on the water. The wind caught a sail, and slowly, the *Maiden's Curse* came into view. Gray watched the pirate ship for a while. It was too far away to see anyone on board. He didn't want to know what the pirate ship was really doing out so late in the evening.

Maybe a mystery rum run, Gray thought. He shook his head to himself. It's probably drugs. What else could it be? he wondered.

*Maiden's Curse* left the Westport dock with a minimal crew. Captain Hamundarson was barking orders, sounding especially harsh and in control. The pirate crew bounced looks between themselves. This wasn't an ordinary sail. Something was up. A few sailors looked back at the dock, wishing they hadn't agreed to these "extra sails," as the captain called them.

Captain Ham had started calling me to go out on the extra sails. I was the only woman on the last couple of extra sails, something that worried me. When he couldn't get me on the phone at the insurance office, he left notes on my apartment door telling me when to be out at Westport for a sail. I didn't ask any questions and did as I was told. I had agreed to the sails, always hopeful that by participating, I would get a break on my dues. I desperately wanted to be part of the pirate world, but without my job, I would have to quit.

The sails always happened near dusk, and always with just a few crewmembers. I felt a sense of dread among the crew. We worked silently, as if we had to maintain a high level of security. Captain Ham blurted out orders and continually scanned the shoreline. It looked like we were headed back to the marina on the Ocean Shores side of the bay.

"Trim the sails," barked Captain Ham.

The ship nudged is way across the channel toward the Bowerman Basin mudflats. There was enough tidal water to cover the mudflats, but the tide was going out and the flats would be exposed within an hour. I could see that some of the other pirates were getting nervous. 'We're too close to the mudflats,' I thought.

"Drop the gangplank," yelled the captain.

"But Captain…," responded one of the pirates.

"Drop it, I said," yelled Ham again. Then he turned to me.

"Ok, you wench," he hissed. "You've gotten to know too much about these sails."

"But I've never said a thing to anyone," I gasped in disbelief.

"I'm making sure you never do," hissed Ham again. "Besides that, you haven't been paying your dues. This is what happens when you violate the code. You're not on this crew or any other pirate ship. Walk the plank!"

"What?" said another pirate with the sound of disbelief in his voice.

"Walk the plank! Don't let me catch you around the docks or any-where else on the bay. If I hear one word about you talking to the police or anyone, I'll make sure you don't have a chance to survive," yelled the captain.

He grabbed my arm and pulled me to the base of the plank. The plank extended out over the edge of the hull. At its far end was a mixture of tidewater, mudflats and grasses.

"Get out there and jump," Ham yelled. "We have to get out of here,"

Ham pushed me to the middle of the plank.

"I can't do this," I gasped again.

"You will or it will be worse," Ham said through his teeth. "I'm giving you this warning. If you survive, I don't want to hear from you or about you again. If I do, I'll find another way to see you in the bottom of the harbor."

The crew stood still in their places on the deck. It seemed unbelievable that this was happening.

I turned toward the end of the plank.

"Jump now, and you've got a chance to make it ashore. Wait another second, and you're caught in the mudflats. Now jump!"

I forced my feet forward until I was at the end of the plank. My head was empty, my stomach clenched, my arms hung lifeless. All the blood in my face and heart had drained away. It was a moment of death. I had no recognition of the people or the place around me.

Suddenly there was a sharp bounding on the plank. Captain Ham stood midway between the keel and the end of the plank. He jumped again, and the plank bounced. I lost my balance and fell.

I could feel the cold, mucky water covering my body. I felt my face surrender into the briny liquid. I sank until I felt the oozing mud of the bottom. Instinctively, I pulled my feet up so that I won't be caught in the mud. My arms reached out, responding with a sense of survival, and pulled me back to the surface. My head rose above the surface and I gasped for air.

Captain Ham turned and looked at the crew. "This could happen to you too if you talk. Now get those sails up."

The ship gained momentum and the wind turned the bow toward deeper water. No one on board looked back at me. I watched for a second before a bit of a small branchless log pushed up against me in the water. I grasped on the log, hoping it would keep me out of the mud.

I clung to the log with all my strength. The log wanted to flow out with the tide. I looked around me to see how far I was from shore. It was getting dark and I had no real idea where I was except within Bowerman Basin. I could see the lights from a hangar at the airport that extended out into the basin. To the south of the airport was the bay and the main channel. To the north, the basin was lined by an extensive stand of alder. The mudflats between me and the alder where becoming more exposed as the tide went out. I had to do something fast or I would die in the mud.

Using my free arm and legs, I half swam half crawled toward the shore and the alder grove. The tidal water pulled harder away for the shore as it left the bay. I was close enough to the shore to see a rocky point. Slowly, I pushed my way to the rocks. There was only twilight now, and I couldn't make out much of anything beyond the point. Darkness soon claimed the bit of land and my cold, wet body. Only more darkness in an already dark and disoriented world.

# 5

# SARON'S SHACK

B ay Timber Company started work at six in the morning. Timber fallers dressed in heavy Carhart jeans, held up around their rounded middles with orange and black suspenders emblazoned with LOGGER down the dual fronts began showing up in the company's maintenance shop area by five forty-five. They stood beside their dented and rusted pickup trucks, plastic to-go coffee mugs in hand, yelling ridicule and discontent with a smile at every arrival.

The faller foreman drove through the parking lot in his company pickup. He slowed the pickup down at a spot where the fallers with their lunches, raingear, coffee thermoses, and water jugs were able to crawl into the six-passenger crew cab. Big Stihl chainsaws, oil and fuel cans were already loaded on top of the cab. Minor bickering about the previous day's work in the woods captured the attention of half of the fallers. The other half sat silently, sipping coffee and shifting their weight looking for comfort on the hard seats.

"Back up the Humptulips?" yelled the faller driving the crew cab to the foreman.

"Yeah, same place on the river," yelled the foreman. The foreman turned his pickup north on US 101 for the hour's drive. He passed McGrath Trucking yard. Log trucks with the McGrath named decorating the cab doors were coming to life. Diesel smoke coughed up the exhaust pipes that framed the cabs. The cabs started vibrating, rumbling with the charge of fuel through their veins. The drivers were warming up the diesel motors, checking their safety chains, pushing the gears through the transmissions. They had the luxury of following the fallers in the mornings. At the end of the workday, the log truck drivers would be the last ones to leave the forest with the day's final cut on the trucks. The drive back into Hoquiam was all about getting the loaded truck weighted at the scale shack.

The monetary value of the day was measured by the weight of the logs in the trucks. Profits were made when the daily haul was greater than the cut. The entire timber sale balanced on the ability of fallers and drivers to deliver a volume of logs that sold for a price greater than the cost of timber sale planning and work in the woods. Like ants going out from their communal mounds each day, the men of Hoquiam fanned out into the forest to harvest trees.

One day, however, the costs dipped below the profits. The cost of leaving snags for spotted owls and merlots inched above the cost of timber falling up. The distance from work areas to the scale shack and the sawmills in town became too far to make a profitable day. Equipment and labor costs were also growing. Cheaper wood products were available from foreign countries. Major forest fires made travel and work in the woods unpredictable. The fallers were laid off, then the foreman, and finally, the log trucks were left in the yards. All agreed on one thing, it would be a long time before they would go back to work. They shook their heads as they slammed their pickup truck doors shut to go home one last time. Individual engines were kicked over as the loggers reached down to the ignition switch with their well-worn keys. They nodded their heads to one another and left the maintenance yard in a slow drive, something like a funeral procession.

The scale shack on Bowerman Basin Road where logs had been

weighted and measured before entering the mill was locked and abandoned. First, dust gathered in the corners of the shack. It piled up behind the counter that ran the length of the ten by twelve-foot building. Then it began to find nooks and crannies, places were once weight tickets had been stored and under the small table that had been used for short meetings and daily lunches. The windows that ran the length of the front of the building became streaked from bird droppings and dust that even the rain could not break down. The doors, one on either end of the shack roofed building became stuck from lack of use. More dust gathered on the industrial lamps that hung from the ceiling. The potbellied stove that had warmed the scale shack in the late autumn and early spring days sat silently in the rear of the shack. Within a few short months, the shack settled, and the gravel walks were covered by blackberry vines. The air inside the shack became musty and dank.

The night air was chilling. Lying on the mudflat, I felt the warmth of the mud on my stomach. I was too exhausted to move. I slept intermittently. I heard waves in the direction I assumed was the bay. There were other sounds I couldn't distinguish coming from the alder grove. Small animals, I thought. I hoped. I slipped back into sleep, unable to raise myself or worry about my sudden presence on the mudflat. I thought I heard a vehicle on a road somewhere beyond the alder grove. I didn't have the energy to find the road or wait for another vehicle. From my knowledge of the land surrounding Bowerman Basin, the only place that was routinely frequented by people was the airport. No one would be there in the middle of the night nor during many days.

Gradually, I became aware of the waves coming closer. The outgoing tide must have turned. In another six hours, I could be drowned, I thought. Still, I couldn't move. The terror of last night's events still paralyzed me. The image of Captain Ham pushing me to the end of the gang plank and giving it one last bounce shocked me. 'This is a warning!' I heard him shout before I sank into the mud.

The incoming tide got closer to my spot on the mudflat. I could feel increasing dampness in the mud below me. There was a bit of light in the eastern sky. I sat up, cakes of mud clinging to my shirt and hair. My face was covered in mud from lying on the flat. I turned to look at the water. The tide was coming in closer and closer. With some difficulty, I pulled myself up and out of the mud. I sank a few inches into the flat. I had to get off the mudflat before it captured me, pulling me down to a suffocating death.

I half crawled, half waddled up to the shore. Here the alder and brush extended their roots out toward the water making it difficult to find a good foothold. Tracing the shoreline in the early light, I saw a bit of a cleared area. I caught a handful of brush and pulled myself towards the area. I pushed apart more brush just past the area. There seemed to be a path leading inland.

I pushed aside brush and downed alder branched to follow the path. Maybe it would take me to the road. I would be too much of a mess for anyone to stop and pick me up. Besides, now I had to worry about being seen by someone who was a pirate by night and a regular person by day.

I crept along the path for some distance inland. I counted 245 paces. The path came to an end at what seemed to be a huge brush pile. I sat down again, tired, cold and hungry. Gradually, the sunlight caught up to my collapsed body by the brush pile. The warmth woke me. Birds were flying overhead, making a bit of a racket. The brush pile, I thought. How am I going to get through this? Where is the road? Maybe I should go back to the shore and try and wash this mud off?

I turned again to the brush pile. In the sunlight, I could see something in the piled limbs and bushes. There was something blue exposed through the bushes in various places. I pulled the bushes apart and wiggled my way towards the blue. Finally, I pulled away tall bush covered in blackberry vines. My mud caked arms were armored against the thorns. The blue was the color of siding. It was a shack, overrun with bushes and blackberries. Alder limbs reached out towards each other over the roof. There it stood, more a part of the grove than of humanity.

I fought my way through the brush and blackberries up to the shack. The dense and dangerous foliage had amazingly created a buffer between the elements and the shack. A heavy metal door was located on one side of the building and another on the opposite side. One door opened outward toward the path I had just come up from the shore. The other door was in the middle of the opposite wall. That door must lead to the road, but dense brush obliterated the view. The shack seemed to an elemental part of the site. Noone has used this shack for a long time, I thought.

I managed to get through the brush and up to the door. Please open, I prayed.

The door handle was rusty. I could move the handle back and forth. It pinged with every twist I gave it. I turned the knob round and round, lifting it up and down as I did. Nothing seemed to be working to open the door. Cautiously, I reached up and felt along the doorway molding. Something slipped down in front of me. I stepped back and examined the ground around my feet. A somewhat rusted key had landed near my feet. Grasping the key, I stepped up to the door and slowly slid the key into lock. Carefully, I turned the key. The doorknob turned as well. I pushed in on the door, and it opened.

The door opened into the single room of the shack. The air was dank and difficult to breath. I left the door open, hoping some fresh air would circulate into the room. I guessed twenty feet by ten feet. Four windows were evenly placed along the roadside of the shack, with one window on either end of the rectangle. The windows were still intact. There was a long counter in the middle of the room. Open shelves ran along the bottom of the counter and drawers along the top. A pot-bellied stove stood in one corner. A folding camp chair sat beside the stove. There was some kindling in a wooden box on the floor on the other side of the stove. A box of matches sat on the window frame above. An old calendar from two years past hung from a nail on the back wall opposite the windows. Another nail held a fly swatter. Two narrow shelves were fit into the corner by the single window on the narrow end of the building. A sweatshirt with a Grays Harbor High School Logger on the back hung from another nail on the opposite end of the building.

I started to sit down on the chair, then remembered how muddy my clothes were. I stood for a moment, wondering what to do. There was not a sound, everything was quiet. No vehicle noise or sounds from the airport. I took stock of my wet and muddy clothes. I desperately wanted to get out of them. I thought about the blackberries and the brush I would have to push through to get back down to the shore.

Grabbing the sweatshirt, size XXX, I stepped outside and worked my way back to the water. The in-coming tide was up to the shoreline when I got there. The small cleared area was protected on both sides. I couldn't see either edge of Bowerman Basin or the road on the far side that went north along the coast. Feeling secure enough, I took off all my clothes and put on the giant sweatshirt. It hung to my knees. I folded up the sleeves as best I could. Standing at the water's edge, I rinsed out my clothes. Gradually, the mud washed out of the clothes, but everything was a shade of brown. Without soap, they wouldn't come completely clean. Least of my worries, I thought.

I took the clothes back up to the shack and hung them on the brush. They would dry in the sun that pierced through the branches and vines. I went back into the shack and looked at the stove. If only I could start a small fire and get warm, I thought. I looked more carefully at the stove. I reached to turn the damper handle on the stove pipe. At first it won't budge, but after some pushing and pulling, it moved. I turned the handle in the position I thought would be an open flue. Then I went back outside and pushed my way around to see if the stovepipe was sticking outside of the shack. I cleared away some brush around where I thought the pipe should be. The pipe stuck out of the side of the shack just far enough to send smoke away from the building.

Looking around the base of the shack, I found some small limbs that looked dry enough. I went back into the shack, pulled open drawers until I found a pad of paper, and started loading the old stove with wads of paper and kindling. The match box held about thirty matches. It took four to finally get the paper to burn. The kindling caught fire. Gradually, I added more kindling and then some of the dry limbs. The stove warmed up and began to send heat waves into the shack. I pulled the chair close to the stove and curled up as best I could in the oversized sweatshirt.

The morning slipped by. I dozed a bit and then put another limb on my small fire. I was getting hungry and thirsty. There wasn't much I could do about either until the clothes dried and I figured out how to get back into town. I slept again and woke up realizing the fire had gone out and the building was starting to get cold. I stepped outside to check on my clothes. The sun was at a low angle on the west side of the building. My clothes were dry enough to put on, still brownish from all the mud. I put the sweatshirt on over my clothes. I won't look too strange on the sidewalks of Hoquiam or Aberdeen.

Lastly, I opened the front door of the shack. There was a graveled area under the brush that enveloped the front of the building. I pushed my way along the gravel and then on to a bit of a trail. I stepped out on the road that connected the airport and the shingle mills across from Randolph's house and dock. My goal was to get into the main part of Hoquiam as fast as I could before anyone would recognize me.

It took nearly an hour to walk all the way from the shack to my apartment. No one seemed to recognize me in the big shirt as I walked through downtown Hoquiam, over the Hoquiam River bridge, and the mile to my apartment in Aberdeen. When I got to the door, a I found a black flag with white skull and crossbones attached to the doorknob. A note was pinned to the flag. In barely legible handwriting it said, "Say anything and you're in the sea. Leave town now." I looked around me to see if anyone were watching. I felt like the whole apartment complex must be but there was no evidence to back up my premonition. I opened the door as quickly as I could and locked it behind me.

I wanted only to take a hot shower and climb into bed. Without turning on a light, I managed the shower, some dinner, and a large cup of hot tea. When I finally climbed into bed, I could only think of being thankful to have a warm, dry place to sleep. Who knows where I will find that again? I thought.

I woke up early the next day. With a cup of coffee in hand, I climbed back into bed. I had to think of a plan. My rent was up in four days, and I had to vacate the apartment. I still wasn't exactly sure where to go. The flag and note were threatening. I didn't have enough money to pay for a place to live. I couldn't bear to think of living on the street after all these years of avoiding this last rung on the social ladder. I felt desperate.

Some parts of my life would go on no matter where found shelter. I would get my mail at the post office. My bank account would be good for receiving the small amount from Social Security. I still had the extra cash Bob had given me. I could expect my deposit back on the apartment. These funds would keep me going for a month or so. I'd need most of it for food and other essentials. That brought me back to no place to live. I looked up at Bruce's photograph. Now what? I asked in tears.

As if Bruce were speaking through the photograph, the shack came instantly into my mind's eye. No, I thought. How would that work?

The possibility grew in my mind like the incoming tide had pushed me ashore last night. I closed my eyes and tried to envision living there. It would be safe if no one found me. It was barely large enough to accommodate a bed and a table. The windows were wonderful for letting in light but would also let in the cold unless they were covered. The pot-bellied stove could be used for heat and cooking. I could just barely afford membership at the Y for hot showers. I would have to be careful not to go there when pirates were about. I could change my looks and hope they would not recognize me.

Slowly, the possibility became a reality. I pulled out my collapsible grocery cart. It could hold a few things, and I had my backpack. I loaded the cart with my rain gear and boots, bits of camping equipment including a sleeping bag, flashlight, and first aid kit. I pushed in sweatpants and a heavy wool sweater. The backpack was filled with odds and ends of clothes and my purse. Last, I put Bruce's picture in my pocket. I looked around the apartment.

I left the apartment well before anyone else was up to see me. The cart was hard to push with the full load and the backpack was heavy. It took longer to get out to the shack then coming into town. When I got to the path, I pulled the cart off the road, unloaded it except for the bottom layer of stuff. I would ferry everything else to the shack. The shack was just as I had left it. Once inside, I arranged what I had brought from the apartment on the counter shelves. I would have to think about a bed.

Tired, but resolute, I pushed the cart back to the apartment. Slowly, the shack came to hold more of my belongings than the apartment. The shack also came to hold my determination to survive. The more I filled my shack with my clothes and favorite things, the more it became a refuge. Every time I shuttled back into town, I walked past the large wooden sign that marked the boundary of the Bowerman Basin National Wildlife Refuge. I was like the birds who sought refuge from imposters that wanted to destroy their habitat. Captain Ham may want to destroy my home in Grays Harbor, but I would not let him. He was in the wrong, not me. My new home in the shack was my refuge, and like the shorebirds and waders who graced the wetlands and mudflats, I was protected from that part of humanity that operated out of evil.

I had used the three days of moving as efficiently as I could. On my return trips to town, I ran errands, went to the bank, made sure I had a post office box, and checking on my Y membership. I had done all these things while I still looked like the person in my driver's license. Next, I focused on changing my looks. I did not want to be recognized by any of the pirate crew or friends. I cut my hair in a drastic way, cropping it close to my head with longish bangs. I bought a pair of non-prescription glasses and another pair of large sunglasses. I got rid of all my dress-up work clothes at a thrift shop in Hoquiam where I knew none of my friends shopped. I found a wool sweater and a Pendleton plaid jacket in the men's section. A pair of Carhart pants and a wool boiler style hat added to my disguise. Every time I pushed the cart back and forth from the apartment, I had gone a different route. I will really be in shape from all this walking, I thought.

Now, my first night in the shack, I forced myself to look forward, to see the promise of surviving. I had to concentrate on making the shack livable yet invisible. I cooked my first dinner, a can of soup, on the pot-bellied stove. I boiled water in my teapot, and contemplated changes I could make to the shack. I would always have to stock up dry wood from the alder grove or driftwood and get bottled water from town. I closed the damper halfway and arranged my sleeping bag and blankets to make at least a pallet for tonight. Tomorrow – figure out a bed!

I had assumed my comings and goings had gone unobserved. I always moved brush back over the trail to the road. I had a bit more freedom going down to the shore, but I was careful to make things look as undisturbed as I had found them. I could go to the rocky point and watch the birds and the mudflats. While they seemed to always look the same for some people, they were a wealth of change with every tide. Just as the mudflats were renewed twice a day, I felt equally renewed with the tide's coming and goings. I religiously marked the tidal shifts on my small calendar and went down to the shore to see each change as often as I could. I kept track of the moment daylight filtered into the shack, and the moment it left. Recording the data seemed to pull me further into my alder grove home, and away from my old life.

Unbeknownst to me, someone else was measuring time and place near Bowerman Basin. Gray began spending nearly all his time on the shoreline of the harbor, across the road from the airport. His walk across Aberdeen and through Hoquiam was along the road to a sawmill where he had worked one summer. The mill had since been leveled. A huge machine that chipped smaller timber was in operation at the site. There were large decks of timber, all the size of saplings, stacked in the old log yard. Once chipped into four-inch squares, the chips were moved by a covered conveyor belt up and over the road, and out to a dock. The dock was midway between the airport and Randolph's old fishing dock. Gray's walks along the road reminded him of the summer days he had worked at the mill, using his lunch break to fish from the rocks that lined the bay. High tide brought salmon in closer to the shore.

Sitting out by the rocks, Gray thought more about his mill working days. The logs were brought in by trucks from as far away as the reservation boundary to the north. Some of the logs were massive in size then. They were the last of the old-growth fir forest that had once covered the entire Olympic Peninsula. Now all these forests and their habitat had been cut by Weyerhaeuser and smaller timber companies. The only places left to see a remnant of the old-growth forest were in Olympic National Park. There were probably some small bits of ancient forest on the reservation, but no one was talking about them.

The Nation held their knowledge close to their chests. Gray knew what he did only thanks to his granny.

Gray thought about Granny for a while. He knew a few things about survival thanks to her. He missed her. She would have a story to tell every time they met. She told her stories as if the characters were still with her. He thought of them as Granny's ghost stories. She did not think of them as ghosts, Gray thought.

One afternoon, Gray decided to walk over to the old mill site. The chipper was not working, so no one would bother him poking around the site and the log yard. He walked around the place where the big saws had worked. Everything had been cleared away; there was no evidence of the mill. The yard, only half used by the chip plant, was now a meadow. On the far end of the meadow was the road out to the main highway. An empty osprey nest occupied the top of a power pole. No osprey this time of year, Gray thought to himself.

Halfway across the meadow, Gray stopped. Something was missing. There used to be something else here, he thought. He looked back at the old mill site, and then back at the road just past the power pole and abandoned osprey nest. He stood for a moment and tried to discern what was eating away at the back of his head. The wind kicked up just then, and a steady rain began to fall. He turned up his collar and looked around for a place to get out of the rain. Just as he turned his head, he caught a glimpse of someone just beyond the road. He looked back again, and the image was gone.

Gray walked back into town, still wondering what was missing at the mill site. He remembered summer days helping to unload the trucks. The trucks came down the road from up north. Before they could be unloaded, the logs had to be counted and 'scaled' before they could be sent into the mill. Logs of different sizes were sent to different sized saws inside the mill. He would wait for the next truck to finish being 'scaled' inside the scale shack. Where is the old scale shack? thought Gray.

# 6

# SARON AND GRAY

*G*ray walked o the Fish Bait Bar in Hoquiam. He sat down at a table in the bar and ordered a bottle of Dick's Beer. The scale shack mystery dogged him. What happened to it? Did they tear it down? Hardly, the lumber company didn't do anything they didn't have to. Did they move it? Where? It was a mystery.

Taking a paper napkin and pulling a pen out of his pocket, Gray began to sketch the abandoned mill site. He drew in the highway that led out to the coast, Ocean Shores, and points north. Then he drew the city street that led out of Hoquiam past old mill sites along the edge of the bay. The street became a road through the light industrial area where cedar shake plants, truck repair shops, and Randolph's house and dock were located. The road made a right angle turn around the chipper work site and the overhead conveyor to a dock that had been built for international ships and barges coming into the harbor for the chips. Past an old log yard, the road made another right turn, went past the pole where osprey had nested for years, and then ran into the coast highway. At the last right turn, there was a smaller road that went straight out to the airport. Along this road, the US Fish and Wildlife Service had a pole barn for storing equipment. They never seemed to be around, they had little time or money to spend on the Bowerman Basin Unit of the Billy Frank Jr. Nisqually National Wildlife Refuge. The airport road terminated at a group of airplane hangars. The point separated Bowerman Basin from the bay and created the basin's southern shore. The point was also a popular place for bird watchers and people seeking a bit of solitude.

After sketching in the road network, Gray drew rectangular boxes on the map to indicate the location of the original mill, where logs had been decked in the yard, and where various equipment sheds had stood. Gray oriented the map so that the airport was to the west, the bay to the south, the coast highway to the north, and Hoquiam to the east. Starting on the north end of the map, he made a dashed line to simulate the route of a log truck bringing logs down from the northern forests. The imaginary truck came alone the coast highway, turned south on the road that led past the osprey nest pole, and then… Gray stopped. The trucks had to pass through the scale shack before they turned into the log yard. Using his pen like a pin, Gray placed the pen on the basin side of the road north of the airport road. Gray sat back and looked at his map. He was sure that he had correctly identified the location of the shack. But where was the shack now? he wondered.

Gray had been so intent on making his map, he didn't hear Roger come into the bar.

"What are you so intent on?" asked Roger in a friendly voice. "Haven't seen you for a while," he said. "Busy fishing or looking for pirate gold?" he laughed.

Gray slowly folded up his map. He wasn't ready to tell Roger or anyone else about the missing scale shack. He tried to act natural and put the map in a pocket before Roger became suspicious.

"Not doing much," said Gray.

"There's not much to do," echoed Roger. They both took a sip of beer and sat silently for a while. Their communal silence was one way that they shared a Quinault Indian of giving each other respect.

As if reading each other's minds, Roger offered the first opening statement.

"Did you hear the latest about the bay?" he asked Gray.

"No," said Gray. "Now what?" he said with wry humor in his voice.

"Port Commission wants to put in a gas export terminal. Say they must dredge the channel for tankers. Hell, they already upgraded the railroad all the way from the main line by Centralia over to the port. Say they can make the port millions of dollars if they can transport fuel from North Dakota and ship it to China. Then we'd be shipping cars and fuel to billions of Chinese."

"That sounds a little risky," said Gray with a frown.

"Risky?" said Roger emphatically. "Risky? It sounds like a bunch of businessmen up on the hill trying to make more money on something that will pollute the bay and ruin the fishing. Sons of bitches, always trying to take one more thing away from the Indians and the bay." Roger took another sip of beer and put his fist down on the table. Then he looked around the room, making sure no one had noticed.

"Anyone doing anything about all of this?" asked Gray. "The Quinault Nation taking a stand?"

"Oh yeah," said Roger with a defiant voice. "The Nation's putting in a letter of protest to the governor and the federal government, not that it will do a lot of good. How many times has the Nation tried to stop them messing up the bay?" said Roger. "It is supposed to be our bay first."

"The Nation has control of the bay and the channel. They work with the Port. Maybe the Nation sees something in letting fuel be stored and shipped here," said Gray. "I'm not in favor of anything that messes up the bay. Let it be."

"I hear you, brother," said Roger. "There are a lot of people up on the res who are making the same statement. There are starting to be protests at meetings and here in Hoquiam."

"Who's doing that?" asked Gray.

"There's a bunch of Evergreeners and local environmentalists are having protests at the Hoquiam boat launch every Saturday now. Somebody from the Nation is coming down this Saturday to speak. Going to be a big deal between those Greener environmental types and Quinault people. I'm planning on going."

"You?" asked Gray with another wry smile. "I didn't figure you for an environmentalist."

"I'm not. I just don't think the Nation should be helping the Port Commission destroy Grays Harbor. If I were you, Gray," he stopped and added emphasis to the Gray, "I would be there too. It's your harbor, too," he said with a tip of his now empty beer glass.

"Well, I got to go," said Roger.

"Writing your protest song?" joked Gray, remembering that Roger was a member of a tribal drumming group that often sang at public events.

"As a matter of fact, I am," replied Roger. "You better show," he said and left the bar.

After Roger left, Gray sat a bit longer and finished his beer. He pulled out the map he had drawn and studied it. The same question came back to him: where was the shack? I guess there's only one way to find out, he thought.

After spending the night talking to other homeless people and dozing on the streets of Aberdeen, Gray walked back out to the mill site. He stopped for a cup of coffee and a sweet roll, not having much money after paying for another prescription of pain killers. His funds from odd jobs were running low. Another rainsquall and wind hit him as he got closer to the place where he thought the shack should be. It was getting to be winter and time to find some sort of shelter. The rain would become incessant in another week or so.

He stood on the road where he thought the gravel turn-off to the shack should be. There was a bit of gravel that disappeared into the brush. The brush and downed alder limbs were thick here, almost too thick to be natural. Gray pushed his way into the brush. At first, he didn't see the peeling walls of the shack but then his eyes recognized the blue paint and the rectangular building.

He approached the long wall of windows that faced the gravel path. The shack should have appeared abandoned, but there were signs that it was not. For one thing, there was a stack of driftwood next to the door. He tried to look in the windows, but they were covered with some sort of fabric. He encircled the shack and found other signs of habitation: a clothesline strung between two alder trees, a path that would lead to the edge of Bowerman Basin, and another stack of firewood at the back door. Finally, he reached up to the stove pipe that pushed out of the shack. He felt heat emanating off the pipe.

Home, sweet home, for someone, he thought.

Just at that moment, he heard something move in the brush from what appeared to be a path to the shoreline.

I had gone down to the to watch the tide recede. A tiny sandpiper ran back and forth at the water's edge, finding a new inch of mud and potential prey with each passing. With an armload of driftwood, I started back to the shack, pushing my way through the brush.

"Who's there?" I heard from someone nearer the shack.

"Who's there?" a man's voice asked a second time.

"Come out of there, now," he demanded.

"Okay," said the man. "I'm coming down the path."

I tried to get ahead of him, but he was faster. He grabbed my arm with enough force to stop my efforts to get back to the shack.

We starred at each other, not wanting to believe that the other was there on the path.

"Who are you?" he asked. "What are you doing here?"

I tried to pull my arm free.

"I'm not going to hurt you," he said. "Just tell me who you are and what you are doing here in my scale shack."

"It's not your shack," I said in a thin but piercing voice. "I found it. No one has used it for a long time."

"Tell me who you are and what you're doing here," he demanded a third time.

"Come on," he said, and pulled me back to the shack. "Open the door," he said. "Let's get out of this wind and rain."

Once inside, he looked around at my efforts to take up residence. The counter was fixed as a worktable. The shelves were carefully stacked with dry goods on one end and clothes on the other. A teapot sat on the pot-bellied stove. A chair was placed beside the stove, and a pallet of bedding was along the opposite wall. A photograph of a young man was placed on a shelf in one corner. Rain gear and sweatshirts lined the other wall.

"Take your jacket off," he commanded. "Sit," he motioned me to the chair.

"Let's make some hot tea," he said. After stoking the coals in the stove and adding some firewood. He filled the teapot from a water bottle, reached for the cups he saw below the counter, and found the box of teabags.

The warmth of the fire encircled me. I took off my hat and glasses. I looked at him more carefully as he poured out the hot water. He looked familiar but I couldn't remember from where. I hadn't thought much about anyone in all the busyness of the last few days. He handed me a cup of tea.

He sat down on the floor beside the stove looking for all the world as if he did live here. He looked at me with some vague sense of memory as well.

"Now," he said. "please tell me what's going on here."

I sipped some tea. My shoulders sagged a bit. With a strong dose of relief in my voice I said, "My name is Saron Lindquist. I've been out here for about four days. I was forced to get out of town, to move away. I found this place after being dumped in the water out in the basin. This is the only place I could think of to hide out. I hardly have any money now; my Social Security is pretty meager."

The man looked at me with more and more questions, his eyebrow raised higher and higher as I told my story.

"What do you mean, dumped in the basin?" he asked.

I took a deep breath. As much as I didn't want to tell any of the details or be linked to *Maiden's Curse*, I wanted, needed, to talk to someone. I knew I had met this guy before without any red flags going up, but I still couldn't place where I had run into him.

"I sailed on *Maiden's Curse*. Apparently, I sailed with them too often doing something illegal. I was forced to walk the gangplank, but close enough to shore that I managed to survive overnight on the mudflats before the tide came back in. What is this place, anyway?"

"This is what used to be the scaling shack for the mill that stood across the road," he said, nodding his head over his right shoulder. "Did Ham really made you walk the plank?"

I nodded, hoping he would believe me. After a minute of pondering silence, he said, "It does make a nice place to get out of sight."

"Yes, that's what I decided. It's the only thing I could think of. I've always lived in Grays Harbor. I won't even know how to move away. I got all the stuff I thought I could use out of my apartment just before the rent ran out. Ham was so nice as to leave me a note on skull and crossbones message at my apartment. He made it pretty clear that he didn't want to see me again." I shook my head and looked down into the teacup.

"You said his name was Ham?" asked Gray.

"Yes, Captain Ike Hamundarson, or just Captain Ham. He's the captain of *Maiden's Curse*."

The man took a sip of tea. "The name sounds familiar, but I don't know why."

"Most of the pirates are people you see every day in Aberdeen or Hoquiam. They just do the pirate stuff for fun."

"Sounds like some of them do it for profit," he said with disdain.

"There was always some sort of profit involved," I said. "That's why I volunteered to go along on the extra sails. I thought I was earning my dues, but apparently not." After a sip of tea, I added, "I lost my job about a month ago. When I applied for Social Security, I found out that I didn't have much coming to me. Always got paid under the table."

The man sat up and looked at me. "That's where I know you from," he said with the sound of recognition in his voice. "I met you at the Social Security office. I was there trying to get on disability, but they lost my paperwork again."

I looked at him for a minute. "Yes," I said slowly. "Yes, that's where I ran into you," my voice softened a bit. "Why do you need disability?"

"Got caught in a bad logging accident. Pretty stove up with arthritis now," he said.

"No real income?" I asked.

"Odd jobs here and there," he said. "Most of my money goes to the pharmacy for pain killers." Gray looked down into his cup of tea. "I can't seem to get by without them, and I need a little bit more all the time. Doc says I just must live with it. He says it's a miracle I survived the accident. I think my old granny helped me get better, she knew how to heal people. But my bones can hurt pretty bad, especially during the winter. Just one of the hazards of living in Grays Harbor County."

"So, you don't have a place to live, you don't have a lot of money, and you can't get much help from the government," I said.

"That's about the size of it," he said.

"Were you thinking of living here?" I asked.

"I thought I would check it out as a possibility," he answered. "You got it fixed up pretty good. It could use a bit more work to hide it from the road. What's your plan for water and staying warm?"

"I have to bring water from town. The stove works well enough, but I have to be careful and not let too much smoke go out the pipe during the day I guess when it gets really cold, I'll spend the day in town at the library or in the coffee house in Hoquiam," I answered. "I really haven't gotten that far in working out the details. Just got this all together in the last four days."

"You shouldn't stay out here by yourself," he said.

Where was he going with this? I wondered. "Are you offering to help me?" I asked.

"I guess you need to keep me around," he said with a bit of a smile. "I could tell Ham where you are."

"Yes, I guess you do have that on me."

He leaned forward and looked more closely at me. Our eyes met with careful deference on both parts. "Look, I can help you out here. I won't tell anyone you are here and I'm willing to take on the risk of covering for you. I just need a place to stay myself."

I didn't think I had any options or anything better for protecting myself.

"Okay," I said slowly. "Tell me how this is going to work. But first, you better tell me your name."

"Gray Quinn," he said. "Part Indian, mostly not. The Indian part makes me part of the Quinault Nation. The Gray," he stopped for a minute, "means I was named after my great great-great-grandfather, the explorer John Gray."

# 7

# BOWERMAN BASIN

*W*e had shared a dinner of canned vegetable soup with a tin of tuna fish between us. More hot tea. I showed him how I used the rest of the hot water to wash out the dishes and, with the last of it, my face in preparation for the night. I could see that it took him a bit of energy to walk from one end of the shack to the other. He sometimes grabbed the counter to steady himself.

He quickly understood the need for efficiency whether it was water use, food or firewood. We put as much wood on the fire as we dared, always conscious that a puff of smoke from the pipe could attract attention. He did not seem to be unhappy with the conditions of habitation. In fact, he began making a mental list of projects to improve the shack and our security in it.

"The first thing I'll work on," said Gray, "is painting the outside. The blue paint could attract attention. If the outside walls were brown, the shack would totally disappear into the alder grove."

As was my new ritual, I wrote down on the calendar the time the light disappeared from the shack. The nights were getting longer. I gave Gray my extra blanket and he made himself a bit of a bed on the other side of the room. I slipped into my pallet of wool blankets. I made a mental a list of things that would make the shack more habitable.

I'm already dependent on him, I thought. I don't even really know him. I rehashed his story and how I had met him earlier at the Social Security office. Maybe this is how street people help each other, I thought. I fell asleep after a while, the list making lulling me into a series of jumbled dreams. I dreamed of the cold, wet mudflat that Captain Ham had forced to on to, and the peaceful rise of a black-billed snowy egret from the water's edge.

When I woke up, I looked up at the ceiling with its cracked and peeling paint. It was warm in the shack. I could hear the fire in the stove. I sat up and looked around. There were no signs of Gray other than the fire. Did he leave already? I wondered. Am I still safe or is he going into town to tell someone, anyone, my wild story and destroy my secret home? What if this all goes sour? So many doubts ran through my mind.

The back door opened, and Gray entered the shack. "Good morning," he said. "I was just out seeing if all the dry wood was going to stay that way. There's a pretty steady rain and wind out there."

"Oh, good morning," I responded. I looked around the shack and took stock of the muted morning light. It was not very bright, gray as Gray said it was.

The rain started to pound more loudly on the roof. "We'll need to do something about the roof, it won't hold up against another winter of storms."

I was relieved to hear him speak of the future and use the plural pronoun.

"Coffee and tea will help us get through the day," I said.

"What day is it?" asked Gray.

"Friday," I said.

We spent the day sharing our lists of things that would make the shack winter worthy. Gray had ideas of trying to paint as much of the shack as possible, brown on the outside and white on the inside. He went over every inch of the shack looking for any spaces that would let cold air or mice in. "Maybe we should get a cat," he offered at one point in the day. "A dog would be good but could make too much noise."

"I've never had a dog or a cat for that matter," I said. "Won't a cat scare away birds?" I asked.

"Indoor cat," said Gray as he worked his fingers along the window sill. "Will keep the mice out. We should try to cover these windows with more than curtains."

"Wish we could move this big counter or cut it in half. It takes up so much room in the middle of the shack," I said.

"Let me think about it," said Gray. "Need some tools."

I half smiled wondering where the money would come from to buy supplies, let alone food and water for two people. I was only counting on one.

As if reading my mind, Gray said, "I'll bring some funds in, I'll get an odd job and help with expenses."

I wondered how he could work with the amount of pain he seemed to be in.

The day went slowly along, the lists grew. We had crackers and peanut butter for lunch, and more canned soup for dinner. The rain held steady all day and into the night. The planning had worn us out. The stove kept us warm and the inside dry even though we were careful to not let much smoke escape. It was the good friend that needed to be fed as much as we did. Keeping dry firewood was going to be a challenge.

The next morning, Gray was first up again. The shack was warm, and coffee was ready when I pulled myself out of the blankets.

"Rain stopped," he said handing me a cup of coffee. "I'm going into Hoquiam. I'll see what I can find in the thrift shop across from the hardware store."

"You mean the one across from the library?" I asked.

"Yes, that one. Cheap left-over paint and tools."

"Do you need any money?"

Gray stopped at the door and looked at me. "I have a few dollars. I'll see what I can find. If I find more stuff than I have money for, I'll let you know."

"OK. I'll go a different way into town. I want to go to the Y, check my mail and bank account. Then I'll buy some food and water."

We parted ways for the day. Gray headed toward Hoquiam along the road past Randolph's. He perused the shelves at the thrift store. He located tools, cans of paint, and an old brown army tent. The tent, he thought, would make curtains for the inside of the windows. The canvas would hold back damp cold air and prevent light from escaping out of the shack at night.

After his search of the shop, he went into the local coffee shop and ordered coffee and sweet roll. He sat for a while, considering how his life had suddenly changed for the better. From the shop window, he could see people starting to gather at the boat launch on the Hoquiam River. Across the river from the landing was Anderson's big tug that helped guide freighters in over the bar at the entrance of the Harbor and then up the channel. 'Looks like they are getting ready to go out,' he thought. Gray saw Roger and the drumming group getting ready to sing.

Meanwhile, I took my cart and pushed it into town via the coast highway. It was a long walk, but I ran my errands and took a shower at the Y. There was a letter in my post office box saying my first Social Security check, all of $358 thanks to federal taxes, would arrive in my bank account in two weeks. I went to Grocery Outlet and spent half of the money I had left on food and water. On my way out the door, I saw a sign describing the Hoquiam food bank. There was another sign offering support and direction for social services at the Catholic Church in Aberdeen. I made a mental note to go to the food bank before I came back to the grocery store. I'll have to get used to this:

two mouths to feed is a lot. It took me a long time to get back to Hoquiam, and then I still had to go out to the shack. The cart was full and hard to push on the old sidewalks.

When I got across the Hoquiam River, I noticed a group of people at the landing. A speaker making a speech over a microphone. There was also a Quinault Nation drumming group and a group of people. Young people seemed earnest, holding up signs and voicing support for the speaker. Older people were solemn and respectfully quiet. Most of them were Quinault Nation people. I pushed the heavy cart over to the outer fringe of the crowd. I was careful to keep my head down just in case my disguise wasn't enough to protect my identity. There was one person in the crowd I did know, Gray.

I watched Gary go up to one of the drummers. They were chatting in earnest when a woman protester approached them. She waited patiently until the two men were forced to recognize her. She appeared to be asking the men questions about the Hoquiam River and then the bay. The men gave short answers that didn't seem to satisfy her. After another round of questions and glib answers, the woman disappeared back into the crowd. Gray said goodbye to the man he had been talking to. Good, I thought. I wanted to warn him not to talk about our current living arrangement. I turned the cart back to the sidewalk and started toward the shack.

Gray left the waterfront and headed back to the thrift shop. He had just enough time to pick up the tools and tent. He also bought an old Kelty frame pack, two half-empty gallon cans of exterior wall paint, a box of nails, a roll of wire, and a large roll of duct tape. That was all he could afford, and all he could carry back to the shack. He stuffed everything except the tent into the pack. He strapped the tent on the top of the pack. Now I really do look like a street person, he thought to himself.

Gray headed back to the shack by way of the road past Randolph's. He knew I would go along the street that became the coast road. He worried there might be birdwatchers trying to look for wildlife in Bowerman Basin and that I would have to walk past them with the cart and disappear into the brush that hid the gravel path to the shack. He walked faster thinking he might be able to cut me off.

He heard a pickup truck behind him just as he got to Randolph's. The truck slowed. Gray turned his back to the road, hoping the driver won't recognize him. The truck came to an idle next to him.

"Is that you?" called a voice from the truck.

Gray turned to see who it was. He let out a bit of a sigh when he recognized Roger. "Taking up street life, I see," said Roger. He lit a cigarette and passed it to Gray. "Looks like you need some work. Ham Gravel is putting in a cement pad and metal pole barn up at the quarry. Come by on Monday. I could use your help."

Gray nodded. "I'll be there. Thanks for the smoke."

Just past Randolph's, Gray heard a rustle in the vegetation beside the road. Peering into the tangle of grass and blackberry bushes, Gray was a bit startled to see two green eyes starring back at him. The creature did not move or utter a sound. It tried to back further into the brush but couldn't, evidently caught by blackberry thorns. Black bits of hair were hanging limp in the thorns surrounding the creature. Carefully, Gray reached into the brush and wrapped his hand around the creature behind the eyes that could not move. Fighting off the blackberry vines, Gray pulled the creature loose, disengaging it from the knot of thorns. Finally, free of the brush, Gray held out a straggly lump of a small cat, limp and soaking wet. The little cat had not the energy to cry or protest Gray's hand around its neck.

Gray patted its head. "You look pretty miserable," he said. "How about coming home with me?" He pushed the little cat into his coat, balancing it with his arm. There was not a struggle from the cat, just a valiant but weak effort to hold on to Gray's sweater with its claws.

I was in the shack unloading the food and water from my cart. At the sight of Gray, I went to the door to help him with his pack.

"I brought you something," he said. He gently pulled the cat out from beneath his coat.

"What is that? I asked.

"I think it's a sad, wet, hungry cat," said Gray.

"I guess!" I said. I reached for a towel and wrapped it around the poor thing. I moved over to the wood stove and got as close as I could to warm the cat. "She needs food," I said.

Gray opened a can of condensed milk. "Let's start with this and see how she does," he said.

Slowly the cat came to life. The warmth of the stove and the milk sparked enough energy for the cat to stretch its legs and make an effort to move beyond my gentle grasp.

"Are you our new tenant?" I cooed to the cat. "What's your name?"

"Haven't a clue," answered Gray. "She was just a mishap waiting to be snatched by a hawk in a tangle of blackberries."

"Well, Miss Hap," I said. "You are welcome here as long as you earn your keep. No mice allowed."

Turning to Gray, "I saw you at the protest. "Who were you talking to?"

"That was my friend Roger."

"And the woman?"

"She said she was an Evergreen student who was going to be working for the US Fish and Wildlife Service out here. She wanted to know the best way to get out into the bay, and document birds and wildlife. We didn't give her much help."

"We have to be careful who we talk to," I said.

"I understand," said Gray. "Roger did give me a tip on a job for next week. I'll be going up to Ham Gravel quarry to help build a metal barn."

"Sounds like a bit of money," I said with a smile. "I don't think anyone at the protest or along the road recognized me."

"I don't think very many people were interested in the protest except those who care about the bay and the mudflats," said Gray.

There were a few more people who knew about the protest, but they were not at the boat landing. Ike Hamundarson watched the protest from his elegant home on one of the highest points above Aberdeen. Looking through binoculars, he watched the gathering of protestors, the arrival of the tribal speaker, and the positioning of the drumming circle.

"What's going on?" asked his wife Christine. She was setting up a display of wines, spirits, cheeses, and crackers. "Don't forget, the Englesons will be here soon."

"Remind me of the occasion," said Ike, still watching the events down on the river.

"Just tasting the best of the local foods. There's Westport Winery wines, Wishkah gin, and cheese from one of the local dairies. Found some of the smoked salmon you like at the wine shop downtown."

The doorbell rang and Christine went to welcome Bert and Barbara Engleson into the room. Christine and Barbara chatted at the table of gourmet foods. Bert came and stood by Ike at the window.

"What are you watching?" he asked.

"There's a protest going on down at the Hoquiam boat launch. Bunch of enviro types and some tribal people raising a fuss about the fuel terminal project."

"Really?" asked Bert. "We don't need that. There's a lot of investment and money to be made with that terminal." The Engleson family owned property all over Aberdeen including large commercial lots along the river. "We need that Port expansion," he said.

"Protest?" asked Barbara.

"Looks like the gas terminal project is getting a little heat." said Ike. "We'll have to raise some public support for it." He put down the glasses and raised his eyebrow as he turned to Bert.

Barbara stepped over to the window. She worked at the county courthouse in the clerk's office. Between her knowledge of property values and sales, and Bert's control of family property, there wasn't much that happened in Aberdeen or Hoquiam that the two didn't know about when it came to development.

"Oh, I wonder if that's why the US Fish and Wildlife was looking for someone to help take an observer out into the bay and around to Bowerman Basin. They were trying to find someone with a boat," she said.

Ike slowly set the binoculars down on the windowsill. "I'll take the observer out on my fishing boat. It's tied up at the dock at Westport. I need to bring it in for the winter, this will be a good chance to run the channel one more time this fall," he said.

"That's generous of you," said Barbara. "I'll let F and W know. Won't the fuel be coming in on the railroad? That would put all those fuel cars in the Walmart parking lot."

"The railroad has been there for nearly a hundred years," said Bert. "Walmart built out there about ten years ago. They knew the risks. Everyone has to cross the tracks to get to the parking lot."

"You knew that could be an issue when you leased the land to Walmart," said Ike.

"Well, we only own the land and we have great insurance," smiled Bert. "I'm not so worried about a bunch of Walmart shoppers, poor stiffs."

The two couples laughed a bit and then poured themselves more wine.

"Let's toast to the gas terminal," said Ike raising his glass. He met Bert's eyes over the clinking of glasses. "Nothing will stop the project."

Well below the heights of the Hamundarson home, Gray and I spent Sunday inside the shack at the edge of Bowerman Basin. It was more likely that people would be driving the roads around Bowerman Basin, either going to the airport, birdwatching out along the bay or in the basin or just using the back roads to get around Aberdeen and Hoquiam traffic. We cut up the canvas tent and made panels of fabric to hang over the windows. Fortunately, Gray had brought all the tools and materials necessary. We rehung the curtains in front of the panels. Now we could open and close the canvas panels and cover them up on the inside of the shack with the drapes.

Gray used the duct tape and wire he bought to secure the stove pipe. I had set out beans to soften in the morning. By late in the day, I set them on the stove and added a bag of frozen vegetable that had thawed. We celebrated our day's work with the soup dinner. There was bread and some store-bought cookies. "Just on Sundays," I said. "If we have to stay inside all day, we should have something to look forward to."

"Almost dark," said Gray. "About time for the tide to start back in to shore."

I made a note of the time on my calendar. "A bit sooner for darkness every day now."

"Let's go down to the shore," offered Gray. We put on our dark colored rain gear and tall rubber boots. "It will do us good to get out of the house," he said, trying to mimic an old couple who had spent years together.

I smiled at him. 'Good to have another soul about,' I thought.

We pushed our way through the brush. Tidewater was returning to basin, covering the extensive mudflats. A blue heron was quietly, gracefully stalking fish on the edge of the mudflat. We settled into a niche in the bushes to watch. After a while, Gray got up and walked along the shore toward the point. He came back with a Styrofoam ice chest that had come in with the tide. The lid was gone but the box was still usable. We carried it back to the shack.

"The canvas panels are helping disguise the shack," I said. "The windows don't reflect any light now, no eyes looking out from the shack."

We set the box inside the door to dry out. The only bit of light in the shack was the banked fire in the stove. We made one last pot of tea.

"I'll tell you a ghost story my granny used to tell me," said Gray. It was an engaging story about a young girl who went for a walk in the woods and never came back, at least, her spirit never did. She was 'stolen' by a bear. When she came home, she was empty, spiritless and a cold person the rest of her life.

"So, the message is, 'don't play with bears?' I said jokingly.

After a while, Gray said, "I think she meant that we can lose ourselves when dark problems appear before us."

"Is there anything dark in your world?" I asked him.

Gray took a last gulp of tea and turned away from me. "Nothing for you to worry about," he said.

I thought about Gray and how he seemed so determined to keep going. But I knew from having seen him walk and carry things that he ached with every step. He tried to hide the fact that he took pain pills often during the day.

"I think we should get a transistor radio," Gray said. "Maybe after I work this construction job."

He went to sleep after that. I stayed awake for a while, wondering how long this would all last.

The next morning, Gray was up early. He handed me a cup of coffee while I curled up in bed to stay warm.

"Rest up today," he said. "I'm going to work at Ham Gravel. I'll be back later in the afternoon unless it starts raining bad."

Gray walked into Hoquiam on the coast road that paralleled the Hoquiam River. He followed the river for another mile until he reached Ham Gravel. The quarry was on the steep slope side of a hill. The river cut away from the hill and had created a flood plain all the way across to the hills that stood above the two cities. The flood plain was divided up into small farms, a trailer court occupied one bend of land that hugged the river. The plain periodically flooded.

Nearly all the rock fill that had been pounded into the mudflats along the bay support construction for the Port, commercial district and housing for mill workers had come from the Ham quarry. The owners of the quarry had been mining there for nearly a hundred years. Sometimes you could hear local people joke that they lived on Ham's Rock.

By the time Gray got to the worksite, there were several older rusting pickups parked toward the back of the graveled yard at the base of the escarpment. Dump trucks and larger rock hauling trucks were parked along one side of the yard. There was a small office building toward the highway and a shed in the middle of the driveway. Every load of rock or gravel that left the yard had to be weighed. The cost of rock was determined by its grade, meaning the size of the gravel, and the cubic yards that left the yard.

Gray saw Roger working at the back of the yard. Roger waved and Gray headed in his direction.

"What are we building?" asked Gray after a few hellos to the other men at the site. He knew most of them. Theyran into each other on job sites over the years.

"Hamundarson wants a place to store his boat over the winter," said Roger.

"He must have a big boat," joked Gray as he looked at the area, they were to clear for a cement pad.

"Oh, it ain't no regular boat," said Roger. "Its that fake pirate ship, *Maiden's Curse*. We'll be cursed if we don't get this all done in the next week or so. Weather is going to set in soon."

Gray stood still for a moment. He surveyed the area they were to clean up and make ready for the cement truck's load. He began to suspect that Ham Gravel had something to do with my plight. He didn't say anything, just put on his work gloves and started shoveling the area with the other men. They worked steady all morning. At noon, they took a break. Gray felt tired and ached from head to foot. He took a pain pill and tried to rest leaning up against one of the old pickups. Roger passed out some sandwiches and bottles of water.

They had just about finished their lunch and break when a bright yellow Hummer came barreling into the yard. Seeing the men at their trucks, it made a fast turn and came to a halt next to Roger.

"How are you guys doing?" asked the driver. His voice was not full of warmth or any sign of true meaning.

"Good, Sir," said Roger. "We'll have this area ready for the cement truck tomorrow."

"Well, keep at it, you don't have much time. The pole barn needs to go up by the end of the week. The barn materials will be coming in on Wednesday. I need this all ready by a week from today."

"Okay, Sir, we'll have it ready. We'll be working right along. Shouldn't be a problem. We'll have to be careful around the concrete pad, but it should all be ready for the ship by next week," said Roger.

Without another word, Hamundarson backed the Hummer around and drove towards the office.

"Nice guy," he said to Roger.

"Yah, real nice," said Roger with a frown. "Expects everything now and is always late to get things going. He'll be a pain to deal with if anything slows this project up. And he won't give us any pay until he's satisfied. Wish we didn't have to work for him but there isn't much work around."

Gray watched the Hummer pull into a parking space at the office building. The vehicle had a specially designed license plate that read CAPT IKE. Gray shoved his shovel into the ground and flung its contents as hard as he could out across the yard. He knew to keep his mouth shut or there would be no work for him again in Grays Harbor. He hated the irony and evil that lurked behind every corner of 'his' harbor. Maybe it was a good thing to live as separate as possible from it all. Maybe a shack hidden in the alder grove was the only way to stay away from it all.

When Gray got back to the shack, he found me sitting on my

bed knitting. It was the one domestic hobby I enjoyed. As soon I saw Gray, I knew he was in pain.

"You look exhausted," I said.

I busied myself making tea and turning the hot soup I had made over again in its pot. Gray took off his work clothes and pulled on a pair of sweat pants and the oversized sweatshirt I had found in the shack. He seemed to have only the two sets of clothes and one because they were in the shack. I made a mental note to look for more warm clothes for him.

"What did you do all day?" he asked once he had the cup of hot tea in his hands. They stopped shaking enough for him to hold on to the cup.

"I did what you told me to do, take it easy," I said with a smile. "Tell me about your day. Was the work okay?"

"Work was fine. Roger's a good crew boss brought us lunch and all," he said quietly.

"What else?" I said, suspecting that something wasn't quite right.

"I found out who Captain Ham is," he said looking at me with a serious face. "In real life, he's Ike Hamundarson."

"Ike Hamundarson?" I ask in surprise. "He owns Ham Gravel?"

"Yes. We're building a big shed so he can store *Maiden's Curse*."

"I remember Gary at Harbor Insurance selling him some sort of liability insurance," I said.

"I'm not surprised," said Gray as he took a sip of tea. "He probably needs it. He's liable for your happiness, at least. Plus, Roger says he's not paying us until the job's done. Usually we get paid in cash every day. Guess pay day will be at the end of the week. Hope we can make it."

I nodded slightly, drank some tea and started to bring out bowls for the soup and a loaf of bread. "We'll be okay," I said. "Just have to watch the water and firewood."

We spent the rest of the hour eating our dinner. When it got dark,

I marked the time on my calendar.

"Tide's in and I am out," said Gray. He slid down into his bed and went to sleep, exhausted.

I lit a small candle beside my bed and took out the only book I had brought out to the shack from my apartment. It was a natural history of the Coast Range. Looking through the pages, I remembered how much I enjoyed watching for wildlife and birds. Knowing the tides was interesting. Now I could spend more time outside if I were careful. I could learn to see what the birdwatchers came out to see.

The candle burned down. Gray seemed to be in a deep sleep. It had become very quiet, no wind or rain beating against the shack. The canvas panels seemed to keep out noise as much as they kept in light and warmth from the stove. The shack was starting to feel homier. Having someone to cook for and chat with was definitely a plus. It seemed a bit riskier having him in on her secret life, but Gray acted like he was on board a hundred percent. What other options do I have? I asked myself.

The next morning, Gray was up and nearly out of the shack when I awoke.

"Here you go, sleepyhead," he said as he handed me hot coffee. "Stay warm and out of trouble."

"Okay," I smiled at him. "Be careful."

Mid-morning, I decided to go to the Y and check my bank account and PO box. It was a nice but chilly day to walk into town. I put on my disguise of glasses, hat, and working clothes. I took my backpack with a rain jacket and crackers and the jar of peanut butter. I walked along the road past Randolph's. Without the cart, I had time to explore a bit. I noticed the piles of unused lumber and construction materials at the shingle mill. There were scraps of various pieces of metal lying around at every parking lot. My mind wanted to find a way to use them at the shack. Gray would have to be involved.

A car was parked in one of the turnouts where people could access the rocks and mudflats out to the channel. The car was an older Subaru with a bunch of The Evergreen State College parking stickers on the back window. I kept my head down and pretended to study the roadway.

I took care of all my errands and started the long walk back to the shack. I went back along the streets and coast road, turning towards the shack at Bowerman Basin. This was always the tricky part. Someone could turn on to the road at any time. I had to be careful about ducking into the brush. The car I had seen over by Randolph's was parked near the path to the shack.

A surge of panic went through my body. I stopped for a moment and looked around. I didn't see or hear anyone. Please, please, please do not find the shack, I whispered to myself. I decided the only thing to do was to walk past the path and go down to the turnoff to the airport. I'd have to wait for the person to leave or for Gray to arrive. This wasn't supposed to happen, I thought.

I walked down to the end of the road and found a place to sit that was fairly well hidden in some brush. I waited for about an hour, getting up to look around and see what I could see. I saw nothing. Finally, I heard a car start. This must be the same car, I thought. No one else has driven past me.

I started to get up when I realized the car was headed toward me. I sank down in the brush as fast as I could. The car drove past me and turned towards the airport. Then it stopped in front of the US Fish and Wildlife Service work area. The driver was a woman. She got out, punched in a code on a lock box, and then got back in her car and drove into the fenced in work area. She unlocked the building and carried in a box of equipment. I sat frozen, wondering what would happen next. She came back to the doorway of the building and sat down. I watched her pull out her cell phone and punch in some numbers. She pulled off her hat and sunglasses while she waited for the call to be answered.

"Hello, John?" she said. "Yeah, I got the basic layout of Bowerman Basin in my head. I didn't see any evidence of peregrine falcons, but I'll keep checking. Yes, I did get all the tidal data and made notes about the shoreline. It's pretty quiet out here." There was a bit of silence while John was apparently giving her information. "Okay, I'll be ready to meet Hamundarson at the chipper boat dock tomorrow at three o'clock. It should be just right for an incoming tide. The mudflats will be filling up. I'll get to see the channel and around Bowerman Point. Thanks for arranging this, I think it will help me know the area."

It didn't take long for her to close the building. She got back in her car, and drove out of the fenced area, making sure the gate locked behind her. She drove past me, her eyes on the road and not on me. When she had made the last turn by the chipper plant, I started to feel a bit more secure. I walked as quickly as I could to the path and ducked inside the brush. I couldn't see that anything had been altered since I had left. Getting to the shack, I opened the door as quietly as I could and let myself in. It was only then that I could breath more normally.

When Gray got back to the shack, I could see that he was very tired. I waited until he had a chance to get cleaned up, something he did outside the back door with a wash rag of hot water and a basin. Something would have to be done about our shower situation before long. The winter rains would make an outdoor shower impossible. Gray came back for hot tea and something to eat.

After we had eaten more soup and bread, I said, "Had a close call today. Found some Evergreen birdwatcher nosing around. I had to hide out and wait for her to leave."

Gray paused and took a sip of tea. "Where was she?" he asked.

"I saw her car over by Randolph's this morning. When I got back to the path, it was parked pretty close, so I went over by the Fish and Wildlife area to hide out and wait for her to leave. I overheard her call somebody named Jen. She gave her some sort of information, something about how she's supposed to meet someone named Hamundarson tomorrow at the chipper dock and go out in a boat with him."

"Great, that's all we need. An Evergreen birdwatcher," said Gray. "Well, we'll have to see what happens. The name Hamundarson is getting to be pretty common around here."

The light went out of the sky and worry replaced the feeling of happiness I had twenty-four hours ago. Do not be defeatist, I thought to myself. This is home.

# 8

# ANDY AND THE HARBOR

*A*ndy Steele left The Evergreen State College on Wednesday morning with a single goal in mind, get to the dock at the chipper plant by two o'clock. She was looking forward to spending the afternoon getting to know Bowerman Basin and the surrounding bay from a boat. Kudos to the US Fish and Wildlife Service for setting up the expedition. The boat owner was supposed to be a nice guy who was interested in helping document the natural history of the bay. 'I hope he understands that my research is instigated by the potential gas terminal,' she thought.

Andy glanced down at the paperwork in the front seat of her Subaru. She had finally gotten all the signatures she needed for her Winter Quarter academic contract. The contract would allow her to continue researching wildlife in Bowerman Basin especially birds that wintered in the Basin. She had worked out the academic side of things with the ornithologist who had apparently helped get Bowerman Basin into the refuge system. She had heard him speak one time in a class she had taken at Grays Harbor Community College. His talk had inspired her to take more classes in natural history at Evergreen.

The other signature she had needed was that of the research co-ordinator at the US Fish and Wildlife Service office in Olympia. Her signature gave Andy the right to conduct field studies at the basin and use the facility the refuge maintained at the basin. Andy felt part of a professional environment. She had a focus and contact with the refuge. She would earn her academic credit through experience and supervision by professionals. Maybe being an older student helps, she thought. She wasn't a young extremist trying to say that port development was wrong, and the environment had to be 'saved' like many young, enthusiastic Evergreen students. I love those guys, but not exactly my style, she thought as she pulled onto Mud Bay Road and headed west.

Andy continued to think about the political and social environment of Grays Harbor as she headed toward Aberdeen. The Grays Harbor Community College class had stressed that the bay and its communities were a system, not a set of compartmentalized entities. Conflict in one part of the system had an impact on another subsystem. The possibility of a gas terminal at the port suddenly illuminated a series of unknowns and potentials for all entities in the bay, both natural and cultural. The wide disparity in beliefs about what was good for the port and the economic agenda for the entire harbor was starting to show the lack of knowledge about the natural communities.

But what is natural? Andy mused. Students and faculty in the class had argued about how to know what was natural. Was *anything* natural? Were people natural? Were their past actions setting up the future? What did it mean to say that nature was socially constructed? Could you set a timeframe to evaluate when something had been natural and now it wasn't? Andy shook her head, not sure how she thought about philosophical possibilities. Her goal was much more concrete: start recording the wildlife that inhabited the mudflats at Bowerman Basin.

The gas terminal proposal was complicated and messy after to a long history of massive resource extraction, exceedingly diverse ecology, and generations of people living in around the bay. Now the resource base was changing, the ecology and economy were being threatened by climate change in places far away from the bay like China, and the local populations were feeling disenfranchised, poor and with few opportunities. The port seemed to be working against them the local population by bringing in globalized industries. And let's not forget the role of the Quinault Nation, she reminded herself.

The drive from Cooper Point at the southernmost end of Puget Sound, where the college was located, to Grays Harbor was fascinating to someone interested in natural history. Despite the distance and the repeated times Andy drove the route, she never got tired of seeing the ecological changes along the way. She started every trip by stopping at Blue Heron Bakery just before the on-ramp to US 101. She ordered a cup of coffee and a vegan chocolate muffin.

Blue Heron Bakery had been serving good food and coffee to students and travelers on the way to the beach since the 1970s. Andy loved to stop in and enjoy the simple ambience of the bakery as much as the coffee and goodies. The workspace behind the counter reminded her of a place she had worked at in Portland years ago. There were the odd bits of memorabilia, posters, a few potted plants, folk music for sale, and signs supporting local poetry readings, political causes, and efforts to save Earth.

The bakery gave Andy a sense of safety. It reminded her of places she had hung out at over the course of many years. She had taken a long time to get to Evergreen State. There had been many years of low-paying jobs and living as a vagabond. She wanted to make the most of the opportunity she had to work out at Grays Harbor. She had hopes and dreams of spending the rest of her life working natural resource management.

Andy left the Blue Heron and headed toward Hwy 101. She crossed the bridge over the mudflats of Mud Bay. Here was the end of Puget Sound. An interpretive sign indicated that Lieutenant Peter Puget, Royal Navy serving under the command of Captain George

Vancouver had explored the massive inland reach of the Pacific Ocean that now bears the name Puget Sound. Puget had reached the southernmost extremity of the sound in 1792, finally satisfied that this was not the long-sought Northwest Passage.

Mud Bay experienced tidal change even though it is nearly one hundred miles south of the Strait of Juan de Fuca and the entrance to the sound. As Andy drove across the bridge, she noted that the tide was slowly reclaiming the mudflats in Mud Bay. The water would be nearing high tide by the time she arrived at the dock in Grays Harbor. Not so good for making observations of the mudflats in Bowerman Basin, she thought.

Andy merged onto the busy highway. She watched traffic in her rear-view mirror jockey for position as the lanes approached the exit for US 101. US 101 turned north to begin its way around the Olympic Peninsula. Hwy 12 had left Interstate 5 north of Centralia and followed the Chehalis River to Elma where it merged with Hwy 8 to become the route to Aberdeen. The major cross-country route ended in Aberdeen. At Elma, the twin towers of the dismantled Satsop nuclear power plant stood on the foothills of the Coast Range to the south of the highway. Andy smiled, recalling the commonly held belief that the towers were the backdrop for "The Simpsons."

Just past Elma, Andy stopped at a gas station. A silver Mercedes was parked at the shop next to the gas pumps. She filled the tank of her car with gas with her debit card and went into the shop to buy a few more items for her backpack. She wasn't sure how long she would be out in the boat. A sudden drop in blood sugar levels would make her a basket case. Waiting to pay for her power bar and package of nuts, she couldn't help overhearing the conversation between a well-dressed couple at the counter and the cashier.

"Could you help us with directions? asked the man. "I'm unfamiliar with this area."

"Where are you going?" replied the cashier. She was a younger woman, probably in her mid-20s. She looked a bit worn out either from having to ring up a cashier all day or being just a bit angry with life.

"We are going to a place called Seabrook. We haven't been there but have heard so much about its beautiful setting on the north coast," spoke the woman.

"Oh," frowned the cashier. "You have to go into Aberdeen and then north."

"Well," said the man. "For how far?"

"About forty miles," said the cashier. She kept her eyes on a set of numbers she pretended to be adding.

"Anything more?" asked the man, obviously a bit annoyed.

"Maybe I can help," Andy said.

The couple turned toward me. "Do you know where it is?" said the woman. "We have an appointment with a real estate agent there and we don't want to be late."

The cashier sniffed loudly and walked towards a small office behind the counter.

Andy pulled a free brochure from a rack on the counter. "Here, let me show you."

The three of us gazed at a map on the brochure as Andy traced out the route to Seabrook. "Follow the signs to Ocean Shores and then watch for US 101 signs. Seabrook also has signs pointing the direction. If you end up at Ocean Shores, just stay on the main road and don't turn into Ocean Shores."

"Why not?" asked the woman.

"Let's just say its not the same class as Seabrook. Seabrook tried to keep people headed north on the main highway," Andy said. "You won't have any problems. Seabrook has big billboards that tell you how to get there."

"Thank you," they both said in unison. They closed the brochure and turned together to walk out the door. They got into the Mercedes and pulled back onto the highway.

The cashier came back to the counter. She looked almost angry.

"You didn't need to help them," she said under her breath.

"Why not?" Andy asked. "They seemed nice enough."

"Nice and rich enough," said the cashier. "Just one more rich couple in a Mercedes stopping in here to ask for directions to Seabrook." She raised her head and looked me straight in the eye. "All these people from Seattle coming over here with there money and buying up our land, I hate 'em!" she said.

"That's pretty strong language," Andy said quietly.

"We used to be able to use the land and hunt up there. Now we can't go there. The environmentalists have closed it all down for a bunch of birds. I hate it!" she said defiantly.

She took Andy's money and pushed the register drawer closed with a bit of a shove.

Andy went back out to her car and slipped the food into her backpack. 'There are some unhappy people out here,' she thought. 'Won't make my job any easier.' She got back out on the highway, driving a bit slower as if to pace herself through uncharted territory.

As Andy crossed the south flowing Whynoochee River at Montesano, the last major tributary of the Chehalis, she could see the up Whynoochee Valley. The valley was framed by tracts of land that had been clear-cut. The second, and in some cases, third growth, timber created a checkerboard of forest cover. Much of this timber land was privately owned or maintained by joint agreements with the US Forest Service and large timber companies. Native American claims had either been extinguished or were supposed to be managed with guidance of the US Forest Service. While to most drivers on Hwy 12, the landscape looked like a patchwork of timber harvesting. To Andy, it looked like ecology interrupted.

Just before the commercial area, Andy turned towards the river, crossed the tracks, and drove into the parking lot of the Rotary Log

Pavilion. The site overlooked the Chehalis River right where the river and the bay met. This was a significant ecological area despite all the industry, bank armoring, and docks that lined the river. From here Andy could see the large swath of the river, the Willapa Hills on the other side of the river and the Port area along the channel of the Chehalis out into Grays Harbor.

Directly across from the parking lot was the Grays Harbor Historical Seaport where *Lady Washington* tied up when they were in port. US 101, that had come down around the Olympia Peninsula and along the east side of the Quinault Nation Reservation. The reservation lands extended out to the coast and they had prevented a national highway to be built through the reservation. In Aberdeen, US 101 crossed the Chehalis River on a hundred-foot-tall span. Below the span were old, abandoned dock facilities and warehouses. Increasingly, more and more homeless people camped under the bridge at the water's edge.

Andy sat for a while in her car, taking a break from the drive. Despite all the development along the river, there was a vibrant ecological community here. The mixing of tidal saltwater with the massive volume of fresh water created a dynamic environment. When the tide was all the way in, it raised the level of the river twenty feet from the low tide mark. The exposed banks were lined by a narrow band of mudflats. While nearly invisible, a magnitude of small creatures waited in the mudflats for the brackish water to return. Narrow bands like these were the basis for nearly all marine life in estuaries and river channels of the Chehalis.

Looking at her watch, Andy decided to head to the chipper dock. It took a long time to drive through Aberdeen. Returning the main street, she turned west crossing the Wishkah River and stopping at the light. Before arriving at the intersection, she went past a series of store-fronts advertising souvenirs for sale. These shops were dedicated to the popular culture icons that had made Aberdeen and the

Olympia Peninsula household word across America. One shop advertised replicas of 'Twilight' clothing from the television series that had taken place in Forks, seventy miles north on Highway 101.

The other shops paid tribute to Aberdeen's most famous resident turned international music star, Kurt Cobain. His rise to fame included musical lyrics about his early life in Aberdeen. The hard-piercing music and words depicted his image of the town as a cold and cruel place, a place that kept reclaiming him every time he seemed to have escaped its clasp on his life. In many ways, his music about the town equaled the power of drugs that continually reclaimed him until they won the battle and took his life away.

Andy followed the main street through Aberdeen. The street and surrounding blocks had once been a major commercial area. Now, due to economic hard times, half the store fronts were empty. Those that remained open had not had the resources to keep up appearances. Paint was peeling off the buildings and signs had not been repaired or replaced. Thrift stores and 'Adults Only' shops had replaced stationary stores, women's dress shops, and offices selling services. In some places, buildings had been destroyed due to fire or the city manager had had derelict and abandoned buildings removed. Empty parking lots were the only reminders of better economic times.

# 9

# ANDY AND BOWERMAN BASIN

*F*ollowing the instructions that Jen at the US Fish and Wildlife Service office had given her, Andy stayed on the truck route through Aberdeen and into Hoquiam. After crossing the Hoquiam River on the old metal lift bridge, she turned left and then left again into downtown Hoquiam. A right turn at the light took her past brick city office buildings, an Art Deco federal building, a marble post office, a newer brick multi-stored senior housing building that could have been a prison, the historic Saron Lutheran Church, and finally, past the restored Hoquiam train depot, now occupied by the Washington State Department of Motor Vehicles. The civic oriented buildings were all that was left a thriving river port.

Andy followed the truck route, turning left to drive past cedar shake mills and truck maintenance facilities. She was watching for a large conveyer belt to pass over the road that indicator of where the dock was located where she was to meet her boat ride on the bay. To her left was the bay and, on the right, a second shake mill that seemed to be abandoned. Gravel parking areas were punched into the shoreline of the bay. A few pickups were parked in these areas, the owners seemed to be down at the water's edge fishing, birding or just killing time. Andy pulled into a vacant parking area and stared out at the bay.

The tide was out, exposing two hundred meters of low grasses and then mud out to the channel of the Chehalis. In fact, she could not see the water in the channel, it was at its lowest point, its natural volume, due to the lack of tidewater. Andy was struck by the massive amount of driftwood that littered the grasses and mudflats. Silver tree trunks with stubby limbs, some half buried in mud, lay in mounds like bleached human skeletal remains, arms and legs flung in every direction and massive knots of feet as if a massive grave had just been excavated. The ghostly image of death caused Andy to take a deep breath and sit back in the seat of her car. The sun, which had until now been shining down on the macabre scene was beginning to falter as clouds moved in from the ocean. A wind blew across the scene before her forced her to wrap her coat a bit tighter around her shoulders.

Andy looked to the east, following the shoreline. She hadn't noticed a place of human habitation along the shore until now. This required turning back towards town to see what appeared to be a small dock only accessible by water during high tide. An old thirty-foot wood fishing boat sat in the mud, tied to the dock pier. Alongside the far side of the dock was a rather large silver-gray building. It appeared to have been built half out of planed lumber but never painted and half out of the deadly driftwood.

At first, Andy thought the building was a fish processing plant but the more she looked at it, the more she began to see that it was inhabited. A pirate's skull and crossbones flag ruffled in the westerly wind from a pole attached to the structure. A curtain hung over half of its only window. A mop stood next to a battered door that led from the dock. Driftwood was stacked against the wall within easy reach of the door.

Andy pulled her binoculars out of her pack and focused on the building. She watched as a man opened the door and stepped out on to the dock. He appeared to be surveying the bay and channel, perhaps estimating the expected arrival of as fishing boat. He lifted a pair of binoculars to his face and looked towards the western end of the bay. Then he turned and pointed his binoculars in Andy's direction. The two starred at each other for a full minute, not expecting to see other and not willing to be the first to blink. Remembering she had to work with residents on the harbor, Andy dropped her binoculars and started her car.

Andy followed the road around a bend. The conveyor over the road rose on either side of the road. To her right were mammoth piles of wood chips the color of freshly sawn wood. A three-story high blue metal chute like something you would see at a grain elevator, was dumping more chips on to the pile next to the road. On the bay side of the conveyer a wooden platform extended out over the shoreline. A dock stretched parallel to the shoreline. Water splashed below the dock, a channel through the mud kept open by dredging. The conveyor extended out over the entire distance of the dock so that it could reach the holds of barges and ships.

Reaching her destination, she turned her car onto the platform and parked. It was here that she was to meet her guide, someone named Ike Hamundarson. She was a few minutes early, just enough time to grab her red backpack with field notebook, water bottle, rain gear, and wallet. She pulled on tall rubber boats and tied a hat beneath her chin. Leaving her car on the dock, she walked over to the water hoping to find the nice gentleman in his recreational fishing boat who had volunteered to take her out on the bay and around into Bowerman Basin.

Ike Hamundarson had brought his personal fishing boat over from Westport on the incoming tide. The boat was a 40-foot North River aluminum boat large enough to cross over the harbor bar and fish for halibut and salmon. The boat had two 50-horsepower external motors, a spacious glassed in deck, and below deck stowage area in the bow. Electronic equipment allowed the pilot to read water depth, water temperatures, weather conditions, and exact location.

Pilots learned to trust their sonar and bathometric instruments when visibility was limited by fog or weather. Getting lost as sea was never fully avoidable. Recklessness, even inside the harbor, could have disastrous consequences.

Ike arrived at the chipper dock about a half an hour before the appointed time to meet the Evergreen student. He pulled out a life jacket from beneath a passenger seat. He didn't like having outsiders nosing around the bay especially someone who had the ability to thwart port development. He leaned back on the cabin, waiting to see what the student would look like. He could put together some strategy for frightening the Greener. Shouldn't be too hard, he thought. They're all a little crazy and prone to stupid grandstanding. That made them vulnerable.

Ike watched as the older Subaru drove onto the dock and parked at a safe distance from the water. What Ike expected when the door opened, and the passenger got out was not what he saw. Instead of a fragile but aggressive young student, he was surprised to see an older middle-aged woman who didn't appear fragile in any way. In fact, she stood solidly on both feet, pulled on rubber boats and a hat, and picked up a large backpack. She checked her car's location against the shape of the dock and its proximity to the water, put a US Fish and Wildlife Service employee sign on the dashboard and made sure the car was locked before turning toward the end of the dock and Ike's boat.

"Hello," she said with a mature voice. "You must be Mr. Hamundarson. I'm Andrea Steele, most people just call me Andy." She held out her hand, expecting Ike to extend his in welcome.

Ike, not used to shaking womens' hands, stood for a second, not sure what he was expected to do. By shaking her hand, he was agreeing to a sense of equality. The thought made him squirm a bit internally. Here was someone who was not going to be easily frightened off. Guilt had never been an emotion for him, he never looked back. With a bit of a jerk and a nod, Ike grasped the woman's hand. "Welcome aboard," he said.

Andy stepped down into the boat. Ike handed her the life jacket. "Better put it on," he said. "There's always someone patrolling the bay."

"I can't imagine ICE will stop us," said Andy trying to be a bit coy.

"We won't worry about ICE. They're watching to see if anybody jumps ship and tries to stay on this side of the Pacific. We'll avoid attracting the interests of the Coast Guard or some county sheriff out for a joy ride," said Ike. So, she's a bit cheeky, he thought with a frown.

Andy tried to reconnect. "I'm really thankful you are able to take me out today. I've been trying to learn as much as I can about the channel and the basin. Getting to see the shoreline from out in the water is a great opportunity."

"Tell me what it is you want to see while we are out here," said Ike as he untied the boat. He stepped into the cabin area, turned on the motors and waited to hear them run smoothly before putting them into gear.

"I am most interested in the interaction between the tidal changes and wildlife on the mudflats," she said. "We really don't know much about the ecology of Grays Harbor, least of all the mudflats. A big development like the fuel terminal could have a major impact on the ecology."

"Okay," said Ike. "We'll go for a bit of ride in the channel and then pull into Bowerman Basin. The incoming tide will help us. I don't expect bad weather or a rolling surf, but you never know."

"I've been on a fishing boat before, so I don't worry about me," Andy said. She sat on a bench along the bow of the boat. She could see 180 degrees around the front of the boat, and the other half of their location by turning toward the aft. She pulled out her Rite-in-the-Rain field notebook and a pencil, ready to take notes, camera was looped around her neck.

The boat left the dock for the channel. At this point in tidal change, the channel was well-defined, the deeper water caught in the dredged channel, the true level of the bay floor evident in the lighter color of the water.

"We'll go out toward Westport so you can see the widest extent of the bay," shouted Ike over the churning of the motors. He steered the boat into the channel and ramped up the speed of the motors. The boat created a wake behind them. Andy held on to the gunnel. They passed a freighter coming up the channel and another moored inside the entrance to the bay.

As they neared the Westport jetty, Ike turned the boat to face the bay and cut the motors. "We can sit here for a bit; the tide will push us up the channel."

"Tell me about yourself," he said. "How did you end up being an Evergreen student and getting out to Grays Harbor? This is pretty much off the beaten track." He was curious about her life history given that she wasn't the student he had expected. She didn't appear to be a crazed environmentalist.

Andy closed her field notebook. "I've lived in different places around the Northwest. Tried various jobs in Seattle and Portland. Never got hooked on a career, just tried to keep my head above water financially. I worked hard enough but sometimes things got a little sketchy," she said looking down at her lap. "I spent a summer out here at Westport working at The Chateau as a maid. Took a class at the community college from some Evergreen professors. I learned about natural history."

"Found my passion," Andy continues with a smile. "Now, I'm hoping this work with the Fish and Wildlife Service will help me get a job doing something I care about."

"What do you care about?" asked Ike, again surprised at his interest in the conversation.

"I care that we, as humans, learn to live with Earth, not just on it," she said.

Andy opened her notebook. From this vantage point, the bay was massive. The port's docks and grain terminals lined the north side of the harbor nearly two miles upstream. Another mile upstream was the bridge span that connected the north and south sides of the Chehalis. The south side was bounded by steeper banks, mostly forested. A few openings revealed the large outdoor sport complex and parks directly across from the north side docks and terminals. Closer to Westport was the large Elk River estuary. Another bridge span crossed over the estuary. At the mouth of Elk River was the largest commercial oyster business on the harbor. The site had once been a whaling station but now only place names reminded travelers of the whaling past.

Ike kept the boat idling in the channel for half an hour as Andy took copious notes based on her observations. Grayish tidal waters were pushing up the channel, meeting the sediment-laden brown waters of the river. The sky was gray with layers of clouds settling in over the harbor. Direct sunlight was rare this time of year, but it was there, above the clouds, fueling the wind. Grays' Harbor is aptly named in so many ways, thought Andy.

Between the east side of Damon Point and the north shore of the harbor was Bowerman Basin. The basin was created by the extension of the Damon sand spit and the extension of a point of land about a half mile east. The point had been extended into the harbor by decades of dredged river bottom material. Years and years of the material had filled in the shallow tidal areas around the point. The bottom material had been compacted until it could support roads and the municipal airport that now stretched out toward Damon Point. The shallows between both points were extensive mudflats. Tides moved back and forth across the mudflats, draining the heart of the ecosystem as they retreated, and filling the heart with life as the saltwater returned. It was in this zone that Andy hoped to record birdlife over the next few months.

The tide was beginning to rush in, deepening the channel and pushing them into the bay. Seawater spread on either side of the channel until Andy was unable to distinguish the channel and the reclaimed bay and mudflats. With the tide and the wind becoming stronger by the minute, the boat was being propelled at a faster and faster rate. The calm afternoon was becoming more animated. A group of brown first year gulls practiced diving for food off the water's surface. Andy pulled her pack closer to her feet to protect it from bits of spray that were now popping up over the edge of the boat.

With Westport behind her, Andy turned her attention to the north side of the harbor. Ike had positioned the boat so that she could see the long spit of sand called Damon Point that reached out into the mudflats towards the Chehalis channel. Damon Point curved around toward Westport and the mouth of Grays Harbor. Freighters coming up the channel sailed past the point. Standing on the end of Damon Point, the freighters appeared to be closer to the north side of the harbor then they were to Westport.

"What do you see?" yelled Ike, surprised to hear his own voice express an interest in the bay other than an economic opportunity.

Andy sat for a minute before answering him. "I see bird habitat and brackish water. I see are layers of energy," she shouted back. "I see the horizon with the sky full of clouds, moisture, wind, and, of course, solar radiation. The sun is our ultimate energy supply."

"Not interested in fuel production?" yelled Ike, hoping to spark a debate.

Instead, Andy responded, "I realize we have an economy based on fossil fuel production. I'm not interested in throwing out the entire economy, but we can conserve. We can use less. We can find alternatives. I know the gas terminal is a big project for the port." She stopped, waiting to see Ike's reaction.

Ike didn't answer. She had shown her hand as a conservationist and sounded like all the other people that came out to the harbor, thinking they knew a better way. Aberdeen and Hoquiam never would have been developed if it weren't for raw materials and the capacity to ship them to markets. The Pacific Northwest would be nothing. He didn't want to get into an argument with her, although it might make things easier when he made his moves.

"Let's go over to Bowerman Basin before the weather and waves get worse. It's not so interesting. I don't know why we should care about it so much," shouted Ike.

Ike followed the buoy markers and then turned to the north to enter the Basin. He kept Damon Spit on the west side of the basin on his left. The highway to the coastal towns of Ocean Shores and Quinault were directly in front of them. The airport and the shallowest part of the basin were on their right. As he turned the boat to face the highway, a gust of wind came in from the ocean and pushed the boat to one side despite the motors' power. Spray bit into Andy's face while water began to pool around her feet.

"Starting to get a bit too stormy to be out here," he yelled at Andy.

Andy pulled on her raincoat, zipping it over her camera, and put away her notebook. She put her pack on just in case things got a little blustery. She didn't want to lose anything. The sky turned dark as clouds moved in from the ocean. The bay turned from a silver-gray expanse into dark rolling waves. The boat began to rock between waves that pushed the boat from side to side.

"Does it always change so quickly?" shouted Andy with a bit of fear in her voice. She hadn't expected an interior bay to become like an angry ocean.

"We don't have much time left out here before I won't be able to get the boat back to Westport," yelled Ike. "I'm going to take you in closer to the shore so you can see the mudflats."

"Okay," shouted Andy. She wanted to see the mudflats, but she didn't like the sudden change in weather. The air smelled more like the ocean as the steady westerly winds pushed in the clouds. The sky, once brighter, was becoming grayer by the minute. The winds were picking up and white caps were forming on the bay.

Andy put on her backpack and pulled her way further towards the bow of the boat. Ike revved the motors again, pushing the boat faster toward the shore. She looked back at him, hoping he would see that she was getting more uncomfortable by the second. The boat suddenly slowed as it moved into the shallow part of Bowerman Basin. Even at high tide, this area of the Basin had only a couple feet of water covering the mud.

"Get out!" yelled Ike.

"What?" shouted Andy in disbelief. She looked at Ike as if he were mad and then peered down at the mudflats.

"Get out now," he yelled. "You wanted to see the mudflats, so here you are Besides," he said, looking up at the incoming storm, "I don't think I can get you safely back to the dock in this sea."

"But I could get stuck in the mud," yelled Andy. She didn't believe his claim that he couldn't get them both safely back to the dock.

"That's your problem," yelled Ike. "You better learn to watch your step around here," he shouted at her. "Better learn who you can trust and who you can't. We don't want people like you nosing around the harbor or putting their oar into business that they don't support. Now get out or I'll make sure you do."

The threat was real. The wind and the in-coming tide were changing the shallow water and mudflats by the second. If she jumped out now, she might have a chance of getting to shore. All the stories of people who got caught and drowned in the mudflats flashed through her mind. She looked at Ike and saw how defiant and evil his face had become. She believed him. He would push her out of the boat.

She put one leg over the gunnel and tried to feel for the bottom of the shallows. Her rubber boat touched down into mud. She pulled her other leg over the gunnel and felt her entire weight sink into the mud. Ike revved his motors one more time and backed away.

"Better watch what you're doing out here. Better watch your back. We're not so friendly to outsiders like you," he yelled. He turned the boat to face Westport. After passing out of the basin, he powered the boat at full speed and headed toward the Westport jetty.

Andy was barely cognizant of his efforts to return to Westport. She tried to keep herself upright in the two feet of water. Her boots were very difficult to move, she could hardly pull them out of the mud. The rising tidal water was nearly at the top of her boots. It had started to rain. The late afternoon sun was very low, sinking below the horizon. It would be dark soon. She tried to take a step forward. The mud and the water were making her boots feel like heavy weights. She looked at the shore. The closest bit of land to her was on the point where the airport and the US Fish and Wildfire Service building was located. While the distance was not that great from where she was mired in the mud, it looked nearly impossible to reach.

With great deliberation, she pulled one foot forward and steadied herself. The rising water was now at the top of her boots. She struggled to pull her other foot forward and keep her balance. She didn't want to fall into the water, she would never be able to get back up. There was no leverage in the thick mud. She saw some grasses just ahead of her. 'If I can just get to the grass,' she thought. Using all her strength, she pulled her right foot forward. If she could just get another few feet toward the point, she thought she could grab on to the grasses.

She was so intently focused on the grass and looking forward to the point that she didn't hear the water behind her. Instead of gradual tide water moving inland, the water in the bay was being pushed by the wind, making waves. Without warning, a large wave engulfed Andy. It pushed her down and forward, into the water. She felt her boots clamp around her feet and then be pulled off by the water as it receded.

All Andy could feel was shocking cold water. She kicked her legs and tried to propel herself toward the grasses. She caught a handful in her right hand. It nearly pulled out of the mud, but then held. With one more kick, Andy was able to grab another bunch of grass with her left hand. Her pack was weighing down as she lay face down in the water. She turned her head, hoping to see someplace on shore that she could get to. The cold water was freezing her hands around the grass. Her legs and feet could hardly move.

Adrenaline kicked into her system. With a burst of energy, Andy pushed and pulled herself to the shore, still on her stomach, crawling now in the mud and water. She pulled herself up onto the shoreline. She collapsed in a niche of some rocks, her pack still on her back, her feet bare at the edge of the water. The rain beat on her back. She was totally worn out, cold and wet, her clothes covered in mud. Except for the red of her pack, she was hardly distinguishable from the rocks and mud.

# 10

# ANOTHER MAIDEN CURSED

ray and I were on the airport side of the point when we saw Ike Hamundarson speeding across the water in his fishing boat.

"How do you know it's him?" asked Gray.

"See that bright blue hat?" I said. "He usually wore that hat when he wasn't in his pirate costume."

"He must be headed to Westport," said Gray. He looked at the western sky, now threatening rain. The wind was coming up. "I wonder what he was doing out here. Pretty close to the point," he observed. "We better get going or we are going to be caught in this weather."

Gray and I had taken a walk around the point to gather firewood. Gathering firewood on the shore was a common enough practice. Some people got all their firewood by collecting driftwood. If the driftwood hadn't settled in a dune or up out of the water, it was free for the taking. Gray had stuffed larger pieces of wood into his Kelty backpack. I carried two large canvas bags now full of smaller limbs and bits of wood that would make good kindling. We had to keep the wood small enough so that the fires in the stove would be small.

"Let's go back around the point and get to the shack," said Gray. He turned and led the way. The light rain was becoming a downpour.

Gusts of wind pushed rain from the west. Waves were forming on the basin. 'It was going to be a long and stormy night,' I thought.

We fought the wind and rain as we plodded toward the path that led to the shack. We were nearly there when Gray stopped. I was so intent on getting into the brush and away from the rain, I ran into him.

"What are you doing?" I said a bit impatient. "Let's get inside."

Gray pointed to the rocks just beyond our hidden pathway. "What's that?"

At first, I couldn't tell what he was looking at in the rocks. Then I saw a red pack.

Gray fought against the wind and the rain to get to the rocks. He grabbed the pack and then the shoulders of someone covered in mud. He turned the person to its side and looked closely at the face.

"It's a woman," he said over the wind. "She's not responding. We better get her inside."

As these words left his lips, he looked at me with some apprehension. "We have to help her," he said. "Maybe we can get her up." He pulled off her pack and slid his arms under her armpits. He pulled hard. I knew this was painful for him. I grabbed her around her waist and tried to help get her to her feet. She was barefoot, completely covered in mud.

"She must be freezing," I said. "She's drenched."

She was upright but bent over at the waist like a rag doll. Slowly, knowing that she was barefoot and barely able to move, we lifted her body up and then down, one step at a time. It took long minutes to get her to the path. Gray, I could tell, was now in real pain.

"Okay," I said. "Let's pull her along the path and get her to the cabin. Her clothes are a total mess anyway."

We pulled her along the path, trying to avoid brush and keep it out of her face. She didn't say anything or make any indication that she knew what was going on. Finally, we got her to the back door of the shack.

"You try to get as much of her clothes off her as you can out here. I'll go inside and get the fire going," said Gray.

I pulled off her raincoat, as if it had kept her dry. Her fleece vest was soaked through as well as her jeans. It was difficult to pull off her clothes, my fingers were getting too cold to work properly. After wrestling with her clothes, I managed to get them off. She started to shiver. Gray came out of the shack with a blanket. We wrapped her in the wool as quickly as we could and then pulled her into the shack. The fire was warming the small space. At least there was no rain or wind. I tried to concentrate on her need for warmth.

"I'm going back to the shore and get her pack," said Gray.

I looked at him in sympathy. "Get back here as fast as you can," I said.

I pulled the woman over to my sleeping space and put as many blankets on her as I could. I washed off her face and tried to get as much mud out of her hair as I could. She started to murmur as I washed off mud from her body. I soaked two towels in hot water from the stove and wrapped them around her feet to warm her as quickly as possible.

"Where am I?" she whispered.

"You're okay," I said. "You are safe here."

Who are you? I wondered. And what are we going to do with you in our hidden shack?

# ANDY AND SARON

*I* pulled the blankets up around the woman's head, hoping she would be warm enough through the night. Her clothes were now hanging on a clothesline strung diagonally across the room. Gray lifted her pack to the countertop. "Guess we'll let her tell us who she is in the morning," he said in a tired voice.

"Did you get enough to eat?" I asked Gray. I hadn't paid much attention to Gray. "You must be cold and achy," I said with concern. I watched him slide a painkiller into his mouth and wash it down with a gulp of tea.

"I'll be okay," he said. He turned toward his bed and pulled off his damp clothes. His boots were below the stove as well. The candle made shadows of his form as he took off clothes and sat down on the bed. Miss Hap jumped up beside him and put a paw on his chest. Gray stroked the cat and then shooed her back to the floor.

"Guess you'll have to sleep with me tonight," he said in a voice half joking and half with sweetness. "And I don't mean you, Miss Hap," he said to the cat.

"Guess I will," I said. "We'll be much warmer together," I said looking into his eyes. He pulled me closer into his body and we slowly entangled ourselves into each other's arms. "See," I said gently. "We're warmer already."

"What will we do with the woman?" I whispered.

"Don't think about that now. We'll figure it out in the morning."

Gray was asleep in seconds. I laid awake for a while. Here I am, just about to feel like we are safely hidden away, and now two people have found this shack. How many more will? Why are people being forced to look for shelter? The questions went around in my head until I was overcome with tiredness. 'Yes, we are safe for tonight,' I thought.

The woman across the room began to stir before Gray or I got up. As quickly as he could, Gray got up, dressed in his work clothes and encouraged the banked ashes in the stove to relight. I pulled on my clothes and set out cups for coffee. I found a tin of oatmeal cookies and a can of condensed sweet milk in our stash of food. I broke up the cookies in our other three coffee mugs and poured nearly all the condensed sweetened milk over the cookies. Gray stirred the fire and got the water boiling. He made coffee in the French press and filled the coffee cups. The last of the condensed milk can got turned upside down into each of the mugs.

The warmth of the fire and the smell of coffee filled the shack with the comforting aroma of a homey kitchen. It was our homey kitchen yesterday. No telling what would happen now, I thought. I took a mug of coffee and a mug of cookies and went over to the woman. There was Miss Hap, curled up beside the woman. I sat down on the floor next to the bed.

She opened her eyes. She immediately tried to sit up but slid back into the bed.

"Where am I?" she asked in a fearful voice.

"You are safe," I said. "You are in the alder grove at Bowerman Basin. It's Okay. Can you sit up?"

She looked at me for a minute. "I don't know. Who you are?" she asked in a husky voice. Miss Hap stood up at the sound of the woman's voice. The cat jumped away from the mattress, surprised that the form on the bed was not mine.

"My name is Saron. And this is Gray," I gestured across to the room. Gray was sipping his coffee and testing the boots to see how dry they were.

"Would you like some coffee and oatmeal cookies in sweetened milk? You must be hungry," I asked. I set a mug of sweetened cookies on the floor beside the bed and handed her the coffee cup. "Be careful, it's hot," I said.

She took a sip of coffee and looked around. "Those are my clothes," she said gazing at the pants, shirt, and jacket hanging from the clothesline.

"I hope you don't mind," I said. "You were awfully wet and muddy when we found you yesterday."

"You found me?" she asked. "Where was I?"

"We found you on the shore on the inside of the point. You must have gotten caught out on the mudflats as the tide was coming in. You're lucky to have survived," said Gray. "What were you doing out there?"

"I was left out there,' she said. She took another sip of coffee and then picked up the mug of cookies and milk. "This is good," she said. "Thank you."

"How did you get left on the point?" I asked with some concern.

"I got pushed off a boat," she said quietly. The memory of the events seemed to be returning to her mind.

"What?" said Gray. "Someone pushed you off a boat and left you out there? That's crazy."

I sat back on the floor and looked at the woman. I was finding it hard to believe that the same set of circumstances that had brought me to the point had brought this woman into our shack and secret existence.

"Who pushed you off a boat?" I asked.

"A guy named Ike Hamundarson. He was supposed to be helping me learn about Bowerman Basin. I guess he doesn't want me asking too many questions about the basin."

I looked up at Gray. He was peering down at the woman with a concerned look, almost anger.

"Ike Hamundarson," he said forcefully, turning back to the stove. "He seems to be pushing a lot of women off boats around here."

"Why do you say that?" asked the woman.

"Ask Saron," said Gray.

The woman looked at me with questions in her eyes.

I gave a brief account of my arrival at the shack. "Gray found me here and we decided to stay here together. No one knows about the shack and no one knows we are living here. Except, now you."

"Who are you?" asked Gray.

The woman ate more of the cookies and milk and sipped her coffee. She emptied her coffee cup. "I'll tell you if I can have more coffee," she said.

Gray busied himself making more coffee for all of us. When the cups were full and the plastic tray of cookies was passed around, she sat back on the bed, propping herself up on the wall behind her.

"I'm Andrea Steele. Andy," she nodded, "I am working as an intern with the US Fish and Wildlife Service. My internship is supporting the agency's efforts to understand more about the wildlife especially birds that use the mudflats of Bowerman Basin during the winter. We're doing this work to make a recommendation to the port as whether the gas terminal project will have an impact on the local ecosystems."

"We've heard about the terminal project," said Gray. "Something Hamundarson wants to see happen."

"How are you an intern?" I asked.

"I'm an Evergreen State student," Andy said. She lifted her mug in the form of a toast. "Go Geoducks," she said with a half-smile.

"Have you worked out here before?" I asked. Something about her was starting to sound familiar.

"I took an Evergreen class out here at the community college a few years ago. I got hooked on studying birds by an old prof who came out from Olympia and took us out to do field observations. I knew it was my passion. So, I enrolled in classes at the Olympia campus. I'm almost done with all my credits. Just finishing up this winter on this contract with Fish and Wildlife. I've applied to go to grad school, but I'm not sure if I've been accepted." Andy looked down into her coffee cup.

"Andy," I said slowly, "I was in that class at the community college. I think we spent that day learning to document birds together. We were, like, the only older people in the class, and we teamed up for the walk around the Bowerman Basin Unit."

Andy looked at me, cocking her head and then sitting up straight. "That's right," she said with astonishment. "That was you!"

We sat and looked at each other for a moment and then grinned in recognition. "We both found our passion that day," I said with a smile.

Gray interrupted us. "I'm going to go to work at the gravel pit," he said. "I'll be back before dark."

I stood up and gave him a hug. "Okay, be careful. Dinner will be waiting," I said.

After he left, Andy gave me a questioning smile. "So, what's that all about?" she said.

"He found me in this shack. It was easier to become friends than enemies," I said. "Now we're sort of used to each other." After a moment, I said, "He's not in such good shape. He was in a bad logging accident and now he's addicted to pain killers. He seems to become more dependent on them every day. I guess the doctors just keep giving him more and more. He pays for them. Consequently, he's as poor as a church mouse. We've started sharing everything and are just trying to help each other get by. I don't know what the future holds for either of us. We barely have enough money to buy water and food. The rest we make up as we go along."

Andy finished her second cup of coffee and all the cookies.

"You guys saved my life last night," she said. "What can I do to repay you?"

"Please don't tell anyone we are here," I said desperately.

"No, I won't tell anyone," Andy said. "Can't I bring you something?" she asked.

"Are you still going to work out here?" I asked.

"I want to finish this contract and earn my credits. I want to go to grad school. I'm not going to let that jerk Hamundarson get in my way," she said defiantly. "I'm going to have to find some way to document the wildlife out here whether he likes it or not."

"Maybe I can help you," I said.

"How?" Andy asked.

"I could do observations every time I go down to the point," I said. "It would give me something to do. Something I love," I added. "I want to do something that will help protect this refuge, now that it's my refuge too."

"Why did you take the class?" asked Andy.

"I love learning about the bay. Taking the class helped me believe that I was, am, capable of so much more than a dead-end job." I looked at Bruce's photograph and winked at him. "I practice watching for birds and documenting their activities. I hope it will help make a difference, and now that port development schemes need help."

"Can you make observations every day?" asked Andy.

"I could, although some days it's pretty windy and stormy. We go out as often as we can to get driftwood. That's what we burn in the stove," I gestured across the room. "And some days we have to go into town to buy water and food."

"How do you get that out here?" asked Andy with a frown.

"We manage," I said. "Gray carries what he can home in a big backpack. I either push a cart or carry a smaller pack. It's harder on Gray then on me, he gets pretty worn out on the days we go to town. He'll be very tired and achy tonight from working outside on a construction project. He's actually working out at Ham Gravel, a business that Hamundarson owns. Gray's building a pole barn for *Maiden's Curse*."

We sat for a while considering the nightmare of social problems that the recession had created in so many people's lives, including our own.

"How about if I bring you guys water every time I come out here?" asked Andy. "I can leave it near the Fish and Wildlife fence, under some brush."

"Oh," I exclaimed. "If you could do that for us, it would help us so much."

"Let's agree," said Andy. "I'll bring you water and you take good notes as often as you can. I won't tell anyone about you and Gray."

"Okay," I said. 'I can't refuse,' I thought to myself. It looked like a win-win situation. Gray and I would not be found out living in the shack and Andy's work would be aided by my observations of the mudflats and birds.

"I better get going," said Andy. "I hope my car is okay. I left it over at the dock."

"It's probably Okay," I said. "Unless they are loading a ship or barge. Let's see if your clothes are dry. I can loan you some boots. You'll never see yours again."

The clothes were dry enough to wear. She gathered up her pack, ready to leave.

"Thanks so much," she said. "I'll bring you water and return your boots in a couple of days."

"I'll show you how to sneak out to the road," I said.

I watched Andy step out on the empty road. She walked briskly down the side of the road toward the chip plant and its dock. She would know if her car was still there soon enough. The plant was quiet, no one around, so I assumed she would find everything as she had left it. I went back to the shack and started to tidy up after the meal of cookies and coffee. I set out some beans to soak in a pot.

Gray would be tired and hungry when got back from the construction site. He had to work tomorrow, Friday, to finally get paid. We could use the money, I thought. I started to make a list of things, but I couldn't concentrate. There were so many things to think about after finding the woman, discovering it was Andy, and now that we were accomplices. I found my field notebook, slipped it into my pack, and left the shack for the shore. Chestnut-backed chickadees announced my progress along the path.

# 12

# BOWERMAN MUD

The tide was out when I got to the shore. A relentless wind blew in from the coast. Winter weather was beginning to settle in over Grays Harbor. Tidal water would cover the mudflats and pull the rainwater out to sea, leaving the mudflats to fill again with rainwater. Wintering shore birds would survive due to their adaptation to varying environments. Those that had not adapted left the mudflats as soon as the rains began. I must be adapting well to mudflats, I thought. I'm staying.

Andy's arrival at the shack had changed my perspective on the arrival of winter. I had been dreading the ever-increasing darkness as the sun sank lower and lower over the southern horizon. Now it seemed like the magical times of the day were dawn and dusk, and I could witness these times just by walking down to the shore from the shack after breakfast and before dinner with Gray. I could hide in the blind and watch each shift in light to see a new meaning to the puzzle of life. It was like seeing a Rubik's cube fit together in a new and surprising way. Each shift in the building blocks of life were revealed in a totally different combination of light and energy. The mudflats and the birds were as much a representation as they were dynamic entities.

I pulled my old field notebook out of my pack. My last entry was written on a day I had spent with Andy during the class and now, I was taking up the practice again as if all the time since had collapsed away. Doing the right thing in the right place, I thought. I could see nearly all the basin in front of me, the shoreline to the north and around the curve of land where the coast highway hugged the base of the hills. In the distance, I could see the long reach of Daman Point out into the bay creating the west side of Bowerman Basin. Nearly all the basin and the mudflats were in my sight.

Pausing for a moment to look out over the mudflats, I tried to focus on the scene before me. Field note taking was all about the discipline of silence. A sense of calm came over me. I became more cognizant of the variations of speed and direction of the wind. The gusts were not all the same. There seemed to be a rhythm to the forced air, like a pattern of sounds that became a song of repeated notes passing over and around me.

The mudflats became clearer. What seemed like a continual mass of congealed detritus and soggy spoils started to take on complexity with distance. Near me and the shore was a band of heavy sediments with grasses and bits of rock that had been pulled out from the shore by the tide. Further from the shoreline was a zone of sediments that had arrived with the incoming tide but were left behind when the tide retreated. Beyond that was the seemingly endless expanse of muds that tidal water flowed back and forth across, unable to lift or carry away no matter how powerful the tides were. Occasionally storms would disturb these muds, but their depth of compacted sediments was stronger than the surf.

Shorebirds know these bands of mud. They know just how far they can stand in the muds without sinking beyond their ability to lift and fly to more stable places across the mud matrix. Large shorebirds like herons stand along the shore, waiting for the tide to bring them fish, fry, and fingerlings. As the tide recedes, smaller birds and ducks begin to take up residence on the nearshore muds until finally, the smallest of the birds roam about the exposed flats.

I drew a map of the mudflats across two pages of my notebook, not just the shoreline and then mud, but of the nooks and crannies along the shore, places were grasses were tall and able to hide a statuesque heron. I drew dashed lines to indicate the differences in the appearance of the muds once the tide had receded. I could begin to map the location of different birds and track their patterns over time. Finally, I added details to the map including cardinal directions, a scale to represent the distances I saw before me and the distance I had marked on my map, I put November 1 in the corner of the map, and across the top wrote "Bowerman Basin Mudflats." I would now be able to keep track of different birds by their location on the mudflats.

The map would help identify what birds used the mudflats during the winter months, where they were on the mud, and what they were doing there during low tides. To answer these basic questions of who, what, where, and when would lead to further questions of how the birds had adapted to the mud environment. If mud was their habitat, then more information about mud would eventually become important. Disrupting the muds would mean disrupting the entire ecosystem. We are all in this mud together I thought. Hopefully, after days and days of observation, I could give Andy the map.

I looked again out over the mudflats. Traces of the incoming tide were already pushing into the nearshore muds. A group of mallards landed at the water's edge to survey their dinner prospects. The colorful male with his green head, yellow bill, and white neckband stood out against the drab brown of the females. With a circled M, I located the mallards on my map. First one is the lucky charm, I thought. The wind gusts became fierce. More clouds rolled into the harbor, drowning out the last bits of light in the western sky. I put my field notebook into my pack and slung the pack over my shoulder. Gray would be coming home soon.

Back at the shack, I put a large saucepan on the back of the stove and heated up as much water as I could. I knew when Gray returned, he would be totally exhausted and hungry. I added wood to the fire and heated a can of hearty vegetable soup and added a can of small potatoes to make a robust stew. After sharing our food with Andy, our larder was beginning to look thin. I looked far into the food cabinet and found a tin of tuna. I mixed the tuna with the last of some onion and mayonnaise that still smelled edible. I buttered slices of bread and then filled them with tuna and slabs of cheese. These I grilled on the woodstove.

It was not long before I heard him on the stoop of the back door. Stepping away from the stove, I opened the door to find him slumped against the doorframe.

"Oh, you look totally worn out!" I cried at seeing him. I took his arm and helped into the shack. "You're soaked," I said in sympathy.

I led him over the chair by the stove. "We have to get you out of these wet clothes," I said. Slowly, I pulled his jacket off and took it back towards the door. It was so wet, it dripped water across the floor. I'll worry about that later, I thought to myself.

Returning to Gray, I unbuttoned his shirt and helped him wrestle the wet flannel from his arms and torso. Then I pulled his thin T-shirt over his head. As quickly as I could, I wrapped hot, wet towels around him. Finally, I reached down and unlaced his boots, pulled them off and set them under the stove. His socks were harder to remove, but I persisted and was able to pull the wet fabric over his heels and off his toes. All that remained were his pants.

"Can you take them off?" I asked gently.

Gray slowly stood up and unzipped his pants. He nearly fell over on to the stove, but I grabbed his arm and steadied him.

"Hold on to my shoulders," I said. When I could feel his weight across my back, I slowly knelt and pulled his pants down to his knees. Standing again, I helped Gray sit back down in the chair and I pulled his pants from his legs. I handed him another hot towel and he wrapped it around his middle.

"Sit there," I said. I pulled a wool blanket from his bed and encased him in it. It was only then that Gray began to shiver. I poured him a cup of hot tea and held it while he sipped from the cup. The shivering stopped, and he took the cup from my hands.

"My pills…" he said in a whisper.

"Eat first and then the pills will get into your system faster," I said. I fed him the hot soup and tuna sandwiches. Color was slowly returning to his face. After he ate, he unwrapped the blanket and towels that had grown cold. I helped him pull on sweatpants and shirt. He didn't say much except that Hamundarsons' North River fishing boat was parked at the gravel pit. After a cup of tea and a double dose of pain killers, he crawled into his bed and was soon asleep. Miss Hap curled up beside him as if sensing his aches and pains.

I sat with a candle for a while, writing and thinking about how the experience with Andy was drawing Gray and me together. We had become a mutual support system, working together to provide for Andy. And now, we were working together to keep each other safe from the outside world. The shack's security seemed to be intact despite the breach with Andy's arrival. Andy and I had made a pact that bound her and me together as well. It was as if Gray and I were living in a parallel universe that was drifting further and further away from a parent planet.

I listened to the wind blowing the alder and brush against the side of the shack. It would be chilly in the shack soon. I left my bed and went to Gray's. He somehow knew I was there without rousing from his sleep. 'He must feel safe here, too,' I thought. He pulled me closer inside his arms as sleep swept through me.

I must have needed the comfort of sleep because I did not hear Gray get up. It wasn't until he sat down on the bed beside me and whispered a good morning in my ear. "You and Miss Hap stay here today. You've had enough excitement for a while. I'll be back from the construction job tonight, hopefully not so wet and tired."

"Come home safe," I said softly. The coffee slowly woke me. Miss Hap curled up beside me as if hearing Gray's orders to stay put. I spent the day in the shack except to go out to the point at midday. I wanted to see the basin when the tide had brought a shallow pouring of water over the mudflats. An eagle flew above the water, scanning for a fish.

Gray returned to the shack mid-afternoon. "We got off early," he said.

He pulled an envelope out of a jacket pocket. "And we got paid, in cash," he said with satisfaction. "It's enough to get us through the rest of this month and then some. Maybe it's time we did something for ourselves, just a bit of fun."

"Fun?" I said jokingly. "What would that be?"

"Well, how about going over to Westport on the bus. We could actually go out to eat at a restaurant and maybe go out to the jetty and do some fishing."

"You don't think anyone would recognize us?" I asked.

"I doubt there are many people about in Westport this time of year," he answered.

"Okay, I said. "It would be nice to eat something different and see the ocean beyond the harbor. We'll go the first day the weather is clear."

Gray counted out the money. "Here," he said handing me half of the cash. He put the rest back in his pocket. "I have to go see the pharmacist for more painkillers."

After Gray left, I made myself another cup of coffee and sat next to the stove. It was Saturday. We tried to keep a low profile and stay in the shack on weekends. There was always the chance that a weekend birdwatcher would get too close to the shack. I wished that Gray had not left to go to town. I tried to make things cheerful. We listened to Saturday radio shows and Sunday morning jazz from a Tacoma station. Our stack of found paperbacks was rummaged through for a good read. We started reading a book out loud and enjoying an entertaining set of characters together. Then there were times of quiet contemplation.

I went out to the shore each day to make observations. I started keeping three lists of birds, those onshore, those in the nearshore muds and those out on the flats. I was starting to create a code for each type of bird. Then I could put the codes on the map. Using the codes, I could map where and when the birds had landed on or near the flats. Better then the pirate code, I thought with a smirk.

Our chance to go to Westport came in three weeks later. We walked into Hoquiam and took the bus. We kept grinning at each other, sharing the secret of adventure and being like any other old couple on the bus. It was as if we were running away from home but only for a day. Gray had a fishing pole and gear bag at his feet. The bus driver did not pay any attention to the gear; besides, Gray had his Quinault ID with him, he had the right to fish wherever and whenever he wanted.

Arriving in Westport, we walked down the commercial strip looking for a place to have lunch. I steered us away from the Buoy. If anyone would recognize me, it probably would be there. There was only one other place open in mid-November, Bennett's Fish Shack. We relaxed over fish burgers and enjoyed the busyness of people coming and going. After several cups of coffee and a shared piece of pie, Gray was ready to do some fishing.

We walked out along the jetty defined the entrance to the harbor. The north side of the channel was created by the jetty on the Ocean Shores side. Once we settled into some rocks, Gray rigged up his fishing pole. He sat for a moment, watching the water and taking in the motion of the water and wind. Usually from the southwest, today the wind was coming from the northwest. The air smelled more like the Quinault forest than the long sandy beaches to the south.

The smell of cedar reminded him of walking the beach with his granny. Walking with her was a slow process. She stopped often to poke into the sand with her walking stick, hoping to discover a clam or some abandoned morsel. Sometimes she swung her stick into the air to disrupt a seagull's maneuvers in the air above her head. "Scavengers!" she would say in Quinault. Still, she kept a close eye on their soaring and diving, letting them do the searching to find edible sea life. At times, the old granny on the beach and the grey seagulls seemed as one, a team of beachcombers interested in the fresh food found at the water's edge.

"Wind's coming from the north," said Gray. "The fish will be looking for warmer water. They'll be in closer to shore."

"You're right," I said. "It does smell like the wind is coming all the way down the coast from Canada."

"Granny would be raising her fist to the north wind," said Gray. "She didn't like the disruption to the normal scheme of things. But she would always find something interesting when the weather turned this way."

"Like what?" I asked.

"Who knows," said Gray with a half-smile. "Maybe a different kind of clam or something on the beach that came all the way from Japan. She'd find something for sure," he said.

Gray reached down and grabbed a piece of driftwood. The stick was long and a bit crooked, but it made a fine poking stick. "I'll see what I can find," trying to imitate his granny. I smiled and shook my head. The image of Gray acting like an old woman made her chuckle. "Let's see what you find," I joked. The humor of the image and Gray's jabbing into the air like an old woman was a delight. "It's good to be out here," I said.

Gray hurled his line as far out into the water as he could. The north wind pushed water up onto the rocks. Gray was busy tending his line, hoping to feel the tug of a rock fish. He cast out again and murmured something about the water moving too fast to let a fish find his line.

I watched a tangle of driftwood push up against the rocks at my feet. Limbs and small tree trunks crisscrossed into a mound. I pulled out a limb the size of my arm. I could put a few pieces of driftwood in my pack for firewood back at the shack. I reached out deeper into the mound and pulled on a white looking limb. It stuck so I pulled at it again. This time the white limb freed itself of the tangle. As soon as saw what I thought was a tree limb, I screamed.

"Ach," I yelled. "What is this?" What I had thought was a tree limb was bone. I dropped the limb and looked, horrified, at Gray. "What is this?" I repeated.

Gray swung around at my scream. He looked down at the white bone. At one end of the bone was a Nike athletic shoe. He bent down to have a closer look as I stepped even further back from it.

After a few moments, Gray looked up at me and said, "It's a human foot."

I gasped and stepped closer to Gray. "But what is it doing here? How did it get into the driftwood? Where did it come from?" I asked, afraid to utter the real question of who it belonged to.

"I don't know," said Gray. He looked at the bone tied to the shoe.

"What should we do?" I asked. "Should we take it to the police?" After a moment I said, "Oh, I guess not. How could we explain where we found it and why we were down here?" It was not really a question but more of a recognition that we could not jeopardize our hidden existence. We had no address and no way to be reached in case of questioning. We could not do anything that would raise suspicion.

"Should we just leave it?" I said.

Gray knelt by the foot. The jagged end of the leg bone indicated it had broken off from the rest of the body by force. The bone was white and cleaned of all flesh. Most likely nibbling fish had had a feast. The foot bones were still intact, held together by the shoe. "The rubber sole must have kept the foot afloat and it all got caught in the flotsam," said Gray.

"What should we do?" I asked again. I looked around the water's edge with questioning eyes.

Gray reached down and grabbed the leg. He hurled the leg and its attached shoe as hard as he could into the deeper water. "Let it go back out with the tide," he said.

I watched as the shoe bobbed in the water. The current pulled the shoe into its orbit and it slowly moved in the direction of the channel. Go away, I thought. I shuttered again, thinking of the broken bone and foot tied together by the shoe.

Gray thought of what Granny would say in such circumstances. She would think it an omen of some sort. 'Probably not a good one,' he thought. He didn't want to fish anymore. He wanted to go back to having a nice time with Saron.

"Let's just go back to the shack," he said. "We're cold and the wind is getting worse. The rain is starting to come from the southwest. I need a cup of tea and the warm fire we left behind. The bus ride will warm us up. We'll be back in the shack in no time," said Gray.

I didn't say much on the way back to Hoquiam. Gray was quiet as well. He didn't say anything about his granny's omen, not wanting to add more distress to the afternoon.

"Let's stop by the Fish Bait and have a beer," he offered. He wanted to change the mood and comfort me.

"Okay," I said. I was willing to follow Gray's suggestion. I didn't have much energy to find my own path after the misadventure on the jetty.

I followed Gray into the Fish Bait. A sign on the window read "Support our Troops." Red, white, and blue stripes decorated the sign. A POW flag was hanging over one of the windows. The vets must like it here,' I thought.

The Fish Bait was one place where Gray felt welcome and no one asked about personal lives. Everyone was equal, equally not a member of normal society. The atmosphere in the bar was about people like

Gray, people eking out a living and finding solace and community in the difficult economic times of the bay. Once inside the door, Gray waved to the men sitting at the bar. They were his 'gang' from youth detention camp days. Martin sat straight up on the bar stool. His long black hair hung down to his waist.

"Too wasted to braid your tresses?" teased Gray. The Indian tipped his beer in Gray's direction. "Good to see you, bro," said Martin. Seated next to Martin was someone Gray knew less well.

"Ted?" he asked to confirm the man's identity.

"Yep," replied the man without looking up, just waving an arm in the direction of Gray.

"Hey Gray," came a voice from the next bar stool.

"Is that you, Roger?" said Gray. "Glad to see you made it out of the joint in one piece."

"It wasn't so hard," Roger replied. Always one to see the bright side, Roger was back in his real element.

Gray stood for a second looking at the three men before he joined them at the bar. Each one wore a plaid jacket that most likely came from Walmart. The greens, browns, and blues all ran together to create a single plaid, greens in one direction, browns in the opposite direction, all on a field of blues. Single strands of white and yellow were woven across the major colors. The total plaid became a tartan for detention survivors.

Gray found a table next to the wall opposite the bar for us. He stepped up to the bar to order beers. "On the house," said Cliff. "Who's your lady friend?" he asked.

"Just a friend," said Gray firmly.

"Cliff's tempting us with the smell of a roasted turkey," said Roger. "He knows darn well we won't be eating turkey this year."

"Not going down to the Gospel Mission for their Thanksgiving plate?" asked Gray.

His question was followed by silence.

"Too much like prison food," said Roger. "Sure would like to find a new chef," he joked.

"You guys going to the Mission?" asked Martin. Ted kept looking at his beer.

Gray contemplated his answer before speaking. "Cliff," he said addressing the proprietor, "you making any contributions to the poor this year?"

Cliff looked at Gray for a second, comprehending the message behind the question. "Yeah," he said. "I'm donating, one roasted turkey. You know somebody in need?"

"Saron needs it," said Gray.

"Saron?" came a voice from the table along the opposite wall. "Saron who?"

I looked at the woman at the table. She was medium height although slumped at the table to look smaller than her thin frame would be if she were standing. She wore a dark blue fleece coat that had bits of leaves and twigs attached to the sleeves and across the back. It was clear she had been sleeping on the ground. Her blond hair was tucked back into a red knit cap. Beneath the cap was a wrinkled face that once would have been thought as 'interesting.' It was Connie. I turned my head toward the wall, hoping she won't recognize me in my altered looks.

To cover my identity, Gray said, "Do you know Saron?"

"If its Saron who once worked for the SOB in the insurance office, yes, I know her. I used to have coffee with her back when we all had jobs and money for coffee. We sailed together under Captain Ham."

"What's your name?" asked Gray

"Connie," she said.

"What happened to being a pirate?" Gray asked her.

"'Captain Ham got rid of a lot of us when we stopped paying dues," she said. A real maiden's curse for me," she said with a laugh.

"I'll ask Saron if she knows you," said Gray. "Nice to meet you."

"I used to be nice," she said in a desperate voice. "Now I just used to be."

"Let's get out of here," he said to me in a low voice.

"Brothers! see you early next week. You too," he said to Connie.

Connie only nodded at Gray. She did not recognize me.

"Today just wasn't our day," Gray said. "First the foot out at the jetty and now a near moment of recognition of you. Granny's omen," he said.

When we got back to the shack, Gray fed the stove. I opened a can tomato soup and stirred in the last onion we had.

We both worked in silence. What had started out as a beautiful, fun day had turned into a near disaster. I hoped our luck was not about to turn. How long can we live like this? I wondered.

"Were you and Connie good friends?" asked Gray. "Sounds like she's fallen on hard times."

"Connie?" said Saron. "I haven't seen her since I moved out here. I used to spend time with her when I worked downtown."

"She doesn't appear to be working downtown anymore. Maybe sleeping on the street downtown now," said Gray as he slid into the chair by the wood stove. "Looks like she's down on her luck."

"I'm sorry to see her like that. And to have suffered from Captain Ike's lack of charity. Connie's a good person."

He lit the lamp on the table and watched as I poured out the meager soup dinner. I put some crackers and cheese on the counter. Darkness fell across the alder grove. Gray pulled the canvas and curtains across the windows. The shack disappeared into the grove and out of sight from the road. I wanted all our cares and worries to fade away into the darkness.

"Don't give in to fear," I whispered. "Don't become angry like Connie."

# 13

# THANKSGIVING

*I* left the shack around ten o'clock the next morning. I wanted to catch the outgoing tide on the shore. I hoped to see more signs of birds as the tide drained out of the mudflats. I went through the brush to the shore and settled into my usual spot. Opening my notebook, I recorded the date and time of my visit. I scanned the shoreline for birds or other wildlife. I had seen a fox come down to the water a few days ago. I wanted to see it again, hoping that it survived crossing the road to get to the shoreline.

Scanning the shoreline, I thought I saw someone out on the end of the point. I focused my eyes and watched for signs of movement. The person turned toward me, as if to be looking for me. It was a woman, and she was starting to walk toward me. I sat motionless for a moment, wondering how to hide or what to say. As she got closer to me, I could see the details of her face. It was Andy. I stood up and waved at her, trusting she was alone. She waved back, and we both picked up our pace and walked toward each other.

"Hi!" Andy said excitedly. "How are you?"

"I'm good," I said. "I'm happy to see you." We gave each other a hug.

"Sit down and tell me what's going on," I said.

Andy and I sat among the tall shore grasses and chatted about recent events in each of our lives. I told her about our disastrous trip to Westport yesterday. She nodded in support and shook her head when I told her about Connie and her treatment by Ike Hamundarson. "That guy's gotta go," she said disdainfully.

"How's the project going?" I asked.

"I'm getting enough data, but it should be more," said Andy.

I pulled my notebook out of my pack. "I hope this will help," I said.

Andy paged through my notes on observations and carefully examined the map. "This is wonderful," she said appreciatively. "I'll have to think of some way to incorporate this into my data. I don't know what Jen will say about this but it's definitely helpful in understanding the ecology of the mudflats and the basin."

"How are you guys surviving out here?" she changed the subject.

"Well enough," I said.

"I brought you gallon jugs of water. I left them in the bushes by the fence so you can carry them into the shack."

"Thank you so much," I said. "This will make things easier for Gray."

"How's he doing?" she asked.

"Went to town today to buy more pills. Takes a lot of money and time to keep that addiction going. He needs them, I can tell," I said.

We both shook our heads a bit.

"Addiction is terrible," said Andy. "I've had to fight it off with family members. Unless they can find a substitute, they never seem to get over it."

"I worry that Gray will give up. He's such a nice guy," I said.

"You really care for him, don't you." said Andy.

"Yes, it's starting to be like that."

"Not to change the subject, but what are you guys doing for Thanksgiving?" she asked.

I shrugged my shoulders. "Not sure."

"Could you come into Olympia?" she asked. "I'm having a real dinner with turkey and potatoes and green beans, pumpkin pie and ice cream. It would be great to have you and Gray."

"Well, I guess we could come in on the bus. I hear it takes a couple of hours and the schedule may be different for the holiday. I can check," I said.

"Oh, please come," Andy said brightly. "Jen is coming. Maybe we can figure out how to use your data."

"But we can't tell him how we met or where Gray and I live."

"We'll just say we met in the community college class. I won't say anything about the shack. He can just believe that you live in Aberdeen or someplace nearby."

"Okay," I said. "Just assume we will be there." She gave me her address and cell phone number.

"Get there by midday. Dinner will be served around two o'clock."

We said goodbyes and went in opposite directions.

Gray was pleased when he heard about the invitation. "I'll get the bus schedule. Maybe we can pick up something like a bottle of wine when we get to Olympia. Miss Hap can take care of the shack."

The holiday plans carried us through the next week. On Thanksgiving Day, we walked into Hoquiam, caught the bus for Olympia at nine o'clock and sat blissfully on the bus for two hours, not seeing anyone we knew or being recognized by anyone. We were free of our cares for the day. After the Westport disaster, we were happy to be able to reclaim our independence.

We arrived in Olympia a bit early, so we walked around the downtown area. All the stores and even the Batdorf and Bronson coffee shop were closed for the day. The only place we found open was the old Chinese restaurant, the Clipper. We were the only ones in the restaurant. It felt a bit weird. We ordered cups of coffee and egg rolls, thinking that it would be awhile before we would be eating turkey dinners.

At noon, we walked back to the bus depot, identified the bus to Andy's house. We sat quietly on a bench in front of the bus we needed to take. A few people were about. Three young men, dreadlocked with backpacks chatted amongst themselves. Bits of their conversation seemed to indicate they were on their way to a friend's house for dinner.

Our bus arrived and we boarded it for the trip to Andy's house. We walked the last couple of blocks from where the bus dropped us off on Boundary Boulevard. Andy met us at the door, and we entered a small apartment. There were people working in the kitchen and others sitting on a couch in the living room.

"Hey everybody," said Andy. "This is Saron and Gray."

People said hello and nodded in our direction. I took off my coat and went to the kitchen to see if I could help. Gray sat on a chair near the couch and was soon engaged in conversation with the living room crowd. Dinner preparations were in full swing, it was clear that it was going to be a tasty meal with interesting conversation.

"Andy," said one of the participants. "What's the status of the terminal project out at Grays Harbor?"

"I think Jen can answer that question better than I," said Andy.

Jen sat for a minute before answering. She chose her words carefully, knowing that she could be inadvertently fingered by someone for talking about agency business outside of work.

"The terminal project carries a lot of interest by the port and the businesspeople of the harbor. Expanding the port's facilities to include a major terminal would mean a lot of construction jobs in a place where unemployment is high. Once the construction is done, there would be a constant stream of fossil fuels coming into the port for export. The facilities would have to be maintained. So, you can see, that the project sounds good for the economy of Grays Harbor."

"But won't the majority of jobs go away once the construction phase is over?" asked one of the dinner guests.

"Yes," said Jen. "That's one of the long-term problems for the Port to consider."

"Isn't the whole thing, the railroad and the terminal, a potential environmental disaster?" asked another guest.

"That's what we are attempting to bring forward in the decision-making process," said Jen. "We are just participating in the scoping of the project as this point. The port is trying to clarify what voices will be at the table when the decision is made. We have a long way to go to get to the final decision."

"What's Andy's role in this?" someone asked.

"She is doing the first ever survey of winter wildlife in Bowerman Basin," answered Jen.

"No one has ever done a survey of wildlife in the Nisqually Refuge?"

"No," said Jen. "We have to start with the survey."

There was a long silence. Gray shifted in his chair. Not looking at Jen, he spoke quietly to no one in particular. "The Quinault Indian Nation has lived near the bay for as long as we remember. We know the bay and all the wildlife that lives around it. By treaty, we decide what happens in the bay, we have rights to the bottom of the bay."

Silence followed his comments.

"Is that true?" asked another dinner guest.

Gray looked into the eyes of the questioner. "Yes."

"Yes," said Jen. "The Nation has a great deal to say about what happens in the bay. I'm sure a spokesperson for the Nation will be participating in hearings and the decision-making process."

"The Quinault Nation has resource managers and lawyers who participate in these kinds of things," said Gray. Slowly, he looked up at everyone in the room. "And the people who belong to the Nation are very much attached to the bay and everything that lives there. We will speak."

"I hope you do," said Jen.

Gray shrugged his shoulders. "We'll see," he said.

After we had eaten, we all moved to the living room. We decided to put off desert until after the dinner. Andy peered around the corner from the kitchen. "Hey, Jen," she said. "I want you to meet Saron."

"I think we've met," she said.

"Well come in here and talk with her for a minute," she insisted.

Jen and I made our way to the kitchen with Andy's prompting.

"Saron, you know Jen is my contract supervisor out at US Fish and Wildlife," said Andy. "Jen," she said, "Saron is an accomplished observer of birds and wildlife. She's keeping a log of observations she's made out at Bowerman Basin. I'm wondering if we can use her data."

I told Jen about keeping a daily log of tidal changes, hours of daylight, and my observations of wildlife in the basin.

"She learned her skills when I did, we met in the Evergreen class I was telling you about out at Grays Harbor Community College," said Andy.

Jen listened carefully to her. I could tell that he valued her ideas and input.

"You gather this data every day?" he asked me.

"Yes, so far."

"That's a real commitment," she said. "We don't have that kind of coverage. Andy's work is only the three days a week that she's out there. It would be interesting to compare your data with hers and then add your data to the record. Do you plan to keep doing this all winter?"

"Yes," I said.

"Well, let's see how this works out," said Jen. "Let's plan to get together after the holidays. The first public meeting is in January, and I'd like to have something to present in terms of ecology of the basin."

Andy and I grinned at each other. I couldn't wait to tell Gray. As soon as we got on the bus to head back to Hoquiam, I told him all about the conversation.

"That's great," he said. "It really gives you something to work at. It's been a good day."

"Yes, it's been a good Thanksgiving," I said.

I thought about all the things I did have to be thankful for instead of all the problems or how I worried about the future. Time out for thankfulness, I thought.

The next day I was totally gung-ho to make observe from the shore. Despite some really bad weather, I wanted to be outside making as many observations as I could. Gray sensed my enthusiasm.

"Look," he said tersely, "You have to be careful. You can't barge off as if no one can see you especially if you are doing the same thing every day. The weather is bad. High wind predictions, rain, and the temperature is dropping." See, I put on an extra sweater and I'm tying down the hood on my jacket. I'll only be out there for an hour."

"I'm going to come out there in about forty-five minutes," he said.

"There's no sense in both of us getting wet and cold. Stay here and make sure there is some warmth in the shack. We can have tea when I get back."

"I'm coming out there," he said again. It was one of the first times we had contradicted each other. I gave him a half smile and left out the back door.

The wind was pushing the brush up against the shack. Alders were swaying in the wind while rain was blowing sideways between them. It's a pretty nasty day I thought. I had to brace myself against the wind to get down to the shore. I buried myself as deep as I could into my favorite spot. For all the effort to get down to the shore, it seemed like I was the only living creature to be out in the elements. I could document only the harsh weather conditions. Even the terns had sought refuge. The sky was very dark even at noon. The tide was coming in with whitecaps crashing on the mudflats. The waves were getting closer all the time. A pair of Canadian geese rose from the choppy water and flew inland to wait out the storm in the tall grasses.

Gray appeared on the shore as he had promised. As soon as he saw the waves and the wind in action, he grabbed my arm and pulled me to my feet.

"You have to get back," he said angrily. "Those waves could suddenly break over you. This is dangerous."

"But," I said.

He did not let me finish my sentence. To prove his point, a larger than normal wave crashed onto the shore and nearly swamped us.

"Move now!" Gray yelled.

I stuffed my notebook into my pocket and grabbed Gray's hand. We took big steps to get into the brush and then crouched our way back to the shack. The trees swayed over our heads and the rain drenched us.

Inside the shack, we peeled off our wet clothes. Gray made tea and we sat as close to the stove as we could. Gray had brought in as much driftwood from our stash as he could pack into the shack.

"This could last a long time," he finally said.

"I'm sorry," I said.

"You have to be more careful out there," he said.

"Okay. Okay. I will. But I have to go out every day."

Gray frowned. We did not speak for a while. "We'll see," he said.

Gray was right. The storm lasted for five days. Wind and rain pummeled the shack relentlessly. Despite Gray's warnings, I went out to the shore every day at noon for an hour. Every day I came back cold and soaked through. I was so proud of myself for keeping to the observation schedule. But on the sixth day, when the storm started to dissipate, I woke with a fever. By noon, I was shaking and could not seem to get warm until I was hot to the touch, and them shaking again.

"You are really sick," said Gray compassionately.

I nodded, thankful that he was not angry or accusing me of not heeding his warnings.

Gray made soup and tried to get me to eat as much of it as possible. He brewed hot tea, adding honey and lemon juice. I was not responding to anything he gave me. I buried myself under blankets and then threw them off when the fever returned.

"You need more vitamins and antibiotics," said Gray.

"We don't have any money for them," I said in a whisper. "Who would give them to us?"

Gray shook his head. "You have to have something, or you are going to get pneumonia."

"Maybe Andy can help," I said before slipping into a restless sleep.

Gray had no real idea how to contact Andy. She had left them water about a week ago. The storm had basically stopped her from coming out to the harbor. Maybe now that the storm was breaking up, she would be back. With no other plan, Gray wrote a note and put it in a plastic bag, sealing it as best he could. He took it out to the spot where Andy left the water jugs and tied it to a low brush with yellow tape. All he could do is hope that she found it, and soon.

I slept off and on for two days. Gray kept trying to feed me hot food and keep the shack as warm as he could. I started coughing. The cough became constant. My lungs were congested. I coughed continually, making it impossible to sleep. Gray slept little. He went to get water, or so he said. I barely noticed when he came and went, the coughing totally exhausted me.

On the third day, Gray looked at me with grave concern. "You have to have some help," he said. "I'm going to try and find Andy."

He went out to the water drop spot. His encased note was gone. In its place was a red plastic envelope. Inside was a message from Andy. 'I've gone into town to get vitamins and antibiotics,' it read. 'I'll be back at 10am.'

Gray took the message and went back to the shack. 'She's coming this morning with meds," he said.

Gray started looking at the door and making a space for Andy at ten o'clock. He kept his eye on their small clock, hoping Andy would keep her word. He hoped he had not gotten something mixed up. He felt helpless and dependent on someone he could only hope to trust.

The clock said ten fifteen and still no Andy.

At ten twenty-five, he heard a knock on the front door. He could only hope it was Andy. He opened the door. To his relief, it was Andy.

"I'm sorry I'm late," she said. "It took longer to get these than I thought. I had to go into Safeway in Aberdeen. The Hoquiam drugstore was out of everything."

Andy pulled off her wet rain gear and came over to my hovel of blankets and scraps of tissue. I tried to smile when she took my hand. She felt my forehead and throat.

"You are pretty sick," she said.

Gray brought a glass of water and doses of vitamins and antibiotics.

"Take these," he said.

"Is she warm enough in here?" asked Andy.

"It's as warm as I can make it," said Gray. "We can't move her."

"I hope these meds will work," said Andy. "We'll just have to be patient. I parked my car inside the fence at the agency work site. I'll stay tonight and make sure you get some sleep. You look exhausted and you have to not get sick, too."

I slept all afternoon. There were more pills and hot tea in the late afternoon. Gray and Andy took turns sitting with me. I somehow knew it was night and we were all sleeping for the first time. My coughing had diminished.

In the morning, I felt better. I wanted to get up, but Andy said no, and Gray shook his head. "You need to stay quiet for a few days. Here," he handed me several pills. "Take these and sit up if you want."

Andy sat next to me. She took a hot towel and washed my face.

"I owe you," she said with a smile, remembering how I had washed off mud from her face months before.

"Is there some way we could insulate this place?" she asked Gray.

Andy and Gray sat drinking tea and discussing the possibilities of insulating the shack. I drifted back to sleep. When I awoke, Andy was gone. Gray was working on a list of materials for insulating the shack.

"I think we can do this," he said. "I can scavenge most of this, it will just take time. It will be our Christmas present to ourselves," he said.

I nodded in agreement. I was beginning to feel better. The weather stayed cold and windy, but the rain had stopped.

"No going outside until next week," said Gray forcefully. "Andy says your health is more important than your daily observations. Let's just focus on making this place warm as possible and you as healthy as possible."

"Okay," I said. It is nice to have someone looking after me I thought.

# 14

# ADVENT

Gray spent the next day looking for cheap rolls of insulation that he could smuggle out to the shack. He was gone all day, walking into Aberdeen to the Habitat for Humanity ReStore. There were some rolls, but they were too wide to fit into the spaces between the studs of the shack. He went to Home Depot and found other options, but still not what he wanted, and nothing he could easily haul back to the shack.

Discouraged, he wandered over to the Fish Bait for a beer.

Roger came in and they joked about the weather, working at Coast Gravel, and what to do about the Christmas and New Year's holidays. Family celebrations were a major part of the holiday season in Grays Harbor County, yet so many people were on the brink of homelessness or living alone. Gray left Roger and the bar feeling lost in the general sense of depression that had moved into the area with the power of a winter king tide.

Out at the shack, I could see that the dull mood of the harbor was beginning to become a way of being for Gray.

I asked about the insulation project. "Nothing yet," Gray said uneasily. "I'm working on it."

December days slipped away, each one shorter than the last as

Earth followed its path toward its winter destination. The encroaching darkness seeped into the shack. It didn't matter if it was morning or night, darkness surrounded the shack. An odd sense of dread nudged up against the memories of late November thankfulness.

"We have to keep focused on the moment when the light begins to return," I said one morning.

"Well, what do you propose to do?" asked Gray. "You can't change Earth. The moon must shine too. The Quinault say that the winter moon purges our bodies and souls so that we may welcome new life in the spring."

"The moon will be full soon," I said. I pointed to the ellipse of light rising above the cloud cover that hung over the basin. "The churches are decked out in greenery for Christmas. They light a new candle there every Sunday of December until Christmas Eve. I think it's called Advent. Maybe Advent means the coming of new life, too."

Gray looked up from his book. He was reading a paperback he had pulled off the giveaway shelf at Catholic Community Services. "We could do that," said Gray.

"What?" I asked.

"Light candles and wait for an advent, something good to happen," said Gray. "Maybe the churches are trying to mimic what we native people have always known."

The thought made me giggle. "I didn't think you were religious," I said. "I remember going to church and seeing a ceremony to light candles that were in a wreath at the front of the church. We would read a part of the Nativity story and light all the candles from the previous Sundays and then a new one for that Sunday. Then, on Christmas Eve, all the Sunday candles were lit and a big pillar candle in the middle of the wreath was lit. The light of all those candles filled the church. I ran outside one Christmas just to see if the light shown through the stained-glass windows."

"Did it?" asked Gray.

"Yep," I said. "All the windows were glowing. The church looked like a giant lantern. I was confused as whether it was a light for baby Jesus to come to Earth or to guide Santa Claus."

"We could have a wreath and candles." said Gray. "Maybe we could be like Granny's story of welcoming the new light. What would we need?"

"Well, I guess we would have to gather some greens to make the wreath. Then we would have to make candle holders for the Sunday candles, plus find the candles," I said. "I'll have to think about where to find all the candles, plus the pillar. Harbor Drug would have the candles, but they would be expensive. "Maybe at the Dollar Store."

Gray was watching my face and must have sensed my desire to make Christmas a happy time for us.

"We can do this," said Gray. "We'll start looking. Act like it will happen!"

"It will take a miracle," I said. "We can believe in miracles."

"Isn't that what Christmas is about?" said Gray. "Miracles? We could use some."

The next day, Gray went across the highway from the shack and located a fir tree with a set of shabby limbs that draped on the ground. No one will miss those limbs, he thought. Any logger would be glad to have a clear view of the base of the tree. He went back to the shack and pulled out his box of tools from under the porch. The small wood saw he had discovered down the road at the metal recycler fit comfortably in his hand. You still have a few good pulls left in you, he said to the saw.

He headed back across the highway and started pulling the saw across the branches where they spiraled away from the trunk. He kept his body close to the trunk on the far side of the tree. He didn't want anyone on the highway seeing him. He listened for traffic and when the road noise was silent, he curved his body into the tree and reached for the limbs on the far side. Slowly, he sawed through four branches.

Now the tree trunk was exposed. He pulled the limbs up to his spot above the tree.

Suddenly, a rush of feathers rose up to his face and then flew over his head. He froze at the rush of feathers. The bird was gone before he could see what it was. He looked carefully into the branches he had sawn and let fall to the ground. Bits of brown and white feathers were caught in the needles along with soft fur. He turned his attention to the limbs above him. There in a mass of limbs where the tree he was working on collided with another tree was a nearly invisible bird's nest.

Gray stepped back from the tree. This was the home of an owl. Owls were common around the bay, but usually unseen. They hid themselves in dense foliage like the tree limbs he had almost disturbed during the day. Their real ability at hunting small prey like chipmunks, squirrels, and other small rodents was nocturnal.

Gray took a few steps away from the tree. Now alert to the activities of the predator, he found more feathers and fur. He picked up each bit of insulation and waterproofing. The owl had been quite successful and left behind a collection of some other creature's weatherproofing. He filled his pockets with the feathers and fur. He knew exactly what his granny would have done with the find. He would follow her example and do the same for Saron.

Gray brought the tree limbs back to the shack. He stomped his feet on the porch to force the mud from the soles. I was putting away the now dried breakfast dishes when I heard his arrival. Opening the door, I was met with limbs and Gray's smile.

"Do we make a round wreath?" he asked.

"Yes, just a circle of greens. I'll try to find the candles that go into the circle," I said. "You found the perfect limbs for a wreath."

"Yes," responded Gray. "And then some," with a bit of excitement in his voice.

"What?" I said, wondering what he meant.

"Oh, you will see," he said with an air of mystery. "Christmas time, you know."

Gray went back outside. He took a deep breath and sat for a moment with the limbs. 'This has to work,' he thought. The thought was more about making the possibilities of Christmas real for me more than any worries about creating a circle of greenery. It was good to have a bit of holiday secrets in the air.

I could tell that Gray was enjoying the moment. I pulled on my coat and stepped out on the porch. "I have to go into town to find apples. I hope there are still some on the old tree in the abandoned lot."

"Okay," said Gray. "Be careful. Remember that old dog that hangs out in the empty lot."

"I will," I said. "I should be back in a couple of hours."

I walked as fast as I could, the rain becoming more intense. No one should be out in this, I thought. All that kept me going was the possibility of a few sweet apples still on the old tree where they had picked apples in the fall. A few apples would dress up the last of the baked sweet potatoes they had had for dinner last night. A tiny bit of pork sausage would taste great with the potatoes and apples. I fingered the two one dollar bills I had brought with me. Maybe there would be a day-old sausage burrito at the Shell station lunch cooler.

The cashier at the Shell station recognized me. "Did you walk here in the rain?" he asked, noticing my dripping coat that now created a puddle around me at the cooler.

"Sorry," I answered. "I didn't mean to mess up your floor." I turned to the cooler, hoping to find something sausage for less than two dollars. Breakfast Sausage Burrito. Ham and Cheese Breakfast Sandwich. Beans and Eggs Burrito. They were all that were left from the morning rush of truck drivers, forest products laborers, and high school students who frequented the station every morning, too rushed to make breakfast, not hungry until mid-morning, and willing to eat mass produced food. All I wanted was a leftover sausage burrito from yesterday. I pushed the fresh burritos aside and felt around in the cold case. I reached as far as I could into the case. In a last moment of disgruntlement, I stood on my tip toes and tried to see as far as I could in the case. My hand touched something that felt like paper. The light created a shadow across the package but there was enough light for me to read the lettering on the package. 'Sausage Burrito' it said, expiration date yesterday. Maybe things could get better, I thought.

"That's pretty old," said the clerk. "I shouldn't sell it to you."

"It's okay," I said with a bit of panic. "It's still good and I plan to cook and eat it today."

"Okay, you can have it. Just give me a dollar for it and don't tell anyone I sold this to you."

"No problem."

With the three-day old sausage burrito in my bag, I headed for the old apple orchard. Only a few people remembered the old trees. I was counting on a few last apples that would have ripened after Gray and I gathered what was ripe back in October. Today, I just wanted two or three, enough to make the sweet potato and sausage casserole. With the last of the raisins from a food box Gray had brought home from the food pantry, the dinner would cheer us up.

Now what had Gray said about this place? I thought to myself. Oh yeah, watch out for the dog. As I rounded the corner of the abandoned city lot that led to the orchard, I heard a barking dog. The closer I got to the path that led across the lot, the louder the barking became. I reached down and grabbed a fallen limb for protection. The barking got louder as I passed by a fence that had seen much better days. Nearly half the boards were gone. Those that were left were barely tacked into the old rail across the top of the fence. The bottoms of the boards that remained were rotted out from years of exposure to mud, rain and mold. Green slime covered most of the boards, making them seem as soft as pillows.

In the space where two boards had once hung, I saw the dog. A real cur, I thought. The dog spied me at the same time and leapt with each bark. I drew back the limb and braced myself. Just as the dog leapt with all his might, he was yanked back to the ground. He was been chained to a piece of trim on the shambles of a house that stood next door to the lot. How long is that going to hold him? I wondered. Holding on to the limb, I moved as rapidly as I could to the edge of the lot. Stepping into the old orchard, I could still hear the dog. Going from one old apple tree to the next, I pulled down five small apples of various condition.

Now to get out of here, I thought. I saw another path that led to the edge of the orchard. I wasn't sure where it would lead but had to be better than going past the dog again, the chain could only hold him for so long. This path was not as well-used as the first. I pushed some brush aside and found myself in some blackberries. Beyond the blackberries was an empty street that led back towards houses and busier streets. I pushed my way through the blackberries, I heard the ripping sound of wood and nails coming from behind the fence where the dog had been chained. Dragging the chain and a long piece of house trim, the dog came running into the orchard and down the path toward me. I pushed with all my strength to get through the blackberries. I could feel the thorns that jabbed at my legs.

The dog was on the other side of the thorny barrier of the blackberry thicket. He made a lunge into the bushes and once again got yanked backward as the chain caught on an exposed piece of fencing. The long piece of trim had anchored itself horizontally along the bushes and the dog was trapped in the middle of a bush by a vine that had found its way into the trees above. He was stuck, unable to move forward. To move backward only entangled him more and more into the thicket. I thought of his predicament for a moment and then remembered my fear. I turned my back on the howling cur and took long strides on the empty street until I reached the houses. It was only then that I felt the thorns that had clung to my pants, and by now had worked their way into my skin.

I hurried past the houses and finally reached the sidewalk that ran past the firehouse. At the corner, I kept going straight and avoid the cars that would soon become more frequent on the road that went past the path to the shack. My detour required me to pass by Saron Lutheran Church and its parking lot. As always, the church reminded me of my youth and my capacity to believe in ideas like Advent and Christmas. Sharing the same name with the church had endeared the building to me. I wasn't so sure of the people who attended there. They were not so friendly to a girl with absent parents. The late afternoon light covered the stained-glass windows with dark shadows but in my mind's eye, I could see the glowing light that emanated from the church during the candle litghting ceremony.

As I neared the parking lot, I heard the clanging of the trash bin lid. An older woman with gray bangs popping out from below a wool knit cab that matched the woman's plaid coat was dusting off her hands from the garbage bin chore. The woman turned away from the street and headed to a car that was parked at the church's back door. I stopped by the church building and waited for the car to leave. Looking around to see if anyone was watching, I moved along the side of the building until I reached the trash bin. Lifting the lid, I could see a large plastic bag at the top of the trash. I reached into the bin and pulled out the bag. It was light, not full of papers or wet garbage. A quick glimpse inside the bag revealed that the contents were the remains of old Christmas decorations. The woman had probably been cleaning out a church shelf and decided to get rid of it all. Just right for us, I thought.

I walked as fast as I could in the descending darkness. Finally, I reached the path to the shack. I took one last look up and down the road, and seeing no one, I hurriedly walked down the path. I could see that Gray was struggling with the firewood. Every time he tried to center the small axe into the section of log on his firewood stump, the log had already fallen over. He seemed a bit agitated and unable to focus.

"Hey, how's it going?" I asked in a cheerful voice.

He didn't look up. "It's okay. You got what you wanted?"

"A miracle! Apples and then some," I said and held up the plastic bags. "Found something at the Lutheran church. Dinner will be ready in about twenty minutes. Why don't you come inside and have some hot tea?" I hoped the warm house, tea and fragrant scent of apples, sweet potatoes and the hard fought for sausage would cheer him up.

"Okay, I'll be in after I cut up some more kindling," he said.

"We have plenty, don't worry. Besides its dark now."

I let myself into the shack. It was chilly. I started a fire in the stove and put the teakettle on to heat. The cast iron frying pan went on the wood stove top next with a dash of olive oil. While the oil heated, I sliced the sweet potato into thin medallions, and cored and sliced the apples. The orange of the sweet potato and the red of the apple skins mingled with the brown oil from the sausage. I pulled the last of the raisins from the wax paper bag that lined the raisin carton. When I added these to the pan, they immediately plumped up and juices drained into the casserole.

"Gray," I called, "dinner is ready. Time to eat."

While Gray let himself into the shack and pulled off his boots. I poured cups of tea and divided the contents of the pan into the two old china plates. I pulled forks from the basket we used to store flatware. I handed Gray a plate piled high with the hot food. After putting some on a plate for myself, I sat down on a pillow in front of the stove. We ate in silence, not exactly what I was hoping for after all the effort of the afternoon. With tea and the hot food, Gray relaxed and seemed more content. His moodiness was becoming predictable.

"This is good," he said.

"Anything wrong?" I asked.

"Just got too cold out there."

"You shouldn't stay outside for so long. Stay inside tomorrow and we will keep the shack warm and cozy."

"You must have had a good afternoon salvaging in town," he said.

"I almost forgot," I said. "I got this bag out of the Lutheran church dumpster. Some old lady put in in there just as I was trying to cut across their parking lot. I waited for her to drive off so I could see what it was."

"You haven't looked in the bag yet?" asked Gray. He pulled the bag over to the table. "Let's see what's in here."

I usually let Gray open the bags I brought home from various dumpsters or trash piles. Who knew what was in them and he would be better at seeing something dangerous. Gray pulled the bag open and peered inside.

"There's just old Christmas decorations in here," he said. He pulled out a wad of silver tinsel, some white paper angels probably cut by a group of Sunday school kids, a big red ribbon tied into a bow with long ends that had triangles cut at the end of the ribbon, a silver star that was covered in sparkles, and a set of construction paper bells decorated with glitter and tinfoil around the clangors at the base of the bells. At the bottom of the bag were four candles, three purple and one pink. They were of varying lengths, two burned down to half the length of the other two. The pink candle was the least used.

I focused on the candles. "These are Advent candles," I said in a hushed voice. "They must be last year's candles."

"Well, they can be our Advent wreath candles," said Gray in a happier voice. "We can have an Advent wreath. I'll get the wreath I made this afternoon while you were gone."

Gray stepped to the door and opened it wide. "It's going to be chilly tonight," he said. Stepping out onto the porch, he leaned down by the side of the house and pulled up the wreath. A nearly perfect circle, the wreath had been formed from the limbs he had cut from the fir tree. He had used a bit of wire to tie the limbs into a circle. I cleared off the counter and put down a piece of cardboard covered with tinfoil. The wreath covered the tinfoiled board. Gray lit a candle and heated the bottom of each candle so that the melting wax could drip onto the board and the candle, once upright and in place on the board, would be secure. Gray placed the candles around the wreath to form a circle of light.

"We can light the first two for the first two Sundays of Advent," I said. Then with a sense of wonder I said, "I can't believe we found these. "Now all we need is the pillar to make a perfect Advent wreath."

"We'll find it," said Gray. "Have faith."

We sat and watched the candles for a few minutes. The light from the two candles was enough to create a glow around the table. I thought of the glow from the church windows again. I would wait until all the candles were lit on Christmas Eve to see if the shack would glow with as much beauty as the church when the Christmas Eve pillar and the four Sunday candles were all lit.

The days became darker as the sun rose later and set earlier south of the hills that framed the southern edge of Grays Harbor. Only at noon did the full sun appear above the skyline. If clouds and rain dominated the sky, the daylight hours shifted from darkness to grey and then back to darkness. There were no shadows or changes in the temperature. It was as if the sun had all but left the sky, leaving clouds that hung down to the water to surround the shack.

Gray kept the shack heated day and night, forcing chunks of fir studs into the old stove. Kindling and pieces of driftwood were stacked and dried beside the stove. I constantly filled the teapot with water. I divided the teabags in my larder, hoping they would last into January. With rainwater an easy source, it was tempting to fill the metal tub and soak away the cold from whatever chores had to be done outside. I often helped Gray move firewood closer to the house or walk with him out to the road and make sure our shack was still invisible from a passing car. Rain and wind made any thoughts of walking into town seem unbearable in the few hours of daylight.

I maintained my twice daily vigil from the blind on the shore, once in the early morning light and again in the growing dusk. Western sandpipers, red knots and a few Caspian terns seemed to enjoy the early morning light, perhaps to escape the watchful eyes of the larger predators. The resident bald eagle waited until the dawn illuminated the mudflats. Always watchful was the blue heron who hugged the shoreline across from my perch. The dots on my map became repetitive, a pattern of accustomed places for the birds and myself. I pushed myself to look for the unusual bird or something odd out on the mud, but the sense of familiarity lulled me into a calmness that fed my soul.

Walking out past the airport one day, I watched a cargo ship enter the bay. Tugs guided the ship into the narrow channel and pulled it to anchor off Westport, its engines rumbling across the water. The ship flew a South Korean flag. Like so many ships now entering the bay, it would eventually get to berth in the Aberdeen port area. I walked back to my usual spot on the Bowerman mudflats. Here the tide was beginning to recede. The pores and veins of the flats were losing the life-giving seawater that supported the animal and plant life. With the receding tide, shorebirds and seabirds moved into the mudflats to feast on the fat, muscles and organs hidden below the surface. Like a mega-heart, the mudflats throbbed with the tides sending life in and out of the mudflats.

I watched the birds move into the flats. They took their places depending on adaptations of legs, bills, and wings to find their location on the mudflat ballroom. A bird dropped from its airborne flight to hover over an exposed portion of the mudflats. I did not immediately recognize it, it looked like an American golden plover, but was a bit smaller. Paging through my guidebook, I found the plover pages. The characteristic speckled blacks, browns and yellows across its wings and the white crescent above its eye and down its chest matched the plover description, but its size lead me to believe it was an uncommon

Pacific golden-plover. This Pacific plover had flown across the northern Pacific to find refuge in these mudflats. A note at the bottom of the guidebook described the loss of Asian mudflats especially the South Korean Saemangeum mudflats that had been transformed into industrial sites and a major harbor for cargo ships.

So here are two arrivals to Grays Harbor, I thought. One represents the natural world and the other the human constructed world. One sat quietly looking for food in the mudflat and other burning diesel fuel. The ship was expanding a network of trade that required harbor facilities, tugboats, railroads, trucks and every kind of machinery necessary to put the cargo into the world markets. The port expansion in Grays Harbor was part of that expanding global trade network. If the expansion project were approved, the mudflats would be impacted, and the Pacific golden plover would have fewer and fewer places for survival. As much as the ship's success was linked to the Saemangeum mudflats, so was the plover's, and so were the mudflats.

Gray and I often talked about the disruption to the bay's natural environment if the port project became a reality. I continued my mental debate about what was natural and what was not. One thing I did know was that the birds were beautiful. The mudflats were alive and that the birds needed the mudflats as much as I needed my shack. Our daily routine during the long days in the shack became a source of calm. Most of our days were filled with reading or making simple meals from the stored food. Miss Hap added warmth and charm.

Gray went out one day to fish but came back after an hour with nothing in his plastic bucket. "Too cold and the fish are not moving," he said.

I kept an inventory of the canned goods and sacks of dried beans once again. This time I spied a small can of tuna in the back corner of the cabinet. I didn't say anything to Gray, hoping that a tuna and noodle stew with an added boost of a can of peas and carrots would be a nice little surprise for our evening meal. I made some biscuits on the top of the stove and set out a few of the butter pats that had come with a meal the last time we ate at the Fish Bait. Gray appreciated the biscuits and stew.

Each day brought its chores, its challenges for creativity to survive the days leading up to winter. It was as if we were in practice mode for the months of darkness, wet and cold they would have to endure until Earth moved further around the sun on its trek toward the spring track of its orbit.

As Christmas approached, I wondered about my ability to find a pillar for the Advent wreath. Gray disappeared almost every day, always saying there were special errands this time of year. He would leave in a sullen mood and return in a better mood. I didn't ask too many questions of him, but something just wasn't the same. He seemed smaller somehow.

He was starting to act like a trapped animal. "We are fine," I said to comfort and calm him. "We'll get what we need as soon as we can. Maybe the weather will be better tomorrow." But it rained again the next day, and I put out more beans to soften in the morning. What could I add to the pot this time? I wondered. I added one potato, a can of stewed tomatoes, and some spices. When we had eaten the soup and stoked the stove, we crawled into bed and listened to the rain.

"We'll be okay," said Gray. The night was long. Gray got up twice to add more wood to the stove. We were starting to run low on food and firewood. We couldn't stay holed up in the shack without getting out tomorrow. Listening to the rain on the tin roof, Gray tried to think of alternatives and a plan of action. The rain beat out his ability to sort and plan. He hugged me and lay awake for most of the night. Sleep came only when he believed we had survived the night.

We stayed near the shack for a week, Gray went out to replenish the firewood stacked beside the door. In his thick bib rain pants and jacket, he was the only brightness in the otherwise dark days of rain and fog. I watched him from the window that looked out over the alder grove. The alder grove had become a mysterious and threatening place in the gloom. Each tree stood like a stone column in a field strewn with the last known remains of soldiers killed in an ancient battle for what no one any longer remembers. I was quick to open the door to the returning Gray and help him unload the firewood from his pack. Once inside, his wet dripping rain gear hung on the back of the door, I handed him a cup of hot tea and embraced him with love and gratitude for his willingness to step out into the battle field.

With the weather forcing Gray to stay indoors with me, I was having a difficult time finishing his Christmas gift. I had hoped to finish knitting the thick wool mittens I was making for him. I had started this knitting project in early November. Walking through the sweater section of the Salvation Army thrift store last September, I found a dark green wool sweater with bits of white striping across the chest. The sweater was handmade with a tag on the back neckline that read, 'Made by Margaret Speller.' I had no idea who Margaret Speller was. Too bad it's not bigger I thought, 'this would be so nice for Gray.' I held out the sweater at arms-length to inspect it further. The wool yarn was in good condition.

"That's been on the rack for a while," said the volunteer. "I keep hoping someone will buy it, but it's just not moving. I'm marking it down today, fifty percent off. The yarn is at least worth that." She reached out and grabbed the price tag. "There," she said. "If you want it, it just got a whole lot cheaper."

Pushing the sweater into my canvas bag, I left the store and headed back to the shack. While Gray was out fishing or had walked to the Fish Bait to see his friends, I unraveled the sweater and rolled the yarn into ball for knitting. Mittens began to take shape.

Finishing the mittens was not my only concern. The third week of Advent had passed on the last Sunday. They lit the first and second candles first and then touched the match flame to the third.

"What is the third candle for?" asked Gray.

"We light the first candle for hope, the second for faith, and the third candle for joy," I said in a solemn voice.

"You sound so serious," said Gray.

"We have to have something to look forward to," she said. "We should sing a carol."

"Not me," said Gray. "You sing, I'll pray to the Great Spirit."

"Okay, just think positive," I responded. I hummed a few lines of 'O Come, O Come Emmanuel' and watched the three candles for a while. We need the Christmas Eve pillar, I thought for the hundredth time. The whole Advent thing would be wasted without the final flame. Maybe the whole thing was too religious. We should be celebrating the Solstice and getting ready for darkness, I thought.

I looked out the window that faced west and saw a snowflake gently swish back and forth until it landed on the grass beside the shack and completely disappeared as if eaten by the desperate-looking winter blades. I frowned and wondered if I had really seen snow. Snow would mean cold, ice and an even more landlocked existence than we currently lived. Trips to town would be impossible due to impassable roads, slush and often downed limbs. Freezing rain would bring ice and even more broken tree limbs. We would be cut off from town for days.

I looked again. Another flake drifted past the window, headed to its demise in the angry blades of sea grass. Grabbing my coat and boots, I gathered up my field notebook and headed to the door.

"Where are you going?" asked Gray, alarmed at my imminent exit.

"I have to see what the mudflats look like in snow," I said and left before he could stop me.

Falling snow filled the scene before me. What had been an infrequent and seemingly lost snowflake was now a mass of white crystals more like a wedding dress of lace and diamonds than a curtain of white velvet. The last rays of the sinking afternoon sun shone through the snowflakes causing tiny rainbows to radiate from each flake. For just a moment, my entire vision was filled with multitudes of tiny rainbow arcs, each in the same sequence of rainbow colors merging to form one huge rainbow. The point was wrapped in a glistening arc of reds, violets, blues, greens, and yellows. The natural event was transformed into a supernatural experience for those who could perceive its beauty. This is my Christmas joy, I thought.

The sun sank beneath the watery horizon. The rainbow disappeared as quickly as it had appeared. There was no dusk. The light in the western sky disappeared, and darkness moved in from the east.

I found Gray outside sorting firewood and finding kindling for the morning fire. He stepped into the shack with an armload of thin limbs and curled shavings he had found at the base of his chopping block. His beard and hat were wet from the snow. His coat glistened with snow.

"So glad we have the firewood. Dinner is nearly ready except for the cooking. Come inside."

Stiff from his work, he shuffled to his chair and pulled his blanket around his legs.

"Tea first?" I asked. He nodded and pulled the sleeves of his old wool shirt as far over his wrists as he could. I put the kettle on the stove and readied a cup with a tea bag.

"How about an early dessert?" I asked. Soon a plate of cookies and a steaming cup of tea were beside Gray on the tiny chest that served as a coffee table and then a dinner table. It seemed to take Gray a long time to warm up. He sat quietly in front of the fire. The cup of tea was more of a hand warmer than a vessel meant for internal warmth. "Drink the tea," I nudged. "I'll make more for you."

"We drink so much of this damn stuff," he said in uncharacteristic rejection. I cast a long gaze at him. His back was rounded, and his head bowed. Every inch of him said his muscles were in pain from the cold and exertion to bring in the kindling. He reached for his bottle of pain killers.

"How about we just stay inside all day tomorrow and read to each other? I have a great new paperback I got at the Salvation Army last week. I think it could be an interesting read," I offered.

Gray nodded in agreement. "Tomorrow will be a better day. The snow will slow everyone down and we won't worry about our lights or path."

"The snow will keep us safe another day," I agreed. I was counting on the magic I had seen, the connection to a spiritual world beyond the present in time and space. "We will be safe," I said.

I still had to finish my knitting project. While Gray dozed much of the next day, I made real progress. Christmas was three days away. Christmas Eve even sooner, and there was still no pillar for the evening ceremony. I resolved to go to town tomorrow no matter what the weather.

The next morning, I made an offer. "Gray, lets go to the Fish Bait this afternoon. We really need to get out of here for a while.

He nodded in agreement, and we walked to the bar after lunch. Gray cheered up when he saw Roger was there. Cliff brought the two beers. They were engrossed in conversation and had forgotten about me. Now's my chance, I thought. I went and sat at the bar. Cliff came over to my spot.

"What can I get you, dearie?" he asked.

I leaned forward and said in a low voice, "Do you have any spare candles?"

"Candles?" he asked.

"Yeah, not the tall skinny ones but maybe one that is," I measured out four inches tall by two inches wide.

Cliff pierced his lips for a minute and then said, "Let me look in the back. There might be something left from a wedding we had here last summer."

He came back with a brown paper bag. "Will this work?"

I opened the bag and peered inside. "This is perfect!" I said, and then looked to make sure Gray hadn't heard me. "Perfect," I repeated to Cliff in a quieter voice. The bag held a purple pillar, exactly what the Advent wreath needed.

"More beer!" said Roger. We spent the afternoon at the bar, happy to be out of the shack and celebrating Christmas with friends.

Christmas Eve Day arrived in a continuous cold rainstorm. Gray went out to look for firewood over on the channel side of the point. I took the opportunity to put the finishing touches on his gift and wrapped up the wool mittens. We'll exchange gifts in the morning. Tonight is about lighting the final candle, I thought. I was still so happy to have gotten the pillar candle from Cliff. I hoped Gray would be equally touched.

Our wreath sat on the counter atop a bit of white linen fabric I had found in the bag from the church. I straightened the tapers and then placed the pillar in the center of the wreath. The decorations made the shack look a bit more regal. It wasn't the cold, damp place it could be. Still no insulation, but the stove was warm. I set out some orange marmalade in water and hoped it would add a festive aroma to the interior.

Looking into our larder, I found the cranberries and small bag of walnuts. There were also a bag of iced cookies and two envelopes of hot chocolate. Some of this food had arrived in a box of food Gray brought home from Catholic Services, and the rest I had been storing up over the last month. I was busy putting together a dinner to go along with the lighting ceremony. We'll have the best Christmas Eve I can muster, I thought.

Gray came back from the Fish Bait. He threw his empty pack to the floor. Wordless, he went to his bed and turned toward the wall.

I sat motionless, denied of what I had anticipated upon his return.

The room slowly turned to darkness in the waning hours of the holy night.

Eventually, I got up and lit the four Advent candles. I was about to light the pillar, the symbol of Christ, when Gray spoke.

"Connie shot herself full of heroin and died behind the Fish Bait," he said in a toneless voice.

I lowered my hand and blew out the match. Then I blew out the four candles that encircled the pillar.

So, there are not miracles, I thought. Not even on Christmas.

I crawled into my bed with all my clothes on. The room grew colder as the stove's warmth died away. The sky clouded over so that no stars or moonlight shone on the shack or the shore. Nothingness became us.

# 15

# CHRISTMAS

Gray woke me the next morning. He sat next to me on my bed, gently stroking my hair. In his other hand, he held a steaming mug of coffee.

"I'm so sorry about last night," he said apologetically. "I know you were counting on a bit of a ceremony to welcome Christmas to our humble shack. I didn't mean to spoil it for you."

I looked at him for a minute, slowly wakening to his voice and sentiments.

I sat up and took the mug of coffee from his hand. "It's okay," I said quietly. "I was so dumbfounded by your news of Connie's death. She was such a wonderful person and a good friend to me. It took the spirit of Christmas out of my heart."

Gray hugged me while I tried to keep the mug upright.

"Merry Christmas," I said as cheerfully as I could. "Its nice and warm in here this morning. Let's enjoy the day."

"No one will be out this morning," said Gray. "We'll have some warmth in the shack. I'm so sorry I haven't got the insulation project together."

"Let's not think about that today," I said. "Let's light our candles and be happy."

We spent the morning sipping coffee and listening to Christmas music on the radio. A station from Central Park just east of Aberdeen that played Christmas music all year round most appropriate on today. We exchanged gifts. Gray was very happy with the woolen mittens. I was totally surprised by the store-bought wool hat lined with feathers and bits of animal fur he had found. "Granny would have made it that way," he said shyly.

We were about to start putting together a lunch of saved and savory foods when there was a knock on the front door. As it was unexpected and we had let our defenses down by having more of a fire in the stove than usual, we both froze for a moment. Gray finally took a step to the door. "There's no use in denying we are here," he said wearily.

"Gray. Saron. It's me, Andy."

Gray reached to open the door. "Oh, thank god," he said.

"I didn't mean to frighten you," Andy said as she stepped into the shack.

"Merry Christmas," we all said at the same time. There were hugs all around.

"What brings you out here today?" I asked.

"It's the annual Audubon Christmas bird count on the bay," said Andy. "And I wanted to be sure you were having a nice Christmas."

Gray went to the stove and turned down the damper. "Guess we could attract some attention out here," he said.

"I really didn't see any smoke," said Andy. "Super cold front with no air motion right now."

"Can you stay for a while?" I asked.

"How about you come with me to count birds on Bowerman Basin and then I'll come back and join you for a late lunch." She handed Gray a large plastic bag. "Check this out while we go out to the point," she said to Gray. Gray looked in the bag and returned a smile. "I'll make a nice Christmas dinner out of this," he said.

I pulled on my heaviest clothes and boots against the cold and grabbed my field gear. Andy and I pushed our way through the brush to my spot in the rocks. We chatted away about birds and Andy's work on her internship. I showed her my observations since I was sick.

"Thank you so much for the meds," I said.

"Gray looked so helpless when I got them to you," she said.

"I know, he's not doing so well."

"I don't see any insulation in the walls," said Andy.

"I don't feel like I can pressure him about it," I said. "He can barely spend a couple of hours in the cold and damp without cramping up."

Andy and I talked more about her internship. Her work was progressing.

"I just want to thank you for making all these observations on the days I'm not able to get out here," said Andy. "Your work is professional quality. I know Jen is thinking of a way to incorporate your observations into the data base with everything else. You'll see," she said. "Your work is going to make a difference."

I was overwhelmed at hearing her praise. It was the first time anyone had ever said my work was professional quality.

"That's the best gift ever," I said quietly. "Thank you."

"The first public hearing is going to be at the end of the month," she said. "I'll be coming out with Jen for it. You and Gray should come."

"Oh, I don't think so," I said. "there will be too many people there who could recognize us."

"Yeah, I know. Ike Hamundarson for one," said Andy bitterly. "At least I have Jen to protect me."

"I'll mention the hearing to Gray," I said. "He doesn't run the same risks for appearing in public places that I do."

Andy and I went down to the mudflats. The tide was mostly out, revealing the last waves to indent the mud as the water receded. Quick to see their chance at a mid-day meal, western sandpipers, dunlins, plovers, red knots and Caspian terns had landed along the capillaries and arteries of sea water that crossed the wave traces. I quickly pointed out the various species to Andy and she recorded them in her bird census.

"Nothing special here," she said. "But at least they are here. They have managed to hang on despite the problems with cord grass invasion and increasing ship movements in the bay."

Andy studied the mudflats, watching the very last of the seawater slip away. "There's so much we don't know about these mudflats, what birds use them, when the birds are here, what they eat, or even how many birds are here on a permanent basis. We know even less about how the mudflats support the fall and spring migrations. We know this is a major flyway and some of the more frequently seen birds on their way through, but all the species and how they use the mudflats? No, we don't know very much at all about this bay and the birds who find it."

I looked out at the mudflats and the tidal waters beyond them. My mind's eye rose up above the bay to see what I thought a migrating bird would see, a huge cavernous indentation on the otherwise continuous stretch of sand beaches of the coastline. From a soaring height, the bay, with its ring of tall fir and cedar at its entrance and the muddy current of the Chehalis River in its engorged channel to the east would offer the gift of rich nutrients in the brackish water, a place to rest in the shallow waters, and protection from the ocean's storms. The bay was a temporary home, a place of refuge from a journey well-known yet full of constant hazardous and sudden chaos.

"Are there other people out taking the census?" I asked.

"Yes, there's a small but focused group of birders in Aberdeen. Some people come from as far away as Olympia to document the species. It's their way of celebrating Christmas." Turning to me, she said, "And you give your gift for watching these waters to all of us who care about the bay." Turning back to the bay, she said, "We all care!" in a loud voice. "Merry Christmas," we yelled in unison.

"I can't think of a better way to celebrate the day," I said.

"Well, I can!" said Andy with a bit of a smirk. "Let's go eat some Christmas dinner."

We headed back to the shack for the Christmas lunch Gray had prepared. We had fried ham steaks and instant potatoes, canned green beans and rolls. Andy had also brought a pumpkin pie from Shari's. We ate until we couldn't take another bite. Gray made coffee and we sat awhile, enjoying the good food and warmth of the fire. Finally, Andy said she had to go. The other birders would be waiting for her report, and she had to get back to Olympia.

"Be sure to tell Gray about the hearing," she said on her way out the door.

"What is she talking about?" asked Gray as he heated water to do the dishes.

"The first public hearing for the terminal project is going to be in a couple of weeks. She wants us both to go but I don't think I should be out in public especially where Isaac James may very well be."

"I'm not afraid of that guy," said Gray. "He pisses me off, for many reasons."

"Okay," I said. "You go."

"Maybe," he replied. "I'll talk to Roger and see what the Nation is going to do."

I helped Gray with the dishes. We spent the rest of the evening listening to music and telling each other stories of our childhood Christmases. We both had stories of times of fullness and other times that were pretty bleak. We agreed that Christmas was a special day, one we both waited for each year. The saddest feeling in the world was saying goodbye to Christmas, knowing it would take another year to see it again. I wonder where we will be, I thought to myself.

I spent the last few days of the year going out to the shore to make observations, reading library books on shoreline natural history, and trying to make the shack as comfortable as possible. Andy's praise propelled me out the door every morning to watch the mudflats. The nights were particularly cold. Gray was often wrapped in a blanket by the stove to ward off aches and pains. He was also using more and more pain killers. I worried we would run out of money just keeping him in pills.

The dark, cold days slowly trudged on. Gray talked about looking for work. I worried more and more about his health and our ability to stay out in the shack. "Maybe we will have to break down and go to a shelter," I said. Gray was very opposed to the idea. "No," he said. "I'll find work and make some money."

The issue came up again on New Year's Eve. I had hoped we could take the last five dollars we had and go to the Fish Bait. But our conversation about money and struggling to survive in the shack became heated.

"I want us to have a good time tonight," I said.

"Not much fun on five dollars," said Gray. "It's not worth going."

"I think you should go and enjoy being with your friends," I said.

"Not wanting to be seen with me?" he said dejectedly.

"No," I said nearly in tears. "I want you to be happy."

"Okay," he said in a mean voice. "I'm going,"

I held out the five-dollar bill for him to take.

"Don't need it," he said gruffly. "I've got friends."

Gray pulled on his jacket and boots. "Don't wait up for me."

His mean-spiritedness was heart breaking. I sat next to the stove, trying to stay warm. My small candle made huge images on the brown canvas window coverings. I felt imprisoned in the shack and in the grief of losing Gray. He wasn't the same person I had met months before. I blew out the candle and crawled into my bed. Miss Hap curled up next to me but even the cat could not bring me solace. My dreams were filled with images of Connie floating out to sea in her pirate costume.

When I woke in the morning, Gray was in his bed. His arm was uncovered, above his blankets. It was bruised not as if he had been punched by someone. It looked like the collapsed blood vessels. I was afraid to admit that his arm looked like the arm of a drug addict from many shots of heroin.

# 16

# THE GREEN FREIGHTER

*N*ot far from the shack was the large conveyor belt that connected the chipper plant to the pier. Hanging at the end of the belt was a canvas penis, limp in the air waiting to be filled with cells of wood that would shoot continuously into a ship's hold. Usually the ships that tied up at the pier were empty. The Chinese market made it much more profitable to bring the chips to a production site in Chinese where labor costs were a faction of American costs. Chips were also easier to load and became the ballast for ships with deck space for additional cargo.

Loading the ships was an intermittent labor need of the port. Friends would call friends and gangs of "pop-up" crews would assemble at piers for day labor wages. Gray was on several call lists of friends. Since he didn't have a phone, he usually heard about a ship needing help with loading and unloading at the Fish Bait. It was hard work for him, but good money always paid under the table, no taxes, no forms, no addresses. He had helped load vehicles at the Chrysler dock, grain at the terminal, and occasionally logs and lumber at the old mill in the port area.

A couple days after New Year's, Gray went into Hoquiam and settled into his usual seat at the bar. He found enough change in his pocket to order 12 ounces of the cheapest draft beer on tap and began to take a sip. He watched the action behind him on the streaked mirror over the bar. Two men came in the door and surveyed the bar's seating. The one closest to Gray tipped his head toward a table along the opposite wall and the two made their way to the chairs on either side of the table. The one giving directions looked ordinary enough, a regular Hoquiam bar kind of guy. He had on thick Carhart blue jeans, a rain parka opened down the front to show a wool plaid shirt, heavy work boots and a knit hat perched on an unshaven face. The other was not so ordinary. He was a slight build, barely five and half feet tall. His pants were dark gray, as his coat. His hat was pulled down over his ears, there was barely enough room for his nose and mouth. It was a wonder that he could see, thought Gray.

When Cliff delivered two beers to the men, the larger man caught his arm and kept him low to the table. Some words were said before Cliff stood up and walked back behind the bar. Starting at the opposite end of the bar from Gray, Cliff leaned forward and appeared to chat with every man seated at the bar. As he worked his way down the bar, the effect of whatever he was saying to the men changed the atmosphere in the room. The bits of yakking and sometimes bickering between the men quieted down, with careful glances made in the direction of the two seated men. Sips of beer could be heard from along the bar and then men started to leave. A slow but steady stream of wool shirted, Carhart-wearing labors began to drift out the door. At last, Cliff reached Gray's position at the end of the bar.

"Interested in a little work?" he asked.

"Sure," said Gray. "What are we doing?"

"Not exactly sure but promises to be some good pay," said Cliff. "Just follow that crew outside."

By now the two seated men had swallowed their beers and stood up to leave the bar. With a quick glance in their direction, Gray recognized the smaller man as Chinese. A Chinese man in port could only mean one thing, there was a Chinese ship with cargo to be unloaded that the Port didn't know about. Gray sized up the other men who had created a crew outside the bar. He knew some of them well enough to know he wasn't going to be alone in wondering what the cargo was and where the ship was tied up. He caught the eye of one guy he had known while working in the woods. A flicker of recognition passed between them. Okay, thought Gray, if he goes, I go.

There was a van parked outside the bar. The men slowly piled in, nervous but willing to earn better money than they had seen for a long time. Hands went into pockets, including his, where Gray knew every man carried a knife. If the van started off in an unknown direction or the conversation from the front seat when bad, there would be a way out of the arrangement.

The van headed west, took the truck route along the water, and turned left to drive past the shingle mill and pirate's landing. Gray watched carefully, hoping the van kept its distance from the hidden path to the shack. When the van reached the wood chip processing site, it turned onto the pier and drove as far as it could before stopping in front of a green ship. White Chinese lettering was tattooed along the back of the ship.

"This is it, boys," said the van driver. "We've got cargo to unload."

Gray looked at the ship, wondering where the cargo was. The hold doors were open. In front of the doors was a container. Ship's crew-members were untying knots and rolling up heavy ropes.

"We're going to unload the container," yelled the van driver. The Chinese man nodded his head and then hurriedly walked up the gangway to the ship's deck.

Gray looked around, as did others, searching for an answer to their common question about the logistics of their work. What was the cargo they were to unload? Why the lack of information? Where were they to unload the cargo to?

Sensing the apprehension of the crew, the driver pointed to the container. "Open the container, "he yelled. "Unload the crates and stack them at the end of the pier."

"You don't have a forklift," yelled one of the crew.

"No. And don't drop the crates," yelled the driver.

The assembled crew looked at each other with questioning frowns.

"Okay," said one of the men. "Let's get this job done and get our pay as fast as we can."

Even though the men had never worked together before as a crew, they had worked on other crews. They knew when to pull their own weight and when to wait for a signal to pull together. A burly, bearded man took the lead. He positioned himself next to the cargo, eyed the four corners of the massive block that had to be moved, and nodded his head to each man as they took up positions.

"Ropes," yelled the leader. Each man grabbed a rope by its knot and quickly slid the knot into a straightened yard of rope.

"Tarp," yelled the leader. The men grabbed at the edge of the canvas tarp at their side. With a unison effort, the corners of the tarp were pinned together. The men moved their corners to one side of the cargo and crossed the edges of the tarp together until a heavy square of canvas four feet thick was dropped to the deck.

Having liberated the cargo from its tarp, the men were able to see the outline of a large gray metal box packed beneath a wooden crate. Gray reached out to give the crate a shove. But before his hand reached the crate, the Chinese man, who had been watching from the upper deck, yelled out. It wasn't that anyone knew what he was saying, it was the intensity of his shouts that stopped all movement on the deck.

"Keep your hands and eyes to yourself," yelled the van driver.

Gray lowered his hand and eyes. "Let's get this over with," he hissed to no one in particular.

"Where do you want it?" yelled the crew leader.

"Just get it to the pier," was the return yell.

The men moved toward the crate. The slats allowed them to brace their hands midway on the crate. They put their collective weight against the load.

"On the count of three," ordered the crew leader. "We'll push it to the gang plank."

"One, two, three, push!"

"One, two, three, push!"

"One, two, three, push!"

Slowly the crate and its heavy load moved towards the plank. Again, and again the crew leader shouted the order. With each order, the men shoved the cargo, some with their shoulders, others with massive arms. Gray, not used to such intensive physical work, felt the man behind him take up a bit of slack due to his inability to do all his share. He turned and nodded to the man, the man shook his head as if to say, 'no apology necessary.' It was the workmen's' code to help another whenever it was needed. You never knew when you would need the help.

After numerous shoves and pushes, the crate reached the edge of the deck. The incline of the deck, due to the height of the receding tide, immediately became a worse challenge than the distance they already moved the cargo. The crew leader stepped back to analyze the situation. He shook his head with doubt about the crew's ability to lower the cargo at such an angle.

"Ropes," he yelled. Three of the crew took long quick steps to retrieve the ropes that had been coiled up on the deck. They tied the ropes through the crate and wound them around one of the railings attached to the ship's lower cabin.

"Okay, you three stand there and slowly let the ropes feed the cargo," said the crew leader. "The rest of you hold on to the crate. Work together."

The cargo was pushed into place at the top of the planking.

"Now," ordered the leader. The men at the ropes gradually released the roped and the cargo slide forward and down towards the pier.

"Keep it comin'," yelled the leader. The men at the ropes braced themselves against the weight of the cargo that wanted to pull everything down to the pier. The men holding on to the crate pushed up to slow the cargo's progress. The cargo lurched forward, its weight dropping toward the pier. The men at the ropes began to yell, "It's too heavy," they shouted. "It's going to go."

"Keep it in pace," yelled the leader. The van driver and the Chinese man began to yell the same orders. "Slow it down," they shouted.

The men attempted to hold the crate could feel the weight getting the best of them. Gray used all his strength as some power that seemed to come from nowhere. We have to stop this thing, he thought.

Even with all the power of the crew and the shouts and yells from the ship, the crate became a more powerful force. The ropes ripped from their tethering to the ship. The men jumped away to avoid being hit by the flaying ropes and end knots. The men at the crate leapt back to the deck and the crate slid down the plank. When it hit the pier, the wooden crate shattered leaving the metal box on its side. A corner of the box split open.

The Chinese man ran from his perch on the ship down to the deck and clambered down the plank to the metal box. Yelling at the men and waving his arms wildly, the men were at first confused. Then the crew leader yelled, "Okay men, let's tip this box back up."

Gray was standing next to the ripped corner seam of the box. He slowly grabbed the ripped metal, careful not to tear his hands on the exposed seam. He peered into the box to see cardboard with the words Pill Manufacturing and an arrow pointing up. Below the arrow was a list of prescription drugs. Gray read down the list, aspirin, oxycontin, ibuprofen.... Gray recognized the pills the machine was to make, all of them addictive drugs. First, he had become addicted to the pills after his accident, and now he was unloading the machine that created the drugs. All his energy and strength slipped away from him. He had nothing left to give.

"Hey!" yelled the driver. "Get to work, get this upright."

Gray and several of the other men struggled to get the crate to an upright position. There were three more crates with similar boxes. It took the crew of men five hours total to unload the ship. They were all tired, cold, and weary from the labor.

The Chinese man walked around each crate, checking for damages. When he was done, he walked over to the men. Silently, he pulled out an envelope from his jacket pocket. He walked up to each man and handed out a packet of twenty-dollar bills. The men nodded in thanks and began to separate. Gray was careful to take a circuitous route back to the shack. Even though he was near the shack at the chipper dock, he didn't feel safe just walking down the road to the hidden path. Instead, he walked into town and then cut back toward the shack on the old railroad grade that eventually paralleled the coast highway. He finally got to the shack after an hour of walking.

I had anticipated his return, knowing that he would be exhausted and cold. When he came in the door, I jumped up from my warm seat by the stove.

"Come here," I said gently. I leaned forward and gave him a soft kiss. "You must be freezing." His skin was cold. He could barely nod his head.

"Here," I said. "Take off your clothes and sit by the fire." I had heated up as much water as I could on the stove. I poured the steaming water over all the towels we had and started wrapping them around Gray. He jumped at the heat of the first one bu, began to relax. I could tell the hot towels were helping heat his body core. Once all the towels were around his body. I fixed him some hot tea.

"There's hot soup and biscuits with cheese and the last of the packaged meat," I said. I set cups of the soup and a dish with the biscuits and cheese in front of Gray. He seemed unable to eat by himself. I lifted a spoon of soup to his mouth. We sat silently as I fed him. The food and the hot towels were all I had to caress and soothe his weary, cold body. He started to shiver, but the encompassing warmth took hold and he slowly relaxed.

The afternoon light turned to darkness. I lit candles and kept the stove going as much as I could. I carefully pulled the towels from his limbs and torso, rubbing and cleaning as I went from arms to legs. I poured more water on a few of the towels and wrapped his feet in the warmth. At least his body temperature was as warm as mine. The warmth and food had warmed him on the inside. I pulled a clean sweatshirt over his head and he lifted his arms into its sleeves. He pulled on sweats over his legs and up to his waist. Sitting close, he wrapped his arms around me.

"Thank you," he whispered. "The money's in my jacket pocket."

"We'll get it later," I said quietly. "Let's just crawl into bed now and you get some sleep."

I put a few more pieces of wood on the fire, made sure the shack was secure for the night, and put on my nightclothes. I crawled into bed next to Gray.

"You did so much today," I said gently. "You won't have to do any-thing for a long time. We'll get through this cold spell, don't worry."

Gray hugged me and then drifted into a deep sleep. I caressed his body, hoping he won't be in too much pain in the morning. What will become of us in this new year? I wondered. Why does it have to involve drugs?

Gray hardly moved. I kept him covered in hot towels as best I could. I gave him all the vitamins and antibiotics Andy had brought me when I was sick. Gray wasn't sick, but I didn't want his immune system to take a hit. All the painkillers were beginning to take a toll on his own system's ability to respond to stress. The painkillers were both a blessing and a curse. Without them, Gray couldn't make it through a day without pain. With them, he was able to cope. He would never be cured. Worse, he had to put himself in horrible conditions that worsened his pain so that he could afford the pills. I couldn't see an end to the cycle. It seemed hopeless.

I put the cash Gray had brought home from his day on the dock in our mutual 'bank.' The bank was just a coffee can that we could easily hide in the shack. I put cash from my Social Security check in the can and Gray added whatever cash he was able to make on odd jobs. I never questioned the amount he put in the can; I didn't know how much he brought home unless he told me. Since I was the one who fished out the cash from his jacket pocket from this last job, I knew he had brought home as much as I contributed from Social Security.

My check covered most of our mutual costs for food and miscellaneous expenses like toothpaste and soap. I still had a deduction taken out each month for my Y membership. Gray added time to our 'bank' by collecting firewood off the airport jetty while I usually went only so far as my observation blind on the inside of Bowerman Basin. Gray also made major contributions by staying in touch with people. He brought home interesting information about the goings on in the harbor and he heard about work. While I still tried to keep a low profile against the ire of Ike Hamundarson, Gray had more freedom to stay in touch with Roger and his many acquaintances. Roger and most other people had stopped asking Gray where he lived. If asked, he'd say on the street.

My main outside contact was Andy. She was faithful brought water. Sometimes I ran into her on the shore. Other times, like Christmas Day, she would softly knock on the door of the shack and announce her arrival. Her visits were always reviving. She brought sunshine into my dark world of rain, gray water, and the brown canvas that covered the shack's windows. She usually brought a newspaper or something else interesting to read.

Andy also kept me up to date about the project. She told me about her observations, how the data were becoming large enough to begin running statistical analyses, and what seemed to be the message from

US Fish and Wildlife Service. Our last conversation had focused on the upcoming public hearing.

"You really have to attend," she had said.

"No, I'm not willing to risk running into people who believe I've disappeared," I told her. "I'll tell Gray about it," I promised.

Gray and I had talked about the hearing. He had promised to talk to Roger and see what the Quinault Indian Nation wanted to see happen in the harbor. As Gray said, they technically owned the bottom of the harbor. No one could do much to invade that space if the Tribe said no. "But stranger things have happened in Quinault land," he had said.

After two days and nights of sleep, Gray started to recover and return to his normal pace. He asked for more food and water. He even asked for tea, even though he was getting very tired of it. I made him thick tea with sweetened condensed milk and cinnamon. We rarely had alcohol in the shack, so no toddies for Gray. On the third day, Gray sat up and engaged in conversation.

"How long have I been out?" was his first question.

"This is day three since you came back from unloading the ship," I said. "How do you feel?" I asked.

"Okay," he said. Then he pushed back down into his bed and dozed off and on all day. He slept all night.

The next day, Gray was more energized, almost his old self.

"Guess I just needed to sleep," he said almost sheepishly.

I smiled at him. "Welcome back," I said and gave him a kiss on the forehead.

Gray toweled off with hot towels and soap. He pulled on his fleece hoodie and rain jacket, then his pants and last, his rubber boots.

"Where do you think you're going?" I asked.

"I thought I would walk over to the Fish Bait while you are out on your bird watch," he said.

"Are you up for that?" I asked.

"Yeah, I'm okay," he said. Then he reached for the coffee can. "I need some more meds."

After he was gone, I couldn't help but look inside the can and see how much he had taken. Nearly all the cash he had brought home was gone. I looked into the can again, unwilling to believe Gray had taken nearly all the cash.

Sitting back on my bed, I felt the cold hand of eternity reach into the shack to undo everything I had been trying to accomplish. I was sabotaged by the collective and individual pain of homelessness and drug addiction that had become so common in Grays Harbor.

It seemed to take him forever to return. I waited until he was curled up on his bed, drinking tea and munching on cookies before I dared to voice my concerns.

"Gray," I said softly. "Did you need a lot of money today?"

Gray investigated his cup and remained silent.

"I thought we were trying to save the money you earned, so you won't have to go out in the cold again."

"Hah," he said almost candidly. "Don't worry about it, honey-bunch. I already got another job at the car terminal. I'll be out the next three days with those guys, maybe stay in town with Roger for the rest of the week."

I stared at him in disbelief. After a while, I realized I was angry. I was angry that he had taken the money. I was angry that he seemed oblivious to the care he needed after the last job, and now he was going to go out on a three-day job? I wanted to go after him for his selfishness. Instead, I shook my head and refused to look him in the eye.

"Okay, whatever works for you," I said. I sat cross legged on my bed not knowing what to do with myself. After a few minutes, I put on my coat and grabbed my bag of field notes and bird identification books. "I'll be back before dark," I said.

Sitting in my usual spot, I tried to focus on the birds in the mud-flats. A plover was investigating a rivulet with its of seaweed and tiny crustaceans. My thoughts were clouded by my anger. How could he? But maybe I had to admit that I wasn't the only thing in Gray's life, that we hadn't set out to be anymore than a mutual aid society to get through the winter in the shack. Still, he meant a lot to me. He apparently had other things that drew his attention. The hopelessness of drug addiction and homelessness crowded out the warmth of the shack.

I watched the last rays of light settle beneath the dark horizon. A moment of light held the edges of the ocean and the sky separate. Like two completely different realms, they both glowed in the light and then it was gone. Gone like the light that had held Gray and me together. Now we were two different realms, Gray hard and cold like the land and me, like the water, flowing with the tides in and out of safety. The security of life in the shack was so fragile. I wasn't sure what to expect, who Gray may tell or how much longer I could count on his presence. He wasn't the same man I had met last fall. He was cold and hard, with an addiction that needed more and more pills. His excuse for going to the Fish Bait and taking nearly all his money was destroying our relationship. And now he would go away? I didn't know how to even think about it all.

I went back to the shack. Inside, candles were lit, and some food was being warmed on the stove. I looked at Gray, hoping there was some explanation or sign of welcome. I took off my coat and went to sit by the stove.

"I'm sorry if I have upset you," said Gray. "I don't feel right about the money or," he looked around the shack, "or that I haven't insulated this place and that we don't have any options."

I waited quietly, hoping he would say more. I was still angry about the money and his deceit. I wanted to survive this winter. I wanted Gray to survive.

"I did get another job, and I just thought it would be easier if you didn't have to take care of me. If I stay with Roger, I'll be closer to the dock and able to stay in a house for a couple of nights."

"Why do you need the job?" I asked quietly.

"I need more pills," he said not looking at me.

"How much more do you need?" I asked.

Gray became agitated. "I just need more drugs," he said angrily.

"Drugs?" I asked. "Are you taking other drugs beside the pills?" I knew my voice was going up in volume. "Tell me!"

"I do some heroin now and then!" he yelled. "It's just with the guys. You know, it's so cold out here and it's hard to keep things going…" he turned towards me. "I don't like seeing you working so hard to take care of me, and hiding out here, you deserve better."

"Maybe," I said. "But this isn't about me. This is about your choices. If you hadn't used your money for drugs, we could have planned to go to a motel for a couple nights or bought better food or lots of other things. Now we can't. Now you must work and bring home the money because we need it to survive. I don't have any options. My only friend now is Andy. Don't think that your choices are for me, I know what my limits are, and I am going to survive one way or another. You are choosing to give up, to surrender to drugs and people who really can't do much for you except make sure you are always dependent upon them. I was hoping to offer you more than that. When you came here, we agreed to help each other."

Gray worked his way around the shack like a caged animal. He seemed half desperate and half childlike. I half expected him to leave. Half of me didn't care if he did and the other half hoped he would stay.

"Stay with me, Gray," I begged. "Don't let this situation destroy you or us. We are good together. Believe in us."

Gray closed his fist and slammed it into the countertop. I flinched.

Turning to me, he said "Okay, I will try my best to help us get through the winter." He bowed his head, trying to avoid me seeing him sink into unbearable sadness. "Okay," he said again faintly, "But, I really don't know how much choice I have any more."

# *17*

# PUBLIC HEARING

The next day brought a turn of events. Gray slept in. I loaded up the stove as much as I dared during daylight hours. I set the teakettle on the stove, laid out coffee and creamer, bread and peanut butter. There was one orange. I peeled and divided it in half, eating my half. After fixing a peanut butter sandwich for myself, I put a hard-boiled egg and a thermos of coffee in my pack and headed out the door. There was a steady rain coming down.

First, I went to my observation spot and sat for a while, eating the egg and drinking the coffee. I watched for signs of wildlife on the basin. Today, a family of otters played outside their den. I wrote out my field notes and sat for an hour. Gray's Christmas hat kept me warm and the raingear dry. A duck I did not immediately recognize flew into the near shore. After watching it for awhile I decided it must be a long-tail given the amount of white on its face, neck and body. He seemed to be all alone. Were we alike, both alone in the rain seeking to survive on the edge of Bowerman Basin? I wondered.

After an hour or so, I made a committed to a plan for the next few days. I would try to get ahold of Andy and see if I could spend a couple of days with her in Olympia. Gray could go off and stay with Roger while he worked at the car terminal. Maybe some time apart would make things easier. He was right to point out that staying in town would prevent him from getting too cold and wet from the walks back and forth to the terminal. I went back to shack, packed some clothes and necessities into my backpack, and scribbled a note to Gray about my plans.

I headed into Hoquiam along the coast highway. This route was still the best for blending into the landscape. I kept my hat pulled down and my hood pulled around my face. I looked different from the woman Ike Hamundarson had bounced off the gang plank of *Maiden's Curse*. I was much thinner, my hair was shaggy from multiple self-trimming events, my raingear was starting to look a bit frayed and permanently muddy, and my backpack bulged from carrying too much stuff back and forth to the shack. Today, it held my field gear, and everything I thought I would need to stay in Olympia for a couple of nights.

When I got to Hoquiam, I went to the public library. I wanted to be the first one in the door so I could claim a computer. The minute it opened, I stepped as fast as politely possible into the building and headed to the bank of computers.

Opening the screen to my email website, I put in Andy's evergreen.edu address in the address line. I typed out a message:

'Andy, could I stay with you in Olympia for a couple of days? Will you be in town today? Could I meet you at the bus barn at the library in downtown Hoquiam?'

Reading over the message before I hit the SEND button, I wondered if it sounded too desperate. But I am desperate I thought, desperate to maintain a sense of purpose in the face of the odds. I hit the button and sat back in my chair wondering how long I should wait for an answer. I had to stay with the computer for my time allotment. I couldn't run the risk of losing my computer.

While I waited for an answer from Andy, I paged through the social services websites for Aberdeen. They immediately came up on the computer as they were some of the most popular websites at the library. I looked around at the other computer users. Yep, I thought. We are all in this together. I found websites for Catholic Services, the Public Health Department, thrift stores, and one from the Grays Harbor Community Hospital advertising outpatient drug treatment but only on certain days. Apparently, drug overdoses were a scheduled event.

I wondered about the local pharmacies. Did they offer any aid for overuse of painkillers? I ran down a Google search of local pharmacies. There were the pharmacies located in Wal-Mart, Safeway, Rite-Aid, and Walgreens. Not offering anything I thought would help Gray. Next, I looked at private drugstores and their pharmacies. Suddenly the face of the pharmacist I knew from *Maiden's Curse* popped up on the screen. He had been on some of the off-the-record sails. He must know something I thought. And he would be the first to tell Ike Hamundarson he had seen me if I contacted him. It was not a risk I wanted to take.

I went back to my email. Yes! Andy had read my request. Her response was affirmative. I'll be out to Grays Harbor around noon, it read. I'll pick you up at the bus barn.

Leaving the computer, I looked down the aisles of the library until I found the science section. I checked out an old textbook on zoology and headed to a coffee shop about three blocks away. I ordered drip coffee and pulled out my last five-dollar bill to pay for it. Sitting in the coffee shop, reading the book and trying to make sense of biological terms and processes made me feel like my old self. I kept an eye on the door in case anyone I knew came into the shop, but it was quiet. The shop owner who served me my coffee was friendly and offered a real sense of caring. Signs hung around the shop indicated that he believed in sharing goodness.

At eleven thirty, I sipped the last of the coffee, put on my raingear, and headed to the door. I didn't want to make Andy wait for me. She could be early…. I sat under the bus barn shelter and waited. There was a large clock in the square that surrounded the shelter. I tried not to look at it, just sat quietly hoping Gray was okay. He won't really know that I had gone to Olympia, but he won't miss me either.

Andy drove up in her Subaru as planned. I got into the passenger seat clutching my backpack.

"You okay?" she asked.

I smiled, not knowing what to say.

"Spill it," said my friend.

"Gray's staying with a friend for a couple of days. I thought I could sneak away to Olympia at the same time. He won't miss me or need me."

"Need you?" she asked.

"He's having a harder and harder time with pain." I decided not to tell her about his use of heroin.

"You can stay with me in Olympia," she said. "We can work on data for the public hearing later this week. What about Miss Hap?"

"I left her food and water. She'll be okay. Thanks for asking, though. What can I do to help get ready for the presentation?" I asked, not sure I had anything that would be that helpful.

"According to Jen, all your observations are going into the report," she said.

"Really?" I said in astonishment.

"Yes, really," she replied. "You've done great work and it's a real contribution to our report to the port. They are just supposed to be listening at this point in the process. You should testify."

"No, I can't," I said. "I'm still MIA, remember?"

Andy gave me a weary smile. "Well, we'll still use your data."

We started the drive back to Olympia. The warmth of the air in the car and its steady motion put me to sleep. When we got to Andy's house, she gently nudged me.

"We're here," she said.

I followed her into the house. She showed me the extra bedroom, passed out towels and made sure I was comfortable. "Take a shower," she said. "I have some reading to do." Later, we shared a dinner of rice, tofu and vegetables. We drank tea and chatted about her life in Olympia.

"My graduate school applications are all in the works. I've heard back from OSU in Corvallis, my first choice, and the Master of Environmental Studies at Evergreen. I put in an application at the UW but I'm not hopeful. Jen has written me letters of recommendation based on my work with US F and W. We'll see," she shrugged her shoulders with apprehension. "I want to go to OSU, but you never know how they will read an Evergreen transcript. You know, no grades, just long-winded narrative evaluations."

"I'm sure you will get in," I said to encourage her.

"Thanks for your support," she said with a smile. "Now, I have to look at some more reports tonight. We'll go visit Jen tomorrow and work on the agency's presentation at the hearing. You'll see where your data has made a difference. Good night," she said and headed toward her room.

I did the same thing. My last thought of the day was a biology term that I didn't recognize in the zoology book. The warm house, warm bed, and freedom from worry put me immediately to sleep.

Andy was already up and looking at documents while sipping a cup of coffee.

"Help yourself," she said brightly. "We will go over to the office in about an hour. They will be happy to see you."

Our arrival at the office was a mixture of friendly hellos and more serious questions about our work. Andy took every opportunity to introduce me to members of the staff. We eventually got to her desk.

"Take a seat," she motioned. "I'll go see when Jen can spend some time with us."

I sat beside her desk, still holding onto my pack with all my notes and the map. Sitting there gave me an opportunity to look at the books on Andy's desk and papers tacked to her bulletin board. Both the books and papers were about nearshore environments, shoreline ecosystems, and lists of flora and fauna. The bulletin board also had policy and regulation information tacked up in a haphazard way. 'Not something she's really interested in,' I thought.

Andy returned to the office space. "Jen can see us now," she said.

I followed Andy to the corner of the building. Jen's office occupied the corner space, with windows on both walls. It was bright and well-lit in the wintery gray of Olympia.

"Hi Saron," said Jen. "Nice to see you again. Andy says you are keeping up with your observations and documentation of birds on the mudflats. Your work is very important to us, Saron. I hope you will continue to keep your eyes on the mud. This hearing is just the beginning of our biological survey in the basin."

"Thank you," I said shyly. For the first time, I felt like something I was doing really, truly mattered. Being with Andy and Jen was a magic potion for me. I hung on every word they exchanged. I recognized a few words from the zoology book. When they talked about species interdependence and the mudflats as a system, I could follow their logic. I began to see why my daily, unique data was important in the larger context of Bowerman Basin as a place.

Not only did my data seem important, Andy and Jen made me feel important. I had a mission, a reason to get up every morning. I could relate to their excitement and commitment to a project. When Jen would ask me for some specific piece of data and I could give him an answer including the date, time, and weather conditions, I felt part of their team. Riding away from the office after the meeting, I sat silent still enjoying the sacredness of the meeting.

"Penny for your thoughts?" asked Andy.

"I am happy that my work is important and included in the project," I said. "I liked being part of the meeting."

"Your work is important, Saron," she replied. "We couldn't do this without you."

We spent the rest of the day working at Andy's house. Jen had asked Andy to pull together slides for a PowerPoint presentation at the public hearing. I kept reading the zoology book. Later in the afternoon, I showed Andy the book and how it had helped me understand the systems approach to ecological management goals. Andy shared theories and concepts she had learned in a recent Evergreen class she had taken. She pulled out her books from the class. I was surprised to see a mix of books ranging from science to humanities. There were environmental history texts as well as standard ecology textbooks.

"Remember how we read all kinds of books in the Grays Harbor College class? It's the Evergreen way of teaching, or I guess I'm supposed to say learning. Students and faculty are co-creators of knowledge. We're supposed to value experience as much as the scientific method and process. Then we would seminar and try to figure out the meaning of the book or what the author was trying to get across," she said.

"Yeah, I remember," I said with a chuckle. "There were some pretty heated arguments in the seminar."

Andy laughed too. "Sometimes those younger kids could get a little carried away," she said. "But we learned how to communicate and find consensus. We'll see how much communication and consensus we can find at the hearing."

I went to the office the next day with Andy. While she and Jen worked out their presentation, I walked around the halls and read posters and announcements on bulletins boards and office doors. There was an interesting mix of natural history images, policy statements, and humorous cartoons. I noticed more than a few Evergreen State College references, Geoduck mementos on peoples' desks, and Evergreen sweatshirts hung on office chairs. Did everyone go to Evergreen before coming here to work? I wondered.

When Andy and I left the building, I asked her about the predominate presence of the college in the offices.

"No, not everyone went to Evergreen," she said. "There are graduates from the UW in Seattle and some OSU grads. Most of those people are totally into their science. We need people like that. The Greener grads," she continued, "are the ones who seem to pull it all together. They end up writing the reports and talking to the public."

"Why do you want to go to OSU in Corvallis?" I asked.

"I think I have the Evergreen interdisciplinary problem-solving approach under my belt," she replied. "What I want is more science. I think a heavy science master's degree will balance my Evergreen experience. And I want to get back to Oregon."

"Will you study mudflats at OSU?" I asked.

"I hope I will be able to take classes that focus on shoreline ecosystems. OSU has a campus out on the Oregon coast. I've asked to be able to do some work out there."

"When will you hear if you are admitted?"

Andy was silent for a minute. Finally, she said, "I should have heard by now. The clock is ticking."

"Don't give up," I said. "Please keep believing you will get in. You've done so much work on Bowerman Basin."

"Thanks, but it's tough competition."

We spent the afternoon looking at the PowerPoint presentation. Andy showed me how she built the presentation from photographs and text. Every time we went through it, we found an error or thought of a better way to present the information. She had me listen to her as she practiced. Finally, she said it looked presentable. She sent a copy to Jen by email. He would have the last say about the entire presentation.

"Now, I need something professional to wear," she said. "Let's go shopping!"

Andy took me to a consignment shop where we looked through racks of professional clothes someone was trying to sell. Andy would pull a blouse or jacket off a rack and look at it not for its shiny power statement, but for its understatement of past value still dearly loved. The colors tended to be muted and 'environmental' or natural. In the end, she bought a gray wool blazer and a striped white and black blouse.

"Pretty non-descript, as far as fashion goes." I said. "I used to wear much more colorful and expressive clothing to the construction office."

"Ah, we women have given up on that approach to professionalism. We're not there to attract attention. We try to put our brains and effort out there first. It's a fine line between being a woman and being a woman in a male-dominated profession. Gives new meaning to the phrase 'clothing optional.'"

While Andy had been looking on the professional clothing rack, I was attracted to a dark green wool cable-knit sweater. On our way to the cashier's counter, Andy grabbed the sweater. "I'm getting this for you," she said.

"What? No," I exclaimed.

"Yes. It's the least I can do for all your hard work of daily observations and living in the shack."

"Okay. Thank you," I said in a small voice.

"Jen doesn't know I live in the shack, does she?" I asked.

"No," she said. I had a hard time believing her, though. Her voice didn't ring true. I decided I didn't want to know. I couldn't take on one more worry about my current living situation. I wondered how Gray was getting along. Guess I'll find out tomorrow when I go back to Grays Harbor I thought.

Andy and I sat over coffee the next morning. Our conversation went in cycles between my thanks for a warm, happy adventure into her internship world, her angst about the hearing, occasional thoughts of Gray, the meanness of Ike Hamundarson, the uncertainty of survival in the shack, and Andy's ticking clock of graduate school acceptance. By noon, we were talked out and decided to go shopping. We headed to Target in Lacey.

Andy bought twice her regular commitment of water for the shack. I bought canned goods and a few items of fresh food. I was so tempted to buy something pretty, anything bright. The home decorating isles were hard to walk through. The pressure of living in the shack was magnified by my desire to have a pretty home, comfortable and safe. It took all my courage not to cry. Andy put her arm around me on the way out the door.

"Don't worry," she said. "I've been in the same spot more than once. You just must have faith. Something will come your way."

I gave her a weak smile. "It's hard sometimes."

"Don't give up," she said.

I just did not know what to expect from Gray or living in the shack or if I could get thought the winter. Bruce's photograph left out at the shack tugged at my heart. Okay, I promised the image in my mind, I will not give up now. I smiled at Jen, if only reassure her that I would do my best.

We left Olympia and started the hour drive out to Aberdeen. When we got out to Grays Harbor, Andy proclaimed that she needed a good dinner before the seven o'clock meeting. She had agreed with Jen to be there at six fifteen to help set up the room and the projector for their presentation.

"Aren't you worried about making the presentation?" I asked.

"Sort of," she replied. "But my classes at Evergreen all required these types of presentations at the end of classes. I'm as ready as I could be to speak in front of a room of critics."

We ate at Billy's in downtown Aberdeen. It was the old local stand-by. I hadn't been there for months now. I was a little worried that I might be recognized but I had taken some precautions to make sure my disguise was tight. I had sprayed my hair with dark brown temporary hair dye, pulled on the green wool sweater Andy had bought for me, and pulled down a black yarn hat with a bit of brim so that my face was nearly hidden between hat and sweater. I told Andy the story of Billy, a Victorian gang leader who had finally been killed in Aberdeen. The clever Billy, one a respected member of the town and secretary of the local sailor's union, was discovered to be the cause of a series of mysterious deaths, arsons, robberies, and even shootings.

"Maybe our Mr. Hamundarson is a modern-day version of Billy," Andy said. "By the way, you look a bit mysterious."

"I don't want to attract attention," I said.

"No, you don't. Actually, you look like a regular Grays Harbor resident."

"Oh good," I said. "You don't know how hard I tried to get out of the image."

"Be yourself," said Andy. "You have your grace and courage."

We ordered fish and chips, hot coffee and finally, a piece of pie that we split between us.

Andy picked up the check. "My treat," she said when I tried to pay the tip.

"Okay," I said. "I hope I can repay you someday."

"You will," she said.

We drove out to the Port of Grays Harbor administrative buildings. The buildings were located across the road in Hoquiam that led out to the chipper plant. Every mile brought me closer to the shack. Closer to Gray, I hoped.

Jen arrived at the designated time and we went into the building. The hearing was being held in a large room that was set up for meetings. There were about fifty chairs in rows facing a podium and a screen in the front of the room. There were tables set up along the sides of the room. The promoters of the gas terminal project had set up trifolds with photos and texts to tell their story. Another table was covered with maps and aerial photos of the harbor with the proposed terminal outlined on the photos. Jen had brought a series of poster boards with images of the ecosystem at Bowerman Basin. The images included various types of shore vegetation and wildlife. There were also images of the mudflats. They looked so plain and seemingly worthless, yet I knew from my observations they harbored a multitude of life. I felt a bit proud and homesick for the shack at the same time.

While Andy set up the projector and the computer with the PowerPoint presentation, I looked around the room trying to determine where I would attract the least amount of attention. I decided to sit in the very middle of the seats, hoping that all the chairs around me would be filled by people I didn't know.

At six thirty people with various interests in port development began to show up. There were the three port commissioners. Then the mayors of Aberdeen and Hoquiam came in together, deep in conversation. The project manager and stepped into the room. He wore a business suit, totally out of context from the usual Aberdeen jeans, fleece vest, and rubber boots attire.

Other people started drifting in. They walked around the room looking at the posters and materials on the tables. Those who knew each other stepped forward and shook hands or slapped each other on the back in mutual recognition. Others, dressed a bit more nicely in expensive rain parkas and low-cut boots, spoke to each other about the current interest rates, demand for fuel, and economic conditions in the harbor.

I kept my head down, trying to see who was there without making eye contact with anyone. I didn't know if my old boss Gary would be there. I did not want him to make a big deal in seeing me by calling out my name. The last person I wanted to see or have seen me was Ike Hamundarson. Other pirates could be there in their regular personas. I started to wish I had not agreed to attend the meeting, but Andy had insisted, and Jen seemed supportive.

By six forty-five the room was beginning to fill. The seats beside me were taken. I relaxed a little bit thinking that now I was surrounded and lost in a sea of faces. Andy and Jen were sitting in the front row, ready to make their presentation about the work they had done so far on the ecology of the mudflats and basin. More people began to arrive, mostly men from various walks of life in the harbor. The women in the room were some of the elected officials or wives of the men whose livelihood depended on shipping or transportation infrastructure in the port.

The moderator took the podium at seven o'clock. I recognized him as Jake, the pirate who had yelled the loudest at me to jump from the gangplank. He was no friend of mine, yet here he was, the moderator of the hearing that could create the demise of my mudflats. He introduced himself as Bill Simmons, owner of the local radio station, happy to be the moderator of the hearing.

Simmons thanked everyone for coming and then laid out the agenda for the evening.

"First, we will have a presentation by the gas terminal project developer, Bob Wrangle. He will give us an overview of the proposal. His presentation will be followed by statements by representatives of the Port Commission, the mayors of Aberdeen and Hoquiam, representatives of the Economic Development Commission, the US Fish and Wildlife Service, and finally, the Quinault Nation. Last, those of you who signed in to make a five-minute comment will be asked to step to the podium and make your statement. Again, you will have five minutes total including stepping up to the podium."

The hearing began with a presentation by Bob Wrangle. He described the terminal development, the railroad transportation infrastructure needed to carry the tanker cars through Aberdeen and Hoquiam, work and employment the project would create, a timeline for development and the company's contributions to mitigate costs including environmental costs of the project. His presentation was well-received by the crowd with applause and a few supportive "attaboy" yells. Simmons thanked the speaker again.

The next speaker was one of the port commissioners. He spoke about the need for port development, the potential for major international shipping, the potential costs and commitment from the port, and the goal so adding more jobs to the Grays Harbor economy. He made a minor reference to the need to protect the harbor's ecosystem and work in partnership with the Quinault Nation. There was a bit of foot shuffling at the end of his presentation. The political and environmental realities of the project could not be denied. The fact that the Quinault held a voice harbor development was a significant strand in the warp and weave of the region.

Simmons kept the hearing on track. He asked speakers to be ready to approach the podium as soon after the previous speaker. He asked the crowd to hold their opinions and comments to themselves. "We are here tonight to listen," he reminded the crowd.

The next two speakers were the mayors. They basically did a public relation talk about the opportunities that would become available to each town with the new port development. They also described the virtues of each town as attractive places for families and businesses. The crowd listened patiently, knowing that the mayors were more interested in being re-elected then addressing the fundamental issues of unemployment, increasing drug use, and a rise in petty crimes across the harbor. In many minds, the need for port expansion and the new jobs created by the development was the best response to social disintegration that had touched every family.

The emphasis on economic expansion continued in the presentation by the representative from the representative from the Olympia-based Washington State Economic Development Commission. "We haven't forgotten you, Grays Harbor County," said the speaker. "We want to see the terminal development in the state. Grays Harbor is the new, hot port on the entire West Coast. The state wants to this development as much as you do here in the county." The presentation received mixed reviews from the crowd. I heard the person sitting behind me say in a low voice, "As usual, Olympia is thinking about themselves first."

Simmons stood back up and addressed the crowd. "Our previous presentations have addressed the social and economic perspectives on the development. Now, let's hear two presentations that will address environmental and traditional perspectives." People sitting in their seats rearranged themselves as if to be ready to face a bad spirit entering a room. Their shoulders faced the podium like young football players taking their positions on a field when they played for the Hoquiam High School Lumberjacks on a field not far from the meeting.

"Our first presentation will be by the US Fish and Wildlife Service." Simmons nodded at Jen, who made her way to the podium.

"We have a short PowerPoint presentation about the ecology of the harbor," said Jen. Andy got up to take her place by the computer. The room lights were lowered to half intensity as the presentation came up on the screen.

"What we want to emphasize tonight," said Andy in a calm and clear voice, "is that the Bowerman Basin mudflats, while may appear as the dumping ground for sediments dredged from the bottom of the bay, are active, vibrant systems of life. Within the mudflats are millions of living creatures that flow through the muds just like blood flows through our veins. The tides, like our hearts, are the pumps that keep the system moving. The tidal action is the energy that fuels the ecosystems. The tides bring in a constant source of biological life, called the biofilm. This film becomes the source of food for various birds. The birds in turn support the life-force for other forms of wildlife and shoreline environments. Let me show you some slides that demonstrate how the whole system functions. I will close with some examples of birds and wildlife species that are dependent upon the muds especially during the winter."

Andy turned to the screen and began to flash slides that first, depicted the concept of a mudflat ecosystem and then went on to demonstrate of the system functions. Last, she showed slides of birds utilizing different parts of the mudflats during tidal events. She closed her presentation by facing her audience. "I know this is full of biological terms and concepts. I hope my explanation and slides have made the process of mudflat ecology understandable. I hope you recognized elements of the mudflats you see each day as you live beside the harbor. Our goal is to make good policy decisions based on solid research. Thank you," she said.

Jen stood up to speak. She addressed Andy. "Thank you, Andy, that was a good explanation of our survey work." Turning to the audience, she said, "We will be moving forward with a more focused survey of the mudflats. Can I answer any questions?"

Simmons stood up and looked at the crowd. "Any questions for the girls?" he said.

"Yeah, I have a question," came a voice from the back of the room.

"Go ahead," said Simmons.

"Do you mean our hearts of made of mud?"

There were chuckles.

Simmons looked at the crowd. "Let's be nice," he said. "The presentation was informative. I'm sure we will hear more from Fish and Wildlife Service as the project moves forward."

Jen nodded to Simmons and sat down.I smiled to myself. Some of these people have mud for hearts, I thought. But I knew not all. Some cared deeply about their community and the possibility of jobs for the growing unemployed population.

The Quinault Nation offered a short presentation on the role of the tribe in managing the harbor. Their spokesperson emphasized a desire to work with the Port and the project while preserving the ecosystems that created the harbor. The perspective of the Nation seemed to be a gentle reminder that they had a significant, if not the most significant, card to play in any decision-making process. The audience's response felt like grudging agreement to Saron.

Simmons thanked all the presenters. Turning to the audience, I heard him say, "We will now have five-minute comments by those of you who signed up to speak. Please remember that you have only five minutes including the time it will take you to approach the podium. You may want to line up and be ready. While they are doing that, the rest of you could stand up for a couple of minutes. This will be the only break this evening. There are seven people signed up to comment. I hope we can all leave here in the next hour."

After ten minutes, Simmons took the podium again and rapped a gavel. "Okay, time to start the public comment portion of the hearing," he said. The crowd began to settle back down into their seats. A few people had taken off and the seven to speak were lined up at the side of the room. I continued to stare at the floor, having no idea who would speak. Maybe I should have left, I thought. Too late now I grimaced.

The first person to make a comment spoke in favor of the project based on economic development and potential for the port. The second person said basically the same thing, as did the third and the fourth. It was beginning to sound like everyone in the room was in favor of the project. Then Simmons called the fifth speaker. "Gray Quinn," he said.

I was stunned. I had no idea Gray was in the room. I bit my lip and tried not to raise my head too high, but I did want to watch him comment from the podium. It was all a bit surprising. What will he say? I wondered.

Gray stood up tall with a bit of pride. He looked more like his Quinault identity than I had seen him in the past. He took the steps to the podium with his shoulders straight and his head up. When he got to the podium, he took both sides of it as if to brace himself. That's when I recognized the man I had met last fall. But I knew he was holding on to the podium to prevent people from seeing his hands shake. The podium hid his thin body from everyone but me.

"My name is Gray Quinn," he said. "I am a member of the Quinault Nation. I speak for myself, but I think also for many other tribal members. This land was our land for all known time. We lost much of our land when white people came to explore and settle here. Ever since your arrival, our resources and way of life have been reduced. We practice resource management on the reservation the way our elders taught us. We own the land beneath the bay. We want to manage the bay and the mudflats as our elders taught us. This project will destroy the mudflats and the waters of the bay. The bay's ecosystems are ours. The project means nothing but pain to us and our elders. I am opposed to the project."

There was silence as Gray walked away from the podium. I felt nothing but pride in knowing him. I heard a voice give a hoot of support. It sounded like Roger. There were a few who clapped in support. Others in the audience whispered and shuffled their feet. It was the most difficult and tense moment of the entire evening. I hoped Gray was able to withstand the critics. 'I'm so glad Roger is here,' I thought.

The last two commenters spoke in favor of the project, although one did mention the need to protect the bay's ecosystems. When the last person had spoken, Simmons addressed the crowd. "Thank you, everyone, for attending tonight's public meeting. This meeting keeps the community and the project developers informed about issues and potentials. A transcript of the meeting will be available at the port offices. I see a reporter from the "Daily World" here tonight. There will be articles in the newspaper and on the radio. There will be a meeting of the port commissioners to determine the next step towards project approval. Please stay informed. Thank you for your participation."

The crowd began to leave the building. There were conversations between people who knew each other, some of them in praise of the meeting and others hoping for a positive outcome. I tried to exit the meeting as anonymously as possible. I wanted to catch up to Gray, who I could see was talking to Roger just beyond the door of the room. I walked past the rows of chairs on my way to where Gray was standing. As I passed a group of men chatting with each other, a hand grabbed my arm and forced me to stop next to where the men stood.

"I thought that might be you," I heard a familiar voice say in a quiet, threatening tone.

I froze, recognizing the voice of Ike Hamundarson.

"I thought I told you to get out of town," he said in my ear. "You be sure to keep your mouth shut and take the hint to leave."

I pulled my arm away from him. "I'm not leaving," I said in an equally intense voice. Hammundarson stepped back and made a sound like an animal growling. "Watch your step, missy," he said. "I don't know where you've been hiding but I will find you."

I was shaking when I got to Gray. "Gray," I said in a faint voice. He didn't hear me at first. "Gray," I said a bit louder. This time he heard me.

"Saron?" he said. "What are you doing here?" He looked around the room.

"I came with Andy and Jen."

Roger gave me a pat on the back. "Didn't our boy do good?" he said with a smile.

"Yes," I said. "You were amazing," I said to Gray.

Gray pulled me closer to him. "Guess I better get you home," he said.

He and Roger said their goodbyes with promises to meet soon at the Fish Bait. Then he took my arm and steered me out of the building. The parking lot was still bright with car lights and people leaving their parking spaces.

"Let's walk along the other side of the road," he said.

"Are we going to the shack?" I asked. "Andy is dropping off supplies and things I got in town at the fence like she always does. We could get a ride with her if that's where you want to go."

"I do want to go there with you," he said kindly.

We found Andy at her car. "Oh good," she said. "Let me take you over to the refuge compound." We climbed into the car and were soon going down the dark road toward Bowerman Basin.

"You guys going to be okay?" she asked as we unloaded the car in the dark night.

"Yes," I said. "Thanks so much."

"I'll see you soon," she said. "Better get back to Olympia."

We watched her drive away. Taking the sacks of groceries with us, we pushed our way through the brush and got into the shack. Miss Hap would not leave us alone, poor thing.

"Looks like everything is the same," said Gray. He started a fire in the stove, and I put the food away. Then I put away my clothes and things from my backpack.

"How are you?" I asked Gray.

"I'm doing okay," he answered. "I did make us some money while you were gone."

I nodded in recognition. We sat together on one of the beds. It took a little bit of time to heat the shack. Rain started falling and a wind started to blow from the west. It would be a stormy night.

"You made a spoke well," I said.

"I'm surprised you dared to be so much in public tonight," he said.

"Ike Hamundarson recognized me."

Gray frowned. "That jackass. Don't let him scare you,"

"Maybe I should stay here for a few days, not go to town or anything. I can keep working on my observations and keep the shack warm during the day."

"Good idea. I'll stay out here, go to town when we need things. Roger will stay in touch at the Fish Bait."

I nodded again. I didn't really have the energy to speak. The shack was getting warm. I heated some water for tea and had some cookies. Gray went outside and walked around the shack and checked all the windows and doors. When he came back in, he came over to my bed, took off his clothes, and crawled in beside me. Miss Hap purred louder than I had ever heard her. It felt good for all of us to be home.

# 18

# A GREAT SORROW AND A DEEP JOY

The last week of January brought a touch of spring to Grays Harbor. For just a few days every winter, the clouds gave way to a blue sky, the rain disappeared, and the daytime temperatures reached into the mid-fifties. The spring-like weather was the result of the jet stream moving north and allowing warmer air from the subtropical Pacific Ocean to wash over the region. After the rain and wind of December and January, the all too brief days of sunny weather revived the harbor's inhabitants. Shorebirds stalked into the mudflats, and birds of prey circled above the water. People walked about without their slick raincoats. The spring-like weather changed peoples' moods. Smiles lit faces. Kids played outside and small yard projects were quickly accomplished. The sun reminded everyone that better days were ahead.

As celebratory as this late January respite was, the next week brought a return to the dull, dismal dark days of winter. The jet stream returned, bringing large quantities of precipitation off the ocean. Waves of storms blew massive amounts of water into the harbor. The rain overwhelmed the streets and drainage systems. Winds toppled trees over powerlines and streets. When tides were high, the severe weather caused flooding as rivers entering the bay rose above their banks. At times, Aberdeen was be cut off from Olympia by high water in the Chehalis River. Travel up and down the coast was curtailed due to bridge washouts or downed trees on the highways. Darkness and despair settled over the harbor once again.

For me, the storms were just as amazing on the mudflats as the brief bit of sun had been. My daily habit of watching the birdlife on the mud was as much a refuge from the shack as the shack was a refuge from the weather. Although I did not see many birds due to the storms, I did see a change in the configuration of the muds as storm and tidal waters swept over them. Along the shoreline, I could see small changes in the shallow areas between tides and shore grasses. At low tide, the retreating seawater left ripples and dips in the mud that remained full of seawater. These dips and ripples in the mud attracted birds that normally stayed on the dehydrating muds. The birds seemed to know how to take advantage of morsels of aquatic life left in the shallow pools. Any fingerling left in a pool was immediate food for a sparrow hawk. The pooled seawater was actually a boon for the birds. Storms had their advantages.

For Gray, the ups and downs of the weather took their toll on his mental health as much as his aching body. During the sunny hiatus, he spent more time collecting firewood for the shack or fishing along the rocks near the chipper plant dock. He imagined his granny sitting with him, telling him stories of tribal people and ways now all but lost into the trauma of reservation and tribal rights events. Gray thought about the terminal project and how much his granny would have opposed the whole thing not only for its potential to damage the bay's ecosystem but on the basis that the fuel being shipped out of the port would only cause damage to other ecosystems thousands of miles away.

Sometimes Roger joined him, and they fished together. Roger always had news about people Gray knew at Taholah or guys they had worked with. The best news Roger could bring was about a possible job. Gray was becoming more and more dependent on working even though his body was becoming more and more broken and in pain. The money he earned went to pay for more and more pain killing drugs while the pain became more and more intense. He wanted to give the money to Saron, but it never got past his pocket on his way to the drugstore. He became more and more withdrawn, nervous, and disoriented. The cycle had to end. His options for ending the physical pain and heartsickness were getting fewer every day.

Gray's trudge to the Fish Bait became a daily habit. It was the only place he forgot about the pain, even if just for an hour of drinking beer with old friends or making new friends. He became increasingly aware of people in the bar who seemed to have a lot of money yet spent their time chatting with people Gray recognized as those down on their luck much like himself.

One afternoon, when he had Roger's ear while sitting at the bar, he asked "Roger, who's the two guys sitting down at the end of the bar? I keep seeing them in here, but I don't know them."

"I'm glad you don't," replied Roger. "They are not locals. They showed up here around Christmastime. Ever since then, people we know have been losing money or more to them. Remember Connie?" he asked.

Gray nodded.

"I think she got to know them a little too well and look at what happened to her. Stay away from them, Bro," he said.

Gray took another look at the pair. They were laughing about something, yet at the same time seemed to be able to look around either down the bar towards Gray or in the mirror behind the bar. They smiled and said hello to people who passed them on the way to the restrooms. Cliff served them more beers but was not as friendly toward them as he was to the locals he knew. Gray eased the last of his beer down his throat, gathered up his lean body from the barstool, and patted Roger on the shoulder.

"No worries," he said. "See you later," and walked towards the door.

One of the men seated at the bar got up and walked towards the door a few steps behind Gray.

"Hey, Gray," he said. "It is Gray, isn't it?"

Gray turned and watched the man take the last few steps to where he stood just outside the Fish Bait. "Do I know you?" he asked the man. The man was dressed in a bit nicer jacket than most of the others in the bar. His hair was cut neatly, and he wore hiking boots, not work boots like the bar regulars. There was something about him that Gray didn't like.

"I hear you were in a bad logging accident," said the man.

"I was," said Gray, in a measured voice. He didn't like the fact that the man seemed to know his history. A brief image of the shack passed through Gray's mind. The fear of the shack being found out made Gray even more cautious.

The man reached out and gave a gentle shove to Gray's shoulder, the way people who were more familiar with each other sometimes laughed and joked together. Gray stepped back at the touch of the man. "Let me know if you need anything," said the man with a smile.

Gray pulled his head back a bit and looked the man in the eye. "I don't," he said, and walked away, leaving the Fish Bait in the opposite direction of the shortest route back to the shack.

Gray began the long walk back to the shack. Rain began to fall. He walked on without a hat, his work slicker shedding water and his shirt becoming clammy from the inside out. Who would have told the man about his accident? he wondered. Lots of people know about it and my painful existence.

It was all starting to catch up to him. His physical pain and his dependency on strong pain killers, his long walks back and forth to the Fish Bait as much to find companionship as to avoid Saron and his inability to take care of her, the siphoning of money out of the shared kitty, and his regret in not being as inspired to live on the mudflat as Saron seemed to be. She had a mission, a goal, a life thanks to Andy and the terminal project. At least Saron was contributing to the conservation of the mudflats. She was such a good person, and he had nothing to offer her, only more pain, and the need for more painkillers that robbed her in the end.

Gray walked on in the rain. His neck and back muscles began to hurt from the cold and wet. His torso was damp which made him colder. He reached in his pocket and took out the bottle of pills he kept with him. There were only a few pills left in the bottle. He would have to find more work to buy more pills. He felt defeated before he even had more work.

By the time Gray reached the shack it was nearly dark. He could smell a bit of wood smoke that told him that Saron was inside probably making dinner. He stood outside the shack for a while, not knowing what to say to her anymore. She would say something cheerful and offer him tea before their dinner of canned goods and a bit of lettuce or a green vegetable that she had brought from the store. He remembered their dinner in Westport and happier times at the Fish Bait. Now there wasn't enough money to eat out, and Saron was getting down to her last few dollars. He kicked at the brush that hid the shack's door.

I opened the door a few inches and peered out into the rain and darkness. "Oh, it is you," I said in a thankful tone of voice. "I was hoping you would show up soon," I said as she opened the door further. I stepped aside as Gray entered the shack. He noticed that she wore a sweater he hadn't seen before, more likely he hadn't noticed before. Even in the heavy sweater her body was thin compared with the woman he had met in the fall.

Gray took off his wet jacket and then his damp shirt. His body was withered and wrinkled like that of a much older man than he had been in the fall. He found a washcloth and dampened it from the tea water on the stove. Running the washcloth over his body, he could feel his ribs too close to the surface. I found another flannel shirt for him and helped him slip his boney arms into the sleeves. I stood in front of him and buttoned the shirt. He could smell my hair, scented from a rinse in my bathing. He wrapped his arms around me. We hugged each other, holding on to each other out of caring and now months of surviving together in the shack. It was a holding on amid deep sorrow.

We parted after a few moments of silence.

"How about some tea?" I asked, just as Gray knew she would. A pot on the stove and two plates on the counter yielded the dinner Gray had anticipated. They sat close to each other in front of the stove and ate in silence. Without much to say to one another, I turned on the radio and they listened to the evening news and weather report. More rain, as usual in Grays Harbor. After listening to some music and the event's calendar for Aberdeen and Hoquiam, Gray slipped out of his clothes and into his bed. He didn't have anything more to say for himself. His body ached, and he was out of money.

Gray left the shack around noon the next day. I was down at the mudflats and didn't know he was gone until I went back to the shack. Intuition told me that Gray was going into town again. He never stays home anymore, I thought.

I looked around the shack and took a quick inventory. Andy still supplied us with water. I expected to see her or at least the water at the usual drop off site. There was no firewood. Gray had not been bringing it up from the beach as he had in the past. I checked the cubby where we kept food, matches, and toiletries. The space was nearly bare. Finally, I looked in the coffee can that held our cash. I was carefully saving the last one hundred dollars to get us through the month. Of the five twenty dollar bills I had counted at the beginning of the week, only one sat in the box.

The sight of the nearly empty box sent a jolt through my body. I looked up and around, as if to find Gray, but as was more and more common, there was no sign of him. I looked back down into the box. Slowly, I pulled out the twenty-dollar bill and fingered it as if I had the power to make it back into the hundred dollars it had once been a part of. What is Gray doing? I asked myself in desperation.

I decided to walk down to the Fish Bait and see if I could find him. I didn't really want to confront him. I just wanted to be near him, to let him know we were sinking into a hole from which we could not climb out. I wanted to be his friend and his loving partner, but I couldn't let us die out in the shack.

I thought of various things I could say to him as I walked into town in the afternoon rain. There were occasional gusts of wind that wanted to pull my canvas bag out of my hand. I hoped to fill it with firewood on my return to the shack. I would have to do this daily. I couldn't carry the amount of wood Gray had been bringing in his big pack.

The closer I got to the Fish Bait, the more I wanted to erase Gray from the entire scene there. Something wasn't right, he spent too much time there. I sound like an old fishwife, I thought.

As I turned the last corner of my walk to the bar, I stopped and tried to disappear into the side of the building that ran along the street to the bar's entrance. Gray was leaving the bar with two men I had never seen before. They walked along as if they were old friends, but I didn't think they were. The men were on either side of Gray, slapping him on the shoulder and sometimes his rear end. Gray must be telling them jokes or some funny story to keep them in good spirits. I watched them until they turned right onto a street that as far as I knew, went only a couple of blocks before dead ending in a forested area along the railroad tracks that led to the port. Why would they be going there? I wondered.

When I got to the door of the bar, I stopped for a moment. I didn't know whether to try to follow Gray or go into the bar and try to talk to someone who might know something about the men or why they had left the bar. I decided to go into the bar.

As usual, I had to wait a minute or two while my eyes got used to the dim light in the bar. I went up to the bar and took a bar stool, hoping to catch Cliff when he had a minute to chat. He saw me walk in and kept an eye on me as he waited on customers. At last, he wiped his hands on his apron, looked at me, looked back at his apron, and then turned and took slow steps to where I sat at the bar.

"Hello, Saron," he said quietly. "Can I get you something?"

"Hi," I said with a raised eyebrow. "No, thanks, on the drink. I was wondering if you could tell me where Gray was headed, I think I just missed him."

Cliff grabbed the edge of the bar and stood for a moment. Finally, he said "I don't know where he went."

"Really?" I questioned him. "I think he just left here with two guys I've never seen before."

"I don't know where they were going," Cliff repeated. "Maybe you should go home and wait for him."

"Something's not right, Cliff. Is he in trouble?"

"No. At least not yet."

"What does that mean?" I asked.

Cliff took his hands off the bar and wiped them on his apron again. "Gray's pretty stove up," he said.

"I know," I replied. "I don't know what to do for him. He's always in pain and he has taken all our cash to buy pain killers."

"He's caught in a nightmare. There are a lot of guys in here in the same nightmare of pain, poverty, and panic. They don't know what to do for themselves or their families. They are all looking for a way out. Some find a way out on a few beers. Others, well, they need more than pills or alcohol. I try not to think of the next stage of losing their memories, it never helps. Sometimes, it kills."

"Are you telling me that Gray is looking for a way out?" I asked.

Now it was my turn to hold on to the edge of the bar. I looked up at Cliff with sorrow in my eyes.

"He might be," Cliff said softly. "I hope not, but Gray's been slipping into a murky, green, mindless pit for a long time. You've kept him going more than anyone and I was hoping he would make it. I don't know."

Cliff went to the other end of the bar and served guys who looked like Gray beers and the free popcorn he always had on hand. I sat at the bar for a while. Nothing seemed to make sense in my brain. Random thoughts about Gray, firewood, the shack, how miserable the weather was, Andy, the mudflats…but my mind always came back to the sight of Gray walking down a dead-end road with two men who were not really his friends.

Cliff looked at me occasionally. No one came to sit with me. Roger never came into the bar that afternoon. Finally, I got up and made my way to the door. I looked at Cliff one more time and then stepped out into the rain.

I went back to the shack along chipper road. The tide was out, and I picked up firewood from the scraps of driftwood that had been left behind by the receding tide. It would take a bit of effort to dry them out under the stove. I had just enough firewood in the shack to start a fire and heat everything up. Then I would have to use the driftwood. Back at the shack, I got the fire going, stored the driftwood under the stove to dry, and tried to think of something to make for dinner. I had no idea if Gray would be coming back. I heated up a can of soup, drank it down, and then sat with a candle and listened to the wind outside.

I pulled out my field notebook and read through my notes. The mudflats had become my subconscious. Holding on to the notebook made them seem more than another place, now they were my place of sanctuary. I hugged the notebook to my chest and rested my head on the top of the pages. The candle burned down, and the stove's heat began to peter out. I sat for a long time before finally crawling into my bed. Waves of sadness drenched over me as if it was the first night I had crawled out of the water and laid exhausted on the shore.

The next week was as cold and wet as the previous one. Gray left everyday without saying much. He didn't want to eat anything no matter how much I tried to make our simple fare more attractive. Just looking for work, he would say as he left the shack. There was no more sharing of thoughts over a warm cup of coffee. Apparently, he didn't want coffee with me or to share his thoughts.

My thoughts raced through my mind, half about Gray and his moody despondence and the other half about finding enough money to buy food. I waited for Andy one day at the US Fish & Wildlife Service work lot. She had brought the water as usual and I thanked her.

"You okay?" she asked.

I waited a moment before answering. "Not really. We've run out of money and there's not much food until I get my Social Security check. I can barely get enough driftwood to the shack to resupply our dry wood."

"Isn't Gray helping you?" she asked.

I couldn't admit to her that I suspected he was using heroin and not thinking about the shack. "He's trying to find work but there's not much this time of year," I said.

Andy reached into her pack. "Look, take these twenties and buy yourself some food. I can drop you off at the grocery store on my way out of town or help you shop and bring you back here, so you don't have to walk in the rain."

"Okay," I said. We got into her car and headed into Aberdeen.

"Can we go to Safeway?" she asked.

"Better not. Someone might recognize me. How about Grocery Outlet? I don't think the pirate crowd shops there."

We went to the Outlet that straddled the city limits of Aberdeen and Hoquiam. It didn't take long to spend the money on food. Andy drove me back out to the shack.

"I really wish you didn't have to live out here in this horrible weather," she said.

I gave a weak smile. "Its all I've got," I said. "Thanks for helping me out. I'll pay you back."

"No worries," she said. "I'll check in on you the next time I'm out here."

I didn't know what to expect for the future. I did the best I could to keep the shack warm and food ready for Gray. But he didn't always come home, and when he did, he seemed a bit dazed and just wanted to sleep. The lack of food was making his body become like a skeleton. His clothes hung from his shoulders and waist. There wasn't much to talk about.

I spent my days reading to keep my mind off things. My trips to the shore did not bring many surprises. Ducks flew in over the grasses to sit on the tidal waters and eat off the mudflats. Peepers ran about the exposed mudflats sipping bioplankton off the mud surface. Curlews and plovers stalked about pulling worms from beneath the muds. My notes from one day to the next looked the same. When would this all end? I wondered.

After another night of watching Gray curl up on his bed without even saying hello to me, I decided to try to take some action. I didn't know exactly what, but maybe someone could help me find something to bring the old Gray back to life.

The next morning, I walked into Hoquiam and went to the library. I waited patiently until the librarian was free and there were not so many people around her desk.

"Yes? Can I help you?" she asked.

"I was wondering," I felt my voice falter.

"Yes?" she looked at me inquisitively.

"You see, I have a friend who seems to be in trouble," I said.

"What kind of trouble?" she asked with concern in her eyes.

"Well, I think he's using drugs."

"Oh, I see," she said. She reached behind her to a counter that held various leaflets and announcements. "Here," she said, handing me a leaflet. "Maybe this will help you. Honestly, though, if your friend needs help, he needs to ask for the help. You can't commit someone to a process of healing. They have to do that themselves."

"You mean there's nowhere I can go to get help?" I said.

"You can go with him, but he has to be the one to ask for assistance."

I looked down at the leaflet. It was from the Salvation Army promising support for those in drug and alcohol rehabilitation. They also offered help for families with people suffering with addiction.

"Maybe you can attend one of their meetings," the librarian offered with a softer voice. "It can't hurt."

"Okay, thanks," I said. I picked up my pack and headed out the door. I didn't know if I could take sitting in a group of people who at least lived in real houses. I didn't want to have to describe my "current" condition. No one would believe me, and if they did, then my entire existence was at stake.

I wandered around Hoquiam for awhile until I was tired. I didn't have the energy to go further into town to the Y even though the thought of a hot shower was a strong plus to head there. Instead, I walked back out to the shack, took off my cold and wet clothes, and went to bed. Miss Hap curled up against me and we stayed there for the rest of the day.

Gray did not return to the shack until the middle of the next day. He looked horrible. I tried to get him to eat a real meal, but he refused. He left before it got dark.

It was the middle of February and I had no source of food or funds until the beginning of March. I couldn't ask Andy for any more money. I could go to the food pantry at the Catholic Church. I could ask for a loan at the Salvation Army. I could start begging on the street like so many others who sat on corners in Aberdeen. The street code said I wouldn't be welcome on these corners. The corners were already taken by people truly living on the streets. Yes, I could go to the charities. Food and some minor amounts of cash were all they had to offer. They were struggling to help those who struggled on the streets. This was another vicious cycle. Is there ever an end to these cycles of poverty and pain? I wondered. How was I to get out of the cycle I was falling into? I was being drawn into the death trap too. Sitting on the shore in a steady rain, I decided to do one other thing to raise money.

I lingered on the shore, watching the mudflats slowly fill with water. The shore birds flew in to sit and wait for the fish that would float in with the tide. Reoccurring death was all around me. I must get out of this one way or another, I thought to myself. With steady but slow steps, I walked into Aberdeen. I was soaked through by the rain by the time I crossed the street and entered the Rite Aid and headed to the pharmacy.

I walked up and down the aisle at a slow pace not wanting to attract attention. A cheery clerk came up to my twice asking if I needed help. "No thanks, just browsing," I replied both times. With every walk down an aisle, I got closer and closer to the window where the pharmacist worked. He was busy handing white noisy envelopes over the counter to people waiting for drugs. 'Legal drugs,' I thought as I watched him smile and say encouraging words to each customer.

But this was not the man I had come to ask for help. The man I had come to see was Pirate Blu with whom I had sailed with on *Maiden's Curse*. I wondered if he would recognize me as I did him, someone in disguise living an alternative identity out in the bay.

When all the customers had gone, I went up to the counter and stood as close to it as I could. I pushed my head over the counter, hoping to get the pharmacist's attention. For a moment, I stood frozen, trying to focus on just exactly how I would say what I had come to say.

Looking a bit alarmed at my position at the counter, the pharmacist stepped away from the bottle of pills that he had been slowly counting through.

"Can I help you?" he said in a cheery voice so unlike the gruff shouting I remembered from the day Captain Isaac had pushed me off the pirate ship.

I looked steadily and forcefully into his eyes. "I hope so, Pirate Blu" I said in a low, husky voice.

The pharmacist, now pirate, stepped back from the counter. He looked to both sides of him. Then leaning forward, he said, "Who are you? What do you want?"

"I think you know me," I said using my new-found voice of authority and calm. "You left me for dead out in Bowerman Basin. But I am not. Perhaps you have heard," I said, slowly raising my voice.

"Shush," he said with panic in his eyes. "What are you doing here?"

I could feel his growing sense of unease. He was getting more nervous as I stood at the counter in my wet raincoat, muddy street-worn boots and dripping black hair. "I need you to help me. If you don't, I will tell start talking about your extracurricular activities. Do you understand me?" I started to raise the volume of my voice. "I will start here and now talking about the night voyages of *Maiden's Curse* and just who you really are."

The pharmacist's face began to turn red. His eyes moved back and forth trying to make sure there was no one listening to me. The door of the pharmacy opened and the bell that sent out the message to everyone working in the store that a customer was on their way into the aisles of pills, make-up, and Depends shattered the pharmacist's ashen face.

"What do you want?" he said again in a more anxious voice.

"I want money," I said as simply as I could. "Just money. I want three hundred dollars now."

"I can't give you three hundred dollars," he said trying to regain the upper hand.

"No?" I said in a louder voice. "Why not, it's a simple amount of money to cover my needs. Just open the draw and give me the money"

One of the clerks walked toward me. "Everything okay?" she asked in her pseudo-cheery voice.

"Oh, yes," I said before the pharmacist could answer. "He's just filling my prescription now. Aren't you?" I said turning back to the pharmacist. "Aren't you?" I said pertly smiling at him across the counter.

The clerk moved on to straightening up the shelves down the aisle from the counter. The pharmacist opened his cash register. He lifted the drawer and pulled out two one hundred-dollar bills and two fifties. He pushed the drawer closed and stepped up to the counter as close as he could to me. "Take this," he said. "I'll let the captain know you were in," he said in a louder voice. "Its always nice to see you," he said, trying to impress the clerk that everything was all right. Then he leaned closer to me and said, "The captain will make sure you never come back in here."

"Is that part of the pirate's code?" I said in as mean a voice as I could. I turned away from the counter and walked to the door, pacing myself to try to appear normal yet knowing I had better get out of the shop as fast as I could. I had no idea if the pharmacist would sound an alarm.

As soon as I was out of the shop, I walked as fast as I could across the main street of Aberdeen, zigzagged through a parking lot full of cars, dropping my jacket and kicking it under a parked car. I didn't care how wet I got. It wasn't until later that I remembered that the hat Gray had given me was in the pocket of the jacket.

I picked up my pace, and walked across another street, in between gray metal warehouses and out the other side to an old landing site on the bank of the channel. From here, I pushed through some brush and got down on the rocks. There was a path that fishermen sometimes used, hidden behind trees and bushes that grew along the water's edge. I crept along the path, keeping my body as low to the ground as I could. Finally, I came to an old wooden boat that had long been abandoned at the water's edge. I crawled into the carcass of the boat and waited for dark.

I wasn't so worried about the police. I didn't think the pharmacist would rat on me; he had too much to lose if he did. I would blab everything about him, Ike Hamundarson and the night voyages of *Maiden's Curse*. But he would tell Hamundarson. He probably already made the phone call. Hamundarson had seen me at the hearing, and now this event would really push him into making sure I was totally out of the picture. I fingered the money in my pants pocket. I was cold and hungry. No wonder people are driven to do things that eventually kill them. Suicides losing hope, I thought.

The afternoon light faded, and the tide started rising. I had to get to higher ground, find warmth and food, and face the fact that there wasn't much comfort in the shack. I had no idea where Gray was or if he cared about me or us. I crept through the back streets of Aberdeen and over the bridge to Hoquiam. By the time I got to the shack, I was bitterly cold. I started a fire, heated water for tea. I ate the last package of cookies and bits of cheese. I promised myself real food in the morning. Exhausted, I put the last piece of wood on the fire and crawled into my bed. I had no idea what would happen tomorrow or next week or even next month, but I had come this far, and I was not going to quit now.

How can I not survive? I thought.

I thought of the mudflats, how they were alive even when they appeared cold and heartless in the receding tide. I thought about the shorebirds and waders I had come to know, how and where they lived on my map. I thought about the birds in the brush who chipped to each other as I walked down the path. These birds, these mudflats had become my home, a refuge if ever there was one. I wanted to stay out here, I belong out here, I thought. I am part of this ecosystem now. My work for Andy was helping to recreate a sanctuary of safety and beauty not only for the wildlife, but for me. I thrived to the beauty I saw every day. It's the beauty of the place and all of us that live out here that fills my heart with joy.

# *19*

# A DEATH

*A* storm came in from the Pacific during the night. The wind started blowing from the west, at first in occasional bursts that shook the tree limbs over the shack and pushed the brush up against the sides of the shack. The bursts of wind became more constant. The trees creaked and groaned against the force of the wind, the brush swept back and forth against the shack's walls. As time went on, stronger gusts hurled themselves across the mudflats of the Basin, slamming into the alders and shaking the sides of the shack.

Rain followed the wind. It pelleted against the sides of the shack, beat on the windows, and drove rivulets under the door frames. Gnarled fingers of wind forced themselves in around the window frames creating a continual whistling sound. The shrieking and beating of the rain surrounded the shack from all directions. I felt entombed in an eerie grave, waiting for the top of the shack to collapse over me like clods of dirt dropping on my coffin and covering over any existence of my life. I waited for what seemed to be my inevitable death in the shack.

The storm continued through the night and into the morning hours. I knew only that daylight had replaced the black night when I heard one cry of a hawk outside the shack. Having survived the night's storm, I pulled myself up to the counter and turned on the radio to hear any news. Instead, I only found static and scrambled voices across the dial. The storm apparently had knocked out all the transmission towers.

I wondered if the harbor's inhabitants had lost power. Electrical lines would be down and towers leaning away from the wind that had blown so hard in from the ocean. It was so easy to forget that I all lived next to a powerful energy system that we absently referred to as the big water. I lived on the ocean, with the ocean, and often surrounded by the power of the ocean, yet I took it for granted. It was the quiet neighbor until its fury reminded me that there was nothing comparable to its might.

Not caring much anymore if the shack and my presence was discovered, I pulled the canvas off one of the windows that faced the road. Rain still beat on the window and wind blew over the brush and alder that surrounded the shack. I felt trapped by the remnants of the night's storm. I needed firewood, food, and water. It would be very difficult to walk into town and then return pushing a cart of food and a pack of firewood. It would have to be two trips rather than one, I decided.

There was another dark cloud over my comings and goings. Surely Ike Hamundarson knew by now that I was still in the harbor. The pharmacist would have called him as soon as I had left the shop yesterday. All I could hope was that he was too busy taking care of storm-related events, power outages, and downed trees to worry about me. Perhaps this morning was the only chance I would have to find food and fuel. I hoped Andy would be out later this afternoon with water.

I had no idea where Gray was. I hoped he was staying with Roger or had found someplace to wait out the storm. I couldn't really think about him, and yet he was always on my mind, and, if honest, in my heart. I grieved for him, not knowing where he was. "Where are you?" I called out to him. "Where are you?" I cried, shaking my head in sadness for him.

I waited until closer to noon to start my trek into town. Hopefully, the electricity was restored to the grocery stores and traffic would be near normal. I would have to watch out for Hamundarson. I hoped he was still busy at the gravel pit, helping his crews to recover the pit operations from the storm.

It took some time for me to get out of the shack. Heavy brush had been pushed up against both doors. Slowly, I unlaced the gaggle of limbs and roots that encased the steps. I tried to maneuver the cart out from its storage spot under the shack, but it was too difficult to pull it over the brush and debris. I opted to use just my pack. I would have to ferry things back to the shack to make it through the next few days.

I pushed my way out to the road. Looking back at the path I had made, it seemed pointless to try and hide its existence. I seemed to be operating on the autopilot of finding food and fuel, yet not even caring whether my existence in the shack was discovered or worse, Ike Hamundarson found me. I walked toward the chipper plant and the water's edge in a bit of a stupor.

I walked past the chipper plant and under the conveyor belt to the dock. A strange scene began to unfold on the road ahead of me. Something wasn't right about the way the vehicles were parked. As I walked slowly ahead, a began to make out an ambulance backed up to the water's edge and a police car parked across the road. A policeman was directing traffic back into town, not letting it pass by the spot. There was a pickup parked beside the ambulance. A man got out of the truck and walked toward the ambulance. The man's gait and jacket looked familiar. It was Roger.

I stopped walking forward and stood still, frozen to the road beneath my feet. A car came up behind me and slammed on its breaks. "Get out of the road," I heard the driver yell. I turned to look at the driver with a cold stare. He motioned to me, directing me to step aside. I turned my gaze back at the scene in front of me. The driver, also looking ahead, saw the policeman. Turning his car around, he drove back in the direction from which he had come, spraying me with water off the road. But I hardly felt the ice-cold water as it tore across my legs and pooled around my feet.

The scene in front of me seemed to take place in slow motion. Even the trees, still bending in the strong wind, moved with incredible slowness, back and forth, almost turning over on themselves. I watched as Roger approached the ambulance. Orange-vested EMTs were lifting a long black bag up over the side of the road, hauling it away from the rocky shoreline of the bay. They stopped and opened the top of the bag, unzipping a space large enough for Roger to peer inside. Roger stared down into the opening and then back at the EMTs. He nodded and spoke briefly to the vested men. They closed the bag and lifted it into the back of the ambulance.

Roger walked slowly back to his pickup and got into the cab. He sat motionless until the policeman came up to the cab window and motioned for him to lower it. Roger rolled down the window and spoke with the policeman. He raised his hand in the truck as if to say, I'm okay. But he still hadn't started the truck. The policeman stopped the next car while the ambulance pulled away from the edge of the road and drove toward town. Roger backed his truck up and started to follow the ambulance. Then he stopped his truck next to the car that was waiting in the other lane. He rolled down the window on the opposite side of the cab and leaned forward to talk to the driver of the car.

I recognized the car as Andy's. They exchanged words as if they knew each other. I think they only knew of each other because of conversations with me and Gray.

Gray, I thought. Where was he? But I already knew where Gray was.

I couldn't move. I was standing in the same spot I had been since I had come upon the scene. I watched as Roger drove away toward town and Andy drove toward me. She nearly passed me before recognizing me standing wet and lost on the side of the road. She slammed on her breaks, drenching me with road spray.

"Saron?" she said. "Saron," she repeated in a tearful voice. She got out of the car and put her arms around me. "I'm so sorry," she said, her head close to mine, her voice muffled in my wet hair. "Come on," she said gently. I still hadn't moved my eyes from the place ahead of me where the black bag had been hauled up to the road and Roger bent over to identify the man who I lived with for months.

It was Roger who had gone looking for Gray, and Roger who had had to identify his friend's body. I could only think of the man I knew. I could only identify with the sweet, generous person who had been willing to place our needs before his and go to work in the cold and rain just to earn money for our survival. His generous spirit in the face of the inescapable cycle of pain and drugs is what had taken him from me. The hawk's cry had been his goodbye.

Andy had to propel me over to the passenger's side of the car and push me down into the seat. She closed the door with care and went around to the driver's side to get back into the car. She drove towards the chipper plant and turned into the US Fish and Wildlife Service work area.

"I'm taking you to Olympia," she said firmly. "Let's get what you need from the shack and leave food and water for Miss Hap."

I moved without being conscious of what I was doing. I gathered up some personal items and found my pack with all my work in it. Last, I put out bowls of food and water for Miss Hap. I gave her a hug. I hope she didn't know that she was being left behind. "Later," and whispered to her and gave her a final hug.

Andy got me back into her car and pulled away from the alder grove and my home of the last few months. I didn't look back. Everything I had known for the last five months ended. Death's icy march made its way across Bowerman Basin like the out-going tide that left the muds exposed to the snatching of shorebirds. My heart felt the draining of blood, the draining of love, and the draining of life sloshing and swirling with the current out to the depths of the ocean beyond Damon Point and Grays Harbor.

# 20

# THE HARBOR IS OURS

*I*n contrast to the darkness of death that surrounded me in Olympia, the next day brought a brilliant blue sky over Aberdeen. Commuters driving over the Hoquiam River bridge were treated to a sparkling and radiant view of Mount Rainier in the distance. The pilots of the big tugboats were busy below the bridge, sweeping up the last signs of the powerful windstorm and turning on their engines. Freighters that had waited out the storm out beyond the bar were lining up to be guided into port by the tugs. Stay-at-home wives stepped out of their front doors in their robes and slippers to sweep off their porches and set turned flowerpots right side up. The fresh, dry air had a whiff of spring in it.

Ike Hamundarson poured himself a cup of coffee and stood at his window, surveying the harbor and the port facilities. He, like many other businessmen in the community, was waiting for the decision of the port as to whether the terminal project would proceed. The port would be in business for a long time with the infusion of funds to build the terminal. Then there would be years of servicing the facility, even more money for businesses like Hamundarson's. They controlled Grays Harbor, not the environmentalists or the Indians. Screw them, thought Hamundarson, we're in charge now.

He heard his wife's car back out of the driveway, on her way to buy something, have coffee with friends, and probably drive over to the new distillery and buy gin and whiskey. At least he had something to look forward to besides yard cleanup when he got home.

Hamundarson looked out toward Westport. There was not a ripple of wind on the water. He gulped down the last taste of his coffee and headed for the door. There was only one way to celebrate the sudden sunny day. He climbed into his pickup truck, turned on the engine, revved the motor, and put the engine in reverse. Once out in the street, Hamundarson drove down the hill to the harbor, taking his half out of the middle of the city streets. He turned west as he always did to get out to the gravel pit. The men had worked well yesterday to clear it of debris from the storm. They would be loading the gravel trucks and starting their way to various job sites around the county.

Hamundarson had no intent of stopping in the office or monitoring the men's work at the pit. Instead, he pulled his truck up to the Black River fishing boat. The boat had survived the storm, its two twin motors securely fastened to the stern. Hamundarson slid his truck beneath the boat's hitch mechanism, tightened the crank of the hitch, and pulled away from the gravel pit. Once out on the highway, he turned his truck toward Westport. He couldn't think of a better way to spend such a beautiful day than out on the water, even getting out into the big water beyond the bar.

He drove through Aberdeen, a few jealous drivers honking their horn at his mastery of the day while they had to work or do more yard work. Hamundarson called his wife's phone. He smirked a bit when his call was sent to voice mail. At least he won't have to listen to her suggestions about why going boating so early in the year was a bad idea or that she needed him to help clear more debris from the yard around the house. He had the day to himself and he was going to enjoy it out on the water.

Then his phone rang. Damn, I'm going to have to listen to her anyway, he thought.

He answered the phone. "I'll be back this afternoon," he said, assuming it was his wife. But it wasn't. It was the pharmacist.

"Now look," said Hamundarson in a stern voice. "I told you I would take care of that woman. Don't worry about her. She won't be back asking for more money," he said impatiently.

"That's not the problem," said the pharmacist. "We just got a call from the police. Apparently, some poor guy the police thought had overdosed on heroin probably didn't commit suicide as they thought. When they ran some tests this morning, they found pretty strong fentanyl in his system. The heroin must have been amped up with the drug. That's what killed the guy. They found him out by the chipper plant. We're supposed to keep an eye out for this new batch of heroin with fentanyl coming into the harbor."

"So, what do you want me to do about it?" said Hamundarson.

"I'm just telling you that whatever we're bringing in on *Maiden's Curse* is getting dangerous."

"Well, maybe you'll just have to drop out," said Hamundarson. "I'm not worried about it. I just get it into the harbor. If people want to use the stuff, that's their business, not mine." He pushed the End Call icon and snapped the phone shut. He pushed his foot a bit harder on the accelerator.

When Hamundarson got to the boat launch at the Westport Marina, he was ready to get out on the water. The phone call had not set well with him. He was more interested in smelling the spray from water churned up by the big motors and turning the boat through the current, out past the bar, than sticking around to talk to other boat owners or fiddling with new gear.

He slid the boat into the water, tied it to the pier and parked his truck in his usual spot. Back at the boat, he unrolled the canvas cover and jumped in behind the control panel and steering mechanism. He yanked the line free of the pier, turned on the motors, and put the boat in reverse. His rough actions got the attention of nearby boaters, some checking their engines, some filling their tanks at the fuel dock, and others washing and clearing their boats with hoses, buckets, and brushes.

Hamundarson backed his boat out of the dock area and turned it toward the entrance to the marina. He made himself keep the motors throttled at the five mile an hour speed limit until he was past the entrance. Once out in the open water of the bay, he opened the throttle and waited to hear the roar of the motors. He set the boat to steer into the main channel and turned it to the west when he felt the current beneath the boat.

It was only then that he backed off on the throttle and allowed himself to take in the changes to the channel due to the winter storms. Damon Point, which helped create the shallows of Bowerman Basin, seemed more elongated and narrower due to the loss of sand. The mudflats in the Basin were larger, twisting all the way around the end of the airport landing strip. Apparently, the winter tides had moved the sand over to the Elk River side of the harbor. Mudflats that never existed before had created a buffer around the mouth of the river, and the river had responded by cutting a fresh channel to the bay. The oyster industry will be happy with that Hamundarson thought.

Hamundarson steered the boat into the center of the channel that led out through the jetties and over the bar. It was then that he noticed that the water in the channel was not its usual gray color. It was brown, full of sediment that the storm had washed into the Chehalis River and was now filling the channel with grit, debris, and logs. The added volume of water in the channel was running faster than usual. He had to focus on steering the boat away from dangerous logs that could easily batter the boat and cause major problems. Terns circled around the boat, diving at Hamundarson and squawking for fish guts.

Hamundarson reached across his control panel and turned on the marine radio. He had to turn the dial a bit to find the radio channel from the US Coast Guard station at Westport. Finally, after switching the radio on and off, and turning the dial again, Hamundarson caught the Coast Guard marine forecast.

"Boaters should be aware of a large amount of water in the Chehalis Channel. Severe storms in the coastal mountains have caused excessive debris in the river. Large amounts of silt in the water is causing difficulties for boaters. Boats may become adrift due to motor failure. In addition to the high water volumes running seaward in Grays Harbor, a very low tide is predicted for one o'clock this afternoon. Boaters should avoid the main channel through Grays Harbor."

Hamundarson switched off the radio. He looked out at the bay to see that he was the only boat on the water. The water was carrying a heavy load of trees and branches. He turned his boat from side to side to avoid logs and debris in the brown water. Ahead, he could see the brown bloom of silt moving out over the bar and into the ocean. Maybe I've been a bit careless to get out in the channel, he thought. I shouldn't be out here.

He grabbed the steering mechanism and pulled it to port, thinking it would be a smart move to turn back toward the marina. As he pulled the mechanism, he heard a loud, wrenching howl from the motors. Then the motors stopped. Hamundarson turned the key on the control panel, but nothing happened. He tried again, cursing at the panel. "Come on," he yelled. The motors did not respond. He ran to the back of the boat and tried to lift the motors, but they were locked in place. Running between the two motors was a large log, its branches wrapped around the propellers. The propellers and the motors were useless.

Hamundarson ran back to the control panel. Without the motors, he couldn't steer the boat. The boat had already been turned by the rapidly moving water. It turned again, another ninety degrees so that the bow was facing east while the current was pushing the boat into the jetty area. Hamundarson tried to turn on his radio. He wanted to send an SOS to the Coast Guard, but the radio failed. The batteries were dead, never revived from their winter's sleep. The marine report had used up all the energy that remained in the unit.

Hamundarson sat in the pilot's chair, unable to use the control panel or the motors. He hadn't equipped the boat with oars or even life jackets in his exuberance to get out on to the water. He could not control the boat, and the boat was being pushed by the Chehalis current and pulled by the lowering tide. There was no one on the jetty to see him bounce over the bar and be drawn out into the big water.

As usually happens on a bright sunny inland day, molecules of water vapor began to rise into the air just offshore. The warm air heats the surface layer, and bit by bit, the vapors rise into a profusion of mist and water droplets. Hamundarson had failed to notice the gathering fog just beyond the bar. When he finally got himself turned around to face the ocean, he was horrified to see that he would soon be engulfed in a bank of fog that stretched all along the coast. Once he entered the fog, he couldn't see or tell anything about his location relative to the bay or the coast. Worse, no one could see him. The fog would muffle all sound and created a blanket that wrapped around his boat. Any other vessel near him would not see or hear him, and he would only hear them when they were right next to his location.

Under the influence of the warm fog, the ocean began to move. Waves built up and then passed under the boat. Without the sun, the water took its cues from the movement of energy and currents beneath the surface. The waves began to knock the boat around, sometimes turning it in circles, sometimes pushing it into waves that seemed to appear out of nowhere. Hamundarson had heard stories of other boats lost in fogs for days, men holding on as the waves raised their boats to wave crests and then slammed the boats into deep troughs. Some boats were found at sea, others were not.

The pounding of the waves forced Hamundarson to sit on the bottom of the boat. He clung to the side of the captain's chair. The boat rose and fell repeatedly. He could do nothing but hold on as tightly as he could. Spray from the waves drenched him until he was soaked. He tried to make himself as small as possible, curling up against the chair's legs hoping … he didn't know what for. Hoping it all would end. Soon.

As Hamundarson lay on the boat's bottom, he thought he could feel a vibration coming through the water and passing through the boat. He tried to pull himself up, but a wave pushed him back to the bottom of the boat. He felt the vibration again, a constant rumbling feeling, now stronger than the water's movements. Then he felt the vibration of a something right next to the boat. The sound got louder and louder, a churning of water and a grinding of engines.

Hamundarson looked up into the fog long enough to see the monstrous dark red hull of a freighter before him. He raised both of his arms skyward. He looked upward with a pleading scream. His mouth open and eyes fixed on the red hull, the ship's crashing wake pulled the Black River boat and its paralyzed occupant down into the water, wrenching the boat in two and sending the captain deep beneath the surface of the water. Within moments there was no sign of Hamundarson or the fishing boat.

A flash of light seared into Ike Hamundarson' soul the moment he was thrust beneath the freighter. In that bright light, Hamundarson saw two figures. He recognized Gray Quinn standing as he had at the public hearing. Only this time, Gray was wearing a cedar cape and held the feather of a sea hawk. He wore a wool knit cap with feathers and soft down lining that encircled his face. The hat looked vaguely familiar, reminding Hamundarson of someone else he had seen in the harbor.

Behind Gray stood an old wrinkled, stooped woman. She was completely dressed in cedar. A long skirt was tied at her waist and a cape hung from her shoulders. A cedar conical hat sat on her head. The cape was held together in front with a long brooch decorated with porcupine quills, feathers, and small shells. She stood hunched over holding on to a rounded shaft of cedar wood that had the face of a raven carved into the top of the wood.

Gray stood before Ike Hamundarson, his arms spread out on either side of his torso as if to calm the waters around him and the old woman.

"Remember," said Gray in a loud measured voice, "the harbor belongs to the Quinault people. We will survive, and you will not."

The light faded, and Ike Hamundarson was lost in a deep current of darkness.

# 21

# RENEWAL

*A*ndy took me to Olympia as she said she would on the day they had found Gray's body. I had sat numb and speechless in the car while Andy drove. She turned on the radio just to fill the air. I didn't hear much of it. I was unable to focus on anything. Instead, visions of Gray, the body bag, the police, and Roger kept crowding into my mind. I know we stopped for coffee and huge homemade cookies at the coffee stand in Elma.

"Here," said Andy. "Eat this and drink this coffee. It will make you feel better."

After a while, she handed me a water bottle. I drank it all down, I hadn't realized how thirsty and hungry I was.

When we got to her house, she ushered me back to the room I had used before. She coaxed me out of my clothes and gave me a robe.

"Take a shower and get warmed up," she said softly. "I'll put these in the washing machine," holding my wet and dirty clothes at arm's length. "And then I'll make you some dinner."

I stood in the hot shower a long time. Finally, I found Andy's shampoo and washed my hair. I used a bar of soap to scrap off days of sweat and mud. When the water started to get chilly, I rinsed my hair one more time and then stepped out of the shower. The image that stared back at me from the mirror opposite the shower was hardly one I recognized. My hair had grown out and hung below my chin line. It was black in some places and brown in others due to my efforts to hide my true dishwater blonde coloring. No doubt there would be gray in it now if not for the coloring. My face was very thin and drawn. Wrinkles I had never seen before crowded into the corners of my eyes and spanned across my forehead. My eyes were blacker than the true blue they had once been. Bones stuck out from my collar and thin droopy arms hung at my sides. The last five months had taken their toll on my body.

I wrapped the robe around myself, nearly doubling around me thanks to all the weight I had lost over the winter. I stepped out into the hallway trying to orient myself. Part of me just wanted to go back to the bedroom and crawl into bed forever. Another part of me wanted to be with Andy and let her keep my mind from wandering back to the shack and the images of the morning. I heard her put plates on the table in the kitchen. She poked her head around the corner of the kitchen and peered down the hallway.

"Hey," she said in a lighthearted voice. "How was the shower?"

I nodded, still not able to say anything.

"Well, how about some dinner?" she asked. "I've made a ton of mac and cheese, a salad, and found some nice deli meat in the frig. We can either put it in the mac and cheese or eat it like finger food."

I nodded again.

"Come on and sit down," she said. She poured hot water into mugs that turned a mixture of powdered chocolate, powdered milk, and powdered sugar into a sweet concoction of hot chocolate. "I think you need to start eating again," she said and patted my shoulder. "There's plenty more, so take all you want."

We ate in silence since I still found it difficult to speak.

"How about some hot chocolate for dessert?" she asked. "And I found these in the freezer, tiny frozen pecan pies! I think I made these for Christmas and forgot to serve them," she said.

She piled two pies on my plate and filled my mug with the mixture of chocolate and added hot water. I felt my stomach stretching to accommodate all the food. It had shrunk from lack of big meals over the last five months.

After finishing the dessert, Andy cleared the table. Then she came back and sat down beside me.

"Today's been a rough day for you," she said.

I looked at the kindness in her face and then at my hands as they clutched the mug. Andy took the mug from my hands and held them. Slowly, tears began to run down my cheeks. It was all too much. Gray's death, our hidden home, the fears of being found out, Ike Hamundarson' efforts to scare me out of Aberdeen, even the night he pushed me off *Maiden's Curse* were still so vivid in my mind. I tried to trace the meaning of each situation, but it all became a jumbled chaos. Each one of the situations was enough to shatter any normal person's life. Altogether, it was unfathomable now.

As if reading my mind, Andy said, "I don't know how you have lasted so long out there in the shack. I am so sorry about Gray."

Her saying his name finally broke my silence. I put my head down and started to weep. Andy turned her chair toward me and pulled me up against her shoulder.

"It's okay," she said. "It's okay."

We sat there for a while. I cried, thinking about how unhappy Gray must have been and how he had tried so hard to stop the cycle of pain. I hoped he hadn't decided to stop it, but he was gone. There were things I probably won't know. I missed him. I missed settling into the night at the shack with him. 'Where is he?' I kept asking myself. But there were no answers.

I stopped crying after a while. Andy handed me a glass of water and kept a box of Kleenex close at hand.

"Want to talk about anything?" she asked.

I sipped some water and pulled another tissue from the box.

"I guess I need to find out some things," I said.

"I'll see if I can find out about Gray," said Andy.

"What about the shack?" I asked. "All my field notes are still out there."

"I'll get them the next time I go out to the work site," she said. "I don't think you should go out there for a while. You can stay here for as long as you want."

"Aren't you leaving soon?" I asked.

"I still haven't heard from OSU, so I guess not. I can go to Evergreen for a master's degree."

"I don't have any way to pay you back," I said.

Andy put her hand into her jeans pocket and pulled out three soggy looking bills. "No?" she asked quizzically. "What's this? I found it in the pocket of your pants. Good thing or they would have gone through the wash."

The sight of the three one hundred-dollar bills almost brought a smile to my face. "Oh, those," I said. "I got them from someone who would be in a lot of trouble if I started talking about the extra voyages of *Maiden's Curse*."

Andy looked at me for a minute, about ready to ask me more questions but then decided against it. She put the bills on the table. "We can use this money to buy you some new clothes and food for the house," she said.

I nodded in agreement, my ability to speak having left again.

"I know you must be exhausted," Andy said. "Go to bed and I'll clean up this kitchen." She reached over and gave me another hug. "Things will look better in the morning."

The next morning, Andy organized her pack and made a thermos of coffee to go. "I have to go over to the office and talk to Jen," she said. "I'll be gone only a couple of hours. You going to be okay? There's more coffee, bread and butter for toast, and more pecan pies in the freeze. Eat whatever you want."

"I'll be Okay," I said.

I sat quietly in the living room while Andy was gone. The coffee tasted good with the tiny leftover pies. I found leftover mac and cheese and ate a small bowl of the gooey pasta. I thought about Gray. His memory brought more tears to my eyes. I didn't know how to reach Roger. I didn't know if Gray's body would be taken up to Taholah for an Indian burial. I didn't know how I could ever say goodbye to him. I didn't want to say goodbye. I wanted to say hello and fix him hot tea. The tears kept running down my cheeks and into my lap. I held on to the mug of coffee just to steady my nerves in between wiping my eyes with tissues.

Andy came back as promised. "Well, there must be some news about the project," she said. "Jen wants both of us in his office tomorrow at ten o'clock."

"Me, too?" I said. "Why?"

"I don't really know, but it must have something to do with the project and your contributions to the research end of things."

I looked down at the robe I was wearing instead of my worn-out clothes. Reaching up to feel the ends of my jagged and multi-colored hair, I gave Andy a look of remorse. "I can't go to an office looking like this," I said.

"How about we go into Lacey and get your hair into better shape. We can buy some clothes at the consignment shop or at Target. Maybe find you some new shoes, too."

"Okay," I said.

"Let me see if I have some clothes you can wear this afternoon. They won't let you into a beauty shop wearing the ones you arrive in," she joked.

Finally dressed and primped as much as possible, Andy led me back to her car and we headed into the commercial area of Lacey. An hour later, my hair had been trimmed so that it nearly looked all the same color. The look was flattering and made me feel more my age than the cut I had given myself to appear much younger. We headed over to Target and I shopped for clothing, shampoo, a bit of makeup. Andy kept adding things to my basket. "You might need this," she would say. By the time all the items got rung up by the cashier, the total was $138.19, tax included. I pulled out my cash from the pocket of Andy's jeans I was wearing. The cashier gave me change back. "Have fun with all this stuff," she said with a smile.

"Thanks, I will," I said, managing to smile in return.

"I hope you can find my green sweater you bought me the last time I was here," I said to Andy.

"I'll get it when I go by the shack in a couple of days. Don't worry. Let's go get some food, you look hungry again."

I was, and tired. The food gave me some extra energy, but by the time we got back to Andy's I was exhausted. "I'm going to bed now," I said. "I want to look more rested for the meeting with Jen tomorrow."

The aroma of coffee woke me the next day. For a moment, I thought I was back in the shack with Gray handing me a cup of coffee. Then I remembered I was at Andy's. The momentary sense of Gray's presence slipped away.

"Time to get going so we'll be at the office at ten," said Andy. She went off to shower and to get dressed. I sat at the kitchen table and ate the breakfast of eggs and toast she had prepared for me. The endless supply of hot coffee was what kept everything going in the house. I followed Andy's shower with one of my own, and then got dressed. I pulled on a new pair of jeans, a white cotton turtleneck, and a puffy blue vest I had gotten off a sale rack at Target. My new short haircut dried quickly in the bathroom while I put on a little mascara and lipstick. Last, I wrapped one of the scarves Andy had insisted I buy around my neck.

Andy stood in amazement at my transformation. "You look great!" she said and squeezed my arm. "Now let's go see what's so important that Jen would call us in to his office."

We got to the US Fish and Wildlife Service in Olympia at nine thirty. Andy went into the next-door coffee shop, Laughing Goat, and got more coffee. "Just to keep us going," she said. We got up to Jen's office and stood against the wall across from the door to her office. It was closed. When it opened, two men I recognized as biologists stepped out of the office. They both smiled at us and then walked down the hall to their respective offices. Andy shrugged her shoulders as if to say, 'I haven't a clue.'

Jen saw us from her desk.

"Come in," she said while shuffling some papers around.

Andy and I pulled up chairs to sit opposite her. We both held our cups of coffee and set our packs down on the floor next to our chairs.

"You two act like twins," she said.

"Thanks," we said in unison. That made us all smile.

"First, I want to express my unhappiness at hearing of your partner's passing, Saron. I'm sure it's a loss. I hope this meeting isn't too soon after the events of the last few days. I'm sure Andy is looking after you," said Jen.

"She is, and thanks for your thoughts. I'm doing okay" I said even though I still had moments of panic.

"Well, I wanted to bring you up to date on the terminal project. You've both been instrumental in our efforts to understand the ecology of Bowerman Basin and the potential impact of the project on the mudflats. I was out in Aberdeen yesterday and had a meeting with the port. They had just come from a meeting with the Quinault Indian Nation. The agencies and the local politicians and businesspeople have agreed that we need to do more research before making a final determination as to whether the project will move forward. There is also the fact that the Quinault are threatening a court suit to press their claims of superior ownership and decision-making based on their treaty rights. So, we've all decided to step back from the project until that is finally decided. In the meantime, this agency will continue to do the work that you two have been doing all winter. We need more field observations and then an analysis of the observations. We're talking to the research branch of the Audubon Society in Seattle to see if they will also get involved. As usual, we get to these big projects without the necessary studies. Now we have a project, so now the studies will be funded. Only doing studies in places that need research is entirely backward from doing the studies first, but that's the way it works."

Andy and I smiled at each other. "That's good news," said Andy. "I guess I'll be working here and going to Evergreen in the fall. I never heard from OSU." Her voice showed her disappointment.

"That's not necessarily the case," said Jen.

"What do you mean?" said Andy. "I've never had a letter one way or the other about admission to their grad program."

Jen reached out over her desk that was covered with piles of papers and pulled a long white envelope from one of the piles of papers. "I found this in my mail the other day," she said. "I have no idea why it came to me as it's really for you. Read it," she said with a bit of a twinkle in her eye.

Andy looked at the envelope, especially the return address that said Department of Biology, Oregon State University, Corvallis, Oregon. The envelope was addressed to her care of Jen. Andy looked at both of us and then sliced the envelope open with her finger. She pulled out one sheet of paper and read through the first paragraph. A slow smile began to spread across her face. By the time she had finished the last paragraph, she was beaming. "I'm in," she said in a loud happy voice. "And they want me to come down for the spring and start research at Newport. I'm in!" she said again in an excited voice.

Both Jen and I beamed back at her. "Good going," I said. Jen stood up and reached across the desk to shake her hand. "I know you can do this," she said. "I talked to your new supervisor in Oregon.

He's keen on your abilities and wants you to start as soon as you can. If you don't do an excellent job," she said in a pseudo-gruff voice, "you've got me to answer to."

"Don't you worry," she replied with a grin. "I'll do you proud."

"Good," said Jen. "Now that leaves you, Saron."

"Me?" I said.

"Yes, you. The mudflat project would be nowhere without your daily observations. Andy couldn't be out there all the time, especially after her first day with that boat captain. Saron," she looked intently at me, "you have excellent observation skills. We can teach you how to put together observation diagrams and make sense of the sightings you've made. We want you do keep making the observations."

"But how can I do that?" I asked. "I can't really go back to living there," I hesitated, "I mean sitting in the alder grove at Bowerman Basin."

"We're going to make you a paid volunteer. We're going to give you a real place to live," she said and stole a glance at Andy. "No more living in the shack. We have a small trailer that we can put inside the fence of the work area. You'll have electricity, heat, and water. You can live there as long as we are working on the research, which should be some time, especially if a court case is involved. As a paid volunteer, you will also get some per diem to cover food and other expenses you may have while you are out there. The per diem rate out at Hoquiam is $35.00 a day."

Andy switched from re-reading her letter to look at me with a broad smile. "That's great!" she said.

"I don't really know what to say..., I mean, wow! Thank you," I said.

"Your work is excellent. You've earned this position. We hope to have the trailer set up by the end of next week. The shack is going to be torn down when the weather is a bit better. Turns out the lumber company had totally forgotten about it and would like to have it removed. It's on federal land anyway."

I nodded in agreement. "I don't want to see it again," I said.

"Andy will help you get set up in the trailer and show you a bit more about note taking and using the observations. That is, before she heads out for OSU-land and forgets all about us."

She pulled a pet carrying case out from beside her desk. "And you can have this," she said with a sly smile.

"Miss Hap!" I exclaimed. "How...?"

"We sent a technician out to retrieve her from the shack. You can keep her with you in the trailer but don't let me see her again. Keep her inside. Cats are not so friendly to wildlife, especially birds."

"No worries! She's used to staying inside. Thank you!" I said.

Turning to Andy, Jen said, "I do have my evaluation of your work this quarter for your Evergreen prof. I talked it over with him on the phone. He'll follow whatever I send him for my part of the evaluation. Here's a copy," said Jen as she handed another letter to Andy. "I said you did an excellent job and your contribution to the agency was beyond expectations."

"Thank you, Jen," said Andy sincerely. "I have learned a lot this quarter."

"Well, I guess that's something else you can celebrate," said Jen. "You will graduate from Evergreen."

"Oh yeah, that's right! I completely forgot!" said Andy. "Now I'm a real Greener!"

"I think there's one more piece of news for you two," said Jen turning back to her briefcase. "I got this newspaper in Aberdeen yesterday. You might be interested in the headlines."

Jen passed the newspaper over to Andy who pushed her chair closer to me so I could read it with her. The headlines read "Local Businessman, Ike Hamundarson, Assumed Lost at Sea".

"What?" said Andy. We both looked at the first paragraph of the article that followed.

"Apparently, he got so interested in putting his boat in the water that he forgot to take the usual precautions. They think he must have gotten dragged out through the channel and over the bar and lost in the fog. There's no sign of him or his boat," said Jen. "Everyone at the meeting was talking about it."

Turning toward me again, she said, "You'll be perfectly safe out there in a trailer. There will also be a small pickup for you to use whenever you need it."

I could hardly believe all the news. I was free of Captain Hamundarson and *Maiden's Curse*. I would be living in a safe, warm place doing what I loved in a place I had grown to love. Bowerman Basin mudflats! I would have a steady income plus my small Social Security check. Miss Hap would keep me company. I did it, Bruce, I thought. I am me.

I looked at Jen and Andy, chatting away about her grad school research goals. If only I could tell Gray, I thought. For just a moment, I saw him walking along the shore without pain, celebrating life on the bay with his granny. I knew I would see his spirit in every bird who landed on the mudflats. We would still be together watching over Bowerman Basin. I felt nothing but joy.

Out at Grays Harbor, tidal sea water slowly began its filling of the mudflats. The water pushed into veins and capillaries in the mud. Sea life reentered the abandoned sediments, air hole by air hole, space by space, molecule by molecule re-energizing the center of life. Each gentle wave pulsed back and forth across the core of the mudflats until the entire area was alive, beating as the heart of the harbor. Fingerling fish caught the attention of a circling osprey, tired and weak from its flight north. Diving down, the osprey filled its beak with fry and then soared upward, turning and circling over the nest above the alder grove. A new season of life was about to begin.

# EPILOGUE

The characters in this text began to appear to me during many trips between my house in Ocean Shores and Olympia where I was on the faculty at The Evergreen State College. My commute began in 2008, just at the beginning of the Great Recession. Over the next five, I watched the economy and social fabric of Aberdeen and Hoquiam slowly descend into a relatively high rate of poverty and loss of downtown businesses. I began to see more and more blue tarps tied down over houses whose owners could no longer repair the roofs that separated them from the constant cold rain of Grays Harbor.

As in many parts of the Pacific Northwest, years of debate about the rate of timber harvesting and community survival versus wildlife habitat and public land management stressed Grays Harbor County residents. True or not, their sense of loss from jobs to adequate education for their children was easily blamed on populations that did not live in the county. Hand painted signs began to appear in lawns blaring the fact that it was a "timber family" that was being driven into poverty by the reduced amount of timber harvesting. More signs appeared when the thousands of acres of public lands were proposed for wilderness designation effectively making them off limits for timber harvesting.

While looking for a way to express what I saw happening in the county. A group of esteemed social geographers at the University of Washington asked me to participate in a project with the goal of identifying poverty in communities across the state. I was tempted. But I knew this was not the way I could tell the story of the impacts of poverty on individuals I saw in Aberdeen and Hoquiam. Instead, the two characters of Saron and Gray began to speak to me, especially when I drove the truck route along the industrial harbor out past an abandoned timber scaling shack, and along the mudflats of the Bowerman Basin Unit of the Billy Frank Jr. National Nisqually Wildlife Refuge.

While I appreciated the beauty and mystery of the Basin's mudflats, I had little ability to identify the birds who found its refuge. Over the two years of my writing, I have become much more adept to recognizing bird species and their mechanisms for survival. I owe a great deal to a hiking group that included me in their pursuit of birds. In addition, Michael McCarthy's book *The Moth Snowstorm: Nature and Joy* guided my hopes in writing about birds and mudflats. Most importantly, McCarthy reclaims the tradition of receiving from nature the beauty and joy it has to offer us.

The books main characters became more persistent when Grays Harbor County, as blue a county as you could find based on historic labor unions, immigrant families, and a dose of Scandinavian socialism, voted red in the 2016 election. Reading the Aberdeen "Daily World" alerted me to the increasing poverty in the county. Next to nearly every story of economic loss was a story about the inroads drug abuse was making on all sectors of the county population. Homelessness and begging on street corners became a normal sight.

Other characters in the text took shape as I wrote. I had no intention to write about The Evergreen State College's unique curriculum but in doing so, I was able to introduce Andy and describe the benefits of the learning environment. There are real-life Evergreen graduates like Andy and Jen who have made tremendous contributions to the social and natural sciences of Washington State and beyond. I am most proud of these Evergreen students, blessed to have worked with them, and hopeful that they will create a new Earth.

There are pirates on the harbor. The yearly Westport celebration known as Rusty Scupper's Pirate Daze is a popular community and family event. The actions of the pirates in this text are fabricated to support the storytelling. The local pirates are upstanding citizens, not the villains portrayed in the text.

Grays Harbor is an exceptionally large series of mudflats and river channels. Human interaction with the water and mud has created an evolving life system. Ocean marine life mix with freshwater river environments. Birds come and go, stopping on their twice-yearly migrations route from points in the far north to the far south. It becomes increasingly unclear what is 'natural' and what is human constructed. The Port Commission and the Quinault Indian Nation participate in re-defining what is Grays Harbor. We should not forget that the proper name of the bay was once named Gray's Harbor due to the imperial impulse of nonnatives.

The book is written as of events and conditions in 2010. At that time, there were few resources describing the ecosystem of mudflats. Since then, Peter G. Beninger has edited a scholarly volume entitled Mudflat Ecology (2019). Similarly, Tides by Jonathan White (2017) is a beautifully written text on extreme tidal conditions. Bird inventories of the harbor are made every year during the Audubon Society Christmas Day survey. Major amounts of funding for harbor conditions have created a wealth of information about Willapa Bay to the south of Grays Harbor. However, no extensive survey of Grays Harbor ecology has been completed to this date.

Last, the character of Gray is totally fictional. The story of his experience with medical pain killers and his eventual death from heroin is not unknown in the county. I witnessed body bags being pulled up from the harbor's driftwood-strewn shore as I drove the industrial route. I have tried to write about Gray and his granny with a great deal of respect, remembering their position in the harbor's matrix of social and political history. Their circumstances in this text are fictional, but the power of the Quinault Indian Nation is not. The Quinault Nation also lives in a new Earth, able to see the past and the future with eyes that stay focused on the harbor, the wildlife, and the intricate relationship they have built with Earth over many centuries. We can all benefit from listening to and with them.

# ACKNOWLEDGMENTS

Writing this book was a leap of faith on my part. I am grateful for professional and personal people in my life who pushed me to write and publish this story. Joni Rogers worked with me to develop the plot and characters. She took me under her wing because she believed in the story and my ability to write it. Her familiarity with the Washington coastline contributed to the authenticity of the entire work. Other knowledgeable people of the coast, its bird habitats, and the human-Earth relationships in Grays Harbor are also thanked for their insights and support. James Anderson, Susan Robertson, Dr. Steven Herman made sure my leap was not going to shatter on the rocks below. Thank you. I am also indebted to Les Joslin, geographer, writer, forester, and naval man who read and edited the manuscript. As I sailed over the rocks of writing crisis, friends came to my support including Dr. Julie deWitt, Kathy Malone, Dr. Sarah Williams, Gale Masters, and William Tubesing. I thank Carl John Stout for always assuming I would land with two feet on the ground. Last, Andrea Reiber flew with me across the challenges of writing and publishing. She is the bravest friend and writing companion. All errors are mine alone.